THE EDGE

A RELICS NOVEL

THE
EDGE

A RELICS NOVEL

TIM LEBBON

TITAN BOOKS

THE EDGE
Print edition ISBN: 9781785656101
Electronic edition ISBN: 9781785650352

Published by Titan Books
A division of Titan Publishing Group Ltd
144 Southwark St, London SE1 0UP
www.titanbooks.com

First edition: February 2020

2 4 6 8 10 9 7 5 3 1

A CIP catalogue record for this title is available from the
British Library.

Printed and bound in the United States.

Did you enjoy this book?
We love to hear from our readers. Please email us at
readerfeedback@titanemail.com or write to us at
Reader Feedback at the above address.

To receive advance information, news, competitions, and exclusive
offers online, please sign up for the Titan newsletter on our website
www.titanbooks.com

This one is dedicated to my good friends
Olaf and Yuka Buchheim

PART ONE
BONE

1

"Do you trust me?"

The kid doesn't know. He respects the creature before him. He fears it, is fascinated by it, loves it, and sometimes even finds it intimidating, especially on those evenings when it descends from the caves outside town, moving through shadows like a shadow itself to come and visit his mother. The creature's name is Mohserran, and it is his father. He knows that it troubles his mom as well, but he also realises that there's something else between the two of them, something grown-up and mysterious. Even though he's only eleven years old, he understands love.

But trust? He's not so sure about that.

Especially now, with all the blood.

"It doesn't matter," the creature says. The boy has never seen it like this, or heard it sounding so flustered and panicked. It's only rarely that he has seen Mohserran without his mother also being there, and some of those memories are magical. Now, though, the fact that he doesn't know where she is frightens him. He might be growing up, but a kid his age still wants his mother, especially when something strange is happening. Something bad.

The kid has felt sick for a couple of days. He's vomited everything up, and still dry heaves. He's slept and woken, and confused the two. He's sweating even though the night is cool. And he has thoughts that are unfamiliar and frightening, about blood and broken bones, torn flesh and teeth clogged with meat. He has wandered back and forth through the town, hardly knowing where he is, or sometimes even who he is.

"Where's Mom?"

There are strange noises coming from the surrounding darkness. From one direction something is banging again and again, like a door being slammed over and over. From elsewhere he can hear pained shouts, like someone trying to cry past a blocked throat. From further away, a scream.

Overhead, a gentle *whoop-whoop* noise drifts back and forth over the town, the echoes heavy in his chest. A shadow blots out the stars, moonlight glimmering from dark metal. The boy has seen helicopters before, but never without an accompanying roar. He's finding it difficult to ally the sights and sounds. Confusion twists all of his senses. He wonders if he is still asleep. He blinks and sees teeth again, and his jaw aches with a dreadful need.

"You must listen to me," the creature says. It has taken the boy out into the garden, down past the small pond to that uncertain area where garden ends and countryside begins. There are no fences here in Longford, no distinct breaks between civilisation and wilderness. The boy has grown up with that, and he understands it is an aspect of this place that his mother treasures. She says she likes the sense of the wild.

She likes Mohserran, too. This wild thing. That doesn't stop him being afraid. Even more so now, because its eyes are wider than usual, dripping a strange yellow substance that is luminous in the moonlight, almost afire. Blood is splashed across its skin and fur, and trapped between its teeth he can see dark blots of what might be meat. It's like looking at himself in a future mirror.

"But I want Mom."

"Boy, *listen* to me. It's important. It's..." The creature growls and spits, shaking its head like a wet dog. It looks confused, glancing around, clamping its jaws on a shadow. Shaking, fighting against something the boy cannot see or understand, it takes a few slow, deep breaths to compose itself. It stands still for long, long seconds before speaking again. "Something very bad is happening."

The boy knows. It's obvious, from the *whoop-whoop*ing above the town, and the lights he can now see moving up on the surrounding hills, like distant fireflies with malevolent purpose. He knows from the way he feels—the violent things he imagines, the deep, sick hunger gnawing at his belly—and what he's seen other people in the town doing. Maggie Parks was down by the river, choking creatures and throwing them in. They might have been kittens, or puppies. Albert Roy, the post office manager, was sitting beneath a tree on the town square, carefully threading sharp sticks through the loose skin covering his old thighs. Mrs Carter was naked in her garden, walking in tight circles around a pile of red clothes or meat on the ground.

"I'm scared."

"And you should be scared. Scared will keep you safe. Afraid keeps your senses sharp." The creature talks as if it knows scared and afraid. The boy would never have believed that Mohserran was afraid of anything. Not with those teeth, those claws.

"Where's Mom?"

It avoids the question and says, "I won't let you..." It growls and slams the flat of its big, clawed hand against its head. Its eyes roll, spilling speckles of yellow fire like glitter, then refocus on the boy. It seems he is their *only* focus. Everything else is a blur. "I won't let you fall. I can't look after you for much longer, not with the change, and not now that... now that I have to fight."

"Fight?"

Mohserran does not elaborate. The kid thinks it's because there is so little time.

Something is changing. The world is moving, with shifting lights and a vibration through the ground. There's a strange smell on the air, a sweet burning taint like popcorn popping or apple pie warming in the oven. He hears what might be a scream, but when it comes again he realises it's more like a roar from a human mouth. It sounds so unnatural. It sounds mad.

"There isn't long," Mohserran says. "Trust me. I'll save you. Because I love you."

The kid blinks in the night and the creature comes close.

Teeth and blood and torn skin and flesh and the taste in my mouth and the storm in my head—

Mohserran holds his face between its hands and the boy feels the tackiness of blood. He isn't sure whether it's from his father's strange hands or his own face, but now it's on both.

"Now get ready to run, and hide, and don't stop running and hiding until you're out of the valley. *Never* stop." Mad and covered in blood, still Mohserran looks sad as it holds the boy's cheeks with its soft, downy hands, vicious claws withdrawn, and brings his face close. It whispers, "Hold this breath all the way." It presses its mouth to the boy's and exhales.

He feels himself expand, his senses brightening and sharpening, and his knowledge of the mortal danger all around becomes clearer and more focused. *I'm only eleven years old and this shouldn't be happening to me*, he thinks, and it is a very grown-up thought followed by one so childlike: *It's not fair.*

Mohserran falls to its knees, one hand clawing into the ground, the other waving at him to go.

The boy holds the breath he has been given and runs.

* * *

He does what Mohserran told him. Impossible though it is, he holds his breath all the way up the hillside and out of the valley. He's come this way a hundred times before, sometimes with his mother, occasionally with his father, more often with his friends Jake and Emily, lunch packed in their rucksacks ready to be eaten when they reach the hilltop. Sometimes they are explorers, sometimes soldiers, sometimes astronauts landing on a strange planet and charting each footstep for the very first time. Always, they are adventurers.

As he reaches the top of the slope he wonders where Jake and Emily are now.

He gasps out his held breath—he has been running and climbing for half an hour, at least—and he feels a wrench at letting it go. He understands that it is something exotic and mysterious, but he is a child whose mind is open to such things. He has never known anything different. When he draws in a fresh chestful of air, it tastes of heathers and darkness. It is tainted by the fear that his whole life is about to change.

His mind is now clear of those images of blood and violence. He feels empty.

Still unsure if he is out of danger, he hunkers down beside a pile of rocks and turns to look back into the valley below. He has to rest. More than that, he has to know what is happening.

Like how I can hold my breath for half an hour even when it wasn't really my breath.

That was Mohserran's last breath. He understands

that, at least. And his father gave it to him so that he could survive, and everything he does from now on will be to honour that gift and to treasure that sacrifice.

Down in the valley an uneven ring of lights surrounds Longford, far out from the town's furthest extremes. It's made of vehicle lights and larger, stationary lamps that all shine inwards, illuminating the town's perimeter. He's too far away to make out these lamps, but he guesses they're big barrel-sized apparatus mounted on the backs of trucks, similar to the one they use on TV to send the bat signal into the sky. There are no bat signals here.

He starts to shiver, and not from the cold, because he's warm and sweating from his rapid climb up the hillside. He's shaking because he is afraid. He can't remember ever feeling so alone, and what he can see in the valley reminds him of things he's seen on TV, movies about aliens and the army, monsters and men with guns coming to blow them away. The kid understands the distinction between truth and make-believe well enough, even though a small part of him— perhaps one informed by his experience of television and comics—understands that something about his life might well be regarded as make-believe by most other people.

Caught within the circle of lights, the air above the town appears heavy with something he can't quite make out. It's like mist—although the air is light and dry—rolling and pulsing, moving above and through the town like a living, breathing thing. He can't see where it's coming from. He doesn't know what it is.

This is why he told me to hold my breath.

He thinks of the strange noises he heard in the town, and wonders whether there are still shouts, roars and screams in Longford now. He guesses he won't hear from this distance.

He's not too far away to hear the first crackle of gunfire.

By the time dawn arrives the boy is cold and damp. The horrible thoughts of blood have been purged from his mind, but he knows with a shattering certainty that he cannot go back home. Home is safety and love and warmth, Longford is now just a place.

He has seen people wearing special suits and breathing apparatus sweeping the hillsides with strange gadgets, walking in lines and flushing out any living thing ahead of them. He only avoids detection because he knows these hillsides well, and he hides in an old hollow oak.

From high in the tree he sees a fox in the distance, climbing up out of the valley. It has blood around its mouth and is growling, hissing, head darting left and right as if looking for something to kill. It does not look afraid. It looks vicious.

He sees deer and squirrels and rabbits shot as they're frightened out of hiding ahead of the lines of people.

Not every person carries a gun, but most of them do. They bag up the creatures' corpses, tie the bags and then bag them again. Then they leave them out in the open, attaching a small balloon filled with helium which floats a couple of metres above the ground. *So they can find and collect them later*, he thinks. He used to like balloons.

A scurrying thing runs close by the entrance to the hollow tree. He hears its ragged breathing accompanied by a series of pained grunts, and when he glances down from a crack high in the tree he locks eyes with a Labrador puppy. He thinks it might be Lucas, the Thompsons' dog, but it looks different. Muddy, wet, there is also blood spattered around its nose and across its face. He worries that the dog has been injured, but then he sees its eyes.

This is no longer the friendly family pet he stroked a few days ago. They said they'd named him after the *Star Wars* guy. The boy said they should have called him Chewie. His mother laughed.

Lucas growls and runs at him, and he only just ducks back inside the tree before the dog strikes the opening, scrabbling with oversized puppy paws, growling and spitting as it does its best to get at him.

The boy climbs quickly back up inside the tree. He's done this before, but never with a mad dog trying to bite him. He wants to shout and cry, but a strong part of him he never realised was there takes control, guiding his hands and feet as he heaves himself up and away from the sick puppy. It's inside the tree now, but he's beyond its reach. It cannot climb.

He sits high up for what seems like hours while the dog growls and leaps beneath him. Calling its name does nothing. He even tries "Chewie". There's no sign of recognition, no indication at all that the puppy knows its own name or knows him. Teeth are its only response.

Later, as the sun climbs high, the puppy tires of trying to reach him and leaves. Later still he hears a bark and a single gunshot.

He curls up inside the tree, wishing he had food and water. He wants to cry but will not allow himself the tears. He thinks that once they begin they will not end, because all his fears are backing up inside.

Around noon he looks out from high in the tree to see what is happening back down in the town. He can no longer hear gunshots. A calm has settled over the buildings. The strange mist has gone, burnt away by the sun, and now sunlight glints from a tall fence being erected in a rough circle way outside the town's outer boundary. He hears drills and hammers, and several helicopters drift in from down the valley, heavy platforms laden with building materials swinging beneath them. These are normal helicopters with loud rotors, not the stealthy things he heard over the town last night.

Back inside the oak he remembers Jake and Emily, and how they once climbed this tree together.

* * *

He doesn't know where to go, so he stays close to the only place he has ever known.

A day and a night have passed. The boy spent the night in the tree, and next day he stole some food from a big army truck he found beside a forest track with no one inside. He's seen several army vehicles, and soldiers wander the hillsides looking threatening and important. None of them have seen him.

He has a talent for not being seen. Sometimes his mother said he could flit by the corner of her eye all day long. She told him he was sleek. She said it like it was a special word, a big word, and he always believed there was much more behind it still waiting to be told.

She will not tell him now. He's pretty sure she is dead, along with his father Mohserran and the rest of Longford. That is a truth he keeps to one side and views from the corner of *his* eye, because if he allowed it in close it would break him, and he would no longer be sleek, and they would find him and do the same to him.

None of the soldiers goes down into the valley. The only people going into and back out of the valley are the people in the silvery suits, the ones building the fence. He guesses they're soldiers too, but they're different. Occasionally he still hears a lonely gunshot.

On the fourth day after fleeing Longford and home, he doesn't hear any more shooting at all

* * *

The boy moves around the valley. He pretends he's carried with the breeze, drifting from bushes to trees to rocky outcroppings, hiding in their shadows when soldiers are nearby. He's afraid and alone and confused about what has happened and is still happening, but he is also determined not to be caught. Mohserran didn't give him his last breath just for that to happen.

Sleek, he scavenges food. There are several new camps high up on the hillsides where soldiers live, and the only ones he avoids are the couple with dogs. The others he orbits until he sees an opportunity to slip in, steal food and clothing, and move out again. No one sees him. He is the wind, the whisper of a secret, an errant sunbeam. He likes the feel of moving through the landscape without being seen, and he likes even more the occasional turn of a soldier's head as he or she glimpses something from the corner of their eye. It gives him a sense of comfort, in a situation where comfort is lacking.

I'm only a little boy, he thinks. *I shouldn't be out here on my own.*

The noises from the valley have changed. A mile downriver from Longford there are lots of big machines, diggers and bulldozers and lorries streaming up and down the valley dumping piles of boulders and mud. The piles are growing, meeting, and from high on the hillside he can see soldiers scrambling like ants on a giant nest. Over time—days, maybe weeks, he soon loses track—the surfaces of the piles smooth out, and the undulations between them start to level.

The river's flow has stopped. The boy finds that strange, and sad. It's as if the blood has ceased flowing through the heart of Longford.

With nowhere else to go he remains in the valley. Somewhere deep inside, he realises that a small part of him still hopes that this will end and he'll be able to return home. Logic tells him there's no truth in that, as does everything he has seen and heard. But at heart he is still just a little lost boy.

Against all instincts, he decides to go back down to the town one more time.

He has been living in the hollowed oak tree. He's made quite a home of it, with a comfortable bed of old coats in the base and a convenient look-out perch higher up inside. He has a collection of stolen clothing and food, and he has eased back on his thieving in case it is noticed. He dresses in an oversized camouflage jacket, tying it close to his body with belts, and starts back down into the valley early one morning. As dawn sets the eastern hillsides aflame, he mounts a small rise close to the town and looks down upon his old home.

It is the same, but different. He recognises buildings and streets, the church close to the town square and the park on the far side, beyond which is the house where he has lived all his life. He cannot see the house because it's hidden behind the park's trees, and in a way he is pleased. He thinks that if he saw the pale pink walls and white window surrounds he might lose himself, run, get caught.

Get shot, he thinks.

In the days or weeks since he escaped Longford, he has not seen a single human being who is not a soldier.

And that is why the familiar town is also so different—because there is no one there. The streets are deserted and silent. No dogs or cats wander the pavements and gardens. A few screen doors hang open, a couple banging in the gentle morning breeze, and scraps of litter roll lazily along the main street. He has never seen Longford so silent.

The tall fence around the town makes it impossible to approach any closer. There are cameras topping the fence posts. They are aimed both into the town and away from it—the fence keeps him out, but perhaps it is also erected to keep something in.

With the sun behind him, the boy makes his way back up into the hills. The similarity with Mohserran and the two other creatures that call this place their home is obvious—they, too, would leave the town at sunrise and go back to their domain in the hills. Not everyone in Longford knew of their existence. Not everyone who knew welcomed it.

Perhaps he is tired, or grief is blurring his vision, but he does not see the soldier until he almost trips over her. She is sitting by a tree, and when she sees him she lets out a small cry of surprise, and then a grunt of fear. She kicks backwards and away from him, bringing her gun up and aiming it at his face.

She is the same height as him, slightly built, and her camouflage gear is grubby and stained, her face streaked with sweat and dirt. She looks very tired.

Very scared.

"No," the boy says. It is the first word he has uttered since fleeing Longford.

"Who are you? Stay there. Don't move." She quickly gathers herself and is now in charge, her weapon aimed unwaveringly at his chest.

"What's happening?" the boy asks. *I have to get away,* he thinks. *I have to be sleek.* He does not trust this soldier one bit. She's alone, and flustered, but she's one of them. For all he knows this gun might have shot his mother.

"Let me see your tongue," she says. "Stick it out. All the way."

The boy does so. She squints, looks close, then nods. He closes his mouth.

"What's your name?"

"Robert Bonham," he mutters. He looks left and right, past the tree she's got her back to. He's afraid that others will be close by, and he remembers the shooting he heard, the lines of silver-clad people driving all the living things before them. The bloodied fox. Lucas the mad puppy.

"Eh? Speak up."

He mutters his name again. This part of being sleek,

of being unknown and unseen, is almost instinctive. The soldier frowns and turns her head, leaning in closer.

"Eh? Bone? That your name? Bone?"

Bone, the boy thinks, and then he runs. He dashes towards the soldier and then steps left, sleeking past and darting behind the tree, up the slope, jigging left and right and waiting every moment for the bullet that will take him down.

There is no bullet. There is no gunshot.

With his new name intact, Bone escapes.

Three days later something else changes. The river, running almost dry for the past few weeks, surges back into the valley with a roar. Its path is now blocked by the massive construction that has been worked on day and night, and when it strikes the structure damming the valley it boils and churns, white water turning dark with mud, dark as blood. From his vantage point high in the hollow oak tree, the boy can see ant-like figures scurrying around both ends of the dam, watching as the river flows, flows, and rises.

He stays there for another three days. When the water rises enough to start flooding the streets of Longford, he turns his back on that place and finally walks away. He crests the ridge above the wide valley that was his home, and even as the drowning town drops out of sight behind him Bone will not allow himself to cry.

* * *

Life becomes complex and dangerous, as does Bone.

The first time he returns to the valley is nineteen years after he left. He knows what he will find because he has followed the story of Longford, both the faked public version and the more elusive truth. He is surprised to discover the old oak is still there. He cannot fit inside now, but he shines a torch into the hollow, amazed at how small it seems. There's nothing to reveal that he once made this place his home.

He climbs the outside of the tree instead, and perches on a branch close to the crack in the trunk from which he watched, afraid and alone, all those years ago.

Bone sits and watches for quite some time. It's very peaceful in the valley, as if it has always been this way. Much like him, the reservoir presents a calm surface, hiding the potential for endless chaos beneath.

The next time he returns, another twenty years into the future, that chaos will rise.

2

She flows across this land that she has made her home.

The creature she seeks is down near the valley floor, bathing in a pool and treating its wounds. She has met this one three times since closing the Fold—she no longer acknowledges their names, because now they are simply prey. When it senses her approach it will know what is to come, and she hopes that it will panic and flee, darting away across the landscape seeking somewhere to hide, even though it knows there is nowhere. She hopes, but she is not sure. Even now some of the Kin she brought here are becoming passive in the face of their eternal fate. It isn't what she sought. A fairy needs stimulation, not wan compliance. She craves the hunt.

Grace's new home is not what she intended.

Because of them, she thinks. *They're the reason. They taint the air.*

She runs down a steep grassed slope, leaping over rocks and vaulting a low stone wall one of the others has been building. When she arrives at the pool the bathing creature turns its head, and she is upon it before it can splash its way to the water's edge.

Grace drives it beneath the surface, following it down through the weedy water, pressing it to the pond's bed and then closing her mouth around its shoulder.

The creature squeals in bubbles. Grace bites and twists. A chunk of Kin flesh warms her mouth, blood mixing with dirty water to pour down her throat, and she lets the creature go and surfaces with her raw prize clamped between her teeth.

Sitting beside the pond, Grace chews and watches the creature drag itself onto the opposite bank. It casts a glance across at her, both angry and scared. Then it stands and staggers away into the trees, seeking somewhere dark and quiet to let its wound heal once more.

Never somewhere secret, though. This is her Fold, and she knows every inch of the place. There are no secrets here.

Perhaps that is one of its failings.

She enjoys the sunlight on her skin and her mind wanders, as is its wont, to other skies and more distant times...

The ancient and vast woodlands of Europe, where she and her kind lived for millennia and their interaction with the humans of the time was a source of enjoyment and competition. They were gods or demons, friends or enemies, and sometimes all of those things at the same time. They saw respect and fear in human eyes, and in the monuments built to them they witnessed the base need of humanity to believe in something greater than itself, no matter whether that thing was good or evil. They played on this, and preyed on it. It was a time of plenty. An era of joy.

There are too many humans now. The gods and demons they pander to are too ethereal.

Grace chews and swallows, feeling the strength and heat from the meat coursing through her ancient body and invigorating her senses. After finishing her meal and picking scraps from between her teeth with long nails she walks along the valley floor, knowing where she is heading but in no rush to get there. Something draws her to the Nephilim. She will never speak with him. She could kill him, but he is not a Kin she brought here by choice, and to do so would be to admit that she made mistakes. Besides, she likes him where he is. He sought to command and control her. She enjoys turning the tables on the fool.

She remembers Mallian from the Time, a young creature, as impetuous then as now. They are all still young to her, like children, playthings, hers to control... she wishes... she thinks she might have...

The fairy sighs deeply and takes hold of her mind. It drifts so much now, old thing that it is. Sometimes it wanders so far that she worries she might never drag it back. On occasion she fears that much of it has already escaped the gravity of her being, and that the mind she has left is a congregation of random memories, thought shards, and glimpses of things she once knew. She feels herself slipping away. This place is an attempt to hold onto everything she has left, keep herself together. But it is not perfect.

Summiting a small rise, she looks down on one of the reasons for its imperfections.

Mallian the Nephilim is on the valley floor, arms and legs held fast as they have been since the moment she cast him down. Some time has passed since that confrontation, but Grace does not know how long, nor does she care. The passage of time no longer holds much meaning for her.

He is thin and gaunt, his once-strong body withered. She has never eaten of him. She did not bring him here, and to take a bite of his treacherous flesh would be to honour him too much. Better to see him trapped down there, suffering in the knowledge that everything he dreamt of has come to nothing.

Elsewhere in the Fold, not too far from here, the human lives in a cave. Sometimes he feeds the Nephilim, and Grace finds amusement in the strange bond that has grown between the two of them. She lets them have that.

She could kill them both, but their blood would taint the soil. For now she is happy to ignore them most of the time. They are no threat to her.

Nothing is a threat to her. Her mind is too great...
My mind is in shards.
She is too strong, too sure of her own strength and future...
I'm weaker than I have ever been.

She has everything she wants in here with her...
Except her. *I saw fairy in her.*

The memory of the girl is the one aspect of the world beyond the Fold that refuses to let go. Grace is miles and universes away from the world, but the scent of the girl's flesh, the look in her eye, forms a bridge between her old world and this Folded Land. If Grace could break the bridge, she would.

If she could bring the girl here, nurture her fairy blood, and make her an eternal companion... that would be better.

That would make her already long life, and the eternity still to come, complete.

3

Each morning Angela would wake from a nightmare. She rarely remembered them—that was a blessing, at least—but her sheets were always tangled, her skin damp and hot with nervous perspiration, and sometimes her throat was sore, her eyes stinging, as if she had been shouting and crying in her sleep. If that were the case, Sammi never commented. Sammi was a good kid.

Today was the same. She was used to the sense of rising from somewhere deep and dark, and feeling only mild relief at waking into the real world. The grimness of her nightmares, their dark echoes, accompanied her into the day. It felt so unfair having her mood determined by bad dreams. Plenty about her life felt unfair.

Angela sat on the edge of her narrow wooden cot, rested her elbows on her knees, and looked down at the floor. She was all too familiar with the joints, cracks and knots in the floorboards. Sometimes she looked at the dark lines of the joins and wondered what lay beneath them. The truth was, it was simply the crawlspace beneath the cabin, too narrow for her to enter, home to insects and spiders and perhaps snakes. Nowadays she spent a lot of time looking at familiar objects and spaces—fallen trees, turns in forest paths, dark crevasses in piles of rocks—and wondering what might be beyond.

These were the creatures and places that gave her nightmares and haunted her waking hours.

"Sammi!" she shouted. She knew her niece would be awake and out of bed. She usually saw in the dawn, and sometimes she was already gone from the small cabin when Angela rose. She tried not to feel concerned when this happened. Sammi needed to explore and exist in a world that was anything but safe. Keeping her constrained and wrapped in cotton wool would benefit neither of them.

"Coffee's already on!" Sammi replied from beyond the door.

Angela smiled. She rubbed her face, trying to wipe away the dregs of her nightmares. Although she recalled nothing of her dreams, they dragged her down. Old memories circled her. She could feel the stare of the Kin on the back of her neck. She could almost taste Vince on her lips, and feel the ghost of his hand in hers.

He had been gone for two years, but she would never forget his taste or touch. He was as known to her now as he ever had been, as if her sleep renewed her memories of him and made them fresh again. If the price of that was a gloom hanging over the beginning of each day, it was a price she was happy to pay.

"Lovely day, sunny and cool," Sammi said when Angela walked into the living room. She sat down on a tatty sofa and took the steaming mug Sammi offered, closing her eyes and sighing as she breathed in the coffee, groaning in delight when she took the first taste. For someone who did not like hot drinks, the girl sure made a good cup of Joe.

"I'm going for a walk up to the waterfalls," Sammi said.

"Don't forget we're looking at *Lord of the Flies* again later."

"Aww, Angela." There it was. The teenage drawl. And Angela loved it. It was a normality she had despaired Sammi ever finding.

"It's a great book!"

"It's *boring*!"

"How can you possibly find it boring?"

Sammi was smirking a little as she turned away and went back into the kitchen, and Angela almost called her on it. She knew she was being played. Sammi was the brightest girl she had ever known, and sometimes Angela felt it was her doing the learning and Sammi the teaching.

"Want some scrambled eggs?" Sammi asked.

"Sure. I'll fetch some eggs."

"I'll get them. You're old." Sammi darted from the kitchen and through the front door before Angela could respond and disappeared around the side of the cabin.

Angela leaned back on the sofa and sighed. She wasn't old, but sometimes she felt it. Playing happy families was ageing both of them. They'd spoken about it very openly—about how trying to make things feel normal was the only way to move on—but there was always a falseness to acting like this that remained as an underlying tension beneath and behind every chirpy conversation and light-hearted exchange. Two years might be long enough to begin moving on from loss, but the losses they had both suffered were not so simple to confront.

However much people tried to convince Angela that Vince was gone forever, she did not know for sure that he was dead. In her mind—and perhaps in those deep, dark dreams that bled into and tainted her waking hours—he was still there.

Jay had shown them to this cabin after the confrontation with Mallian and the fairy, the closing of the Fold, and the fighting and killing that had surrounded those events. Jay's Kin lover Tah had died, and Angela would not have blamed the older woman if she'd handed her and Sammi over to the law. She knew that Angela was still wanted by the authorities for her supposed part in the massacre in London, and that would always be the case. Yet Jay still sometimes came to visit, and she did her best to persuade Angela that Vince was never coming back.

Lilou, too. The nymph had suffered her own loss when she'd seen her old friend Mallian swallowed up by the Fold. She had betrayed Mallian, desperate for his plotting of Ascent—an aggressive revelation of the Kin to the human world—to fail before it had begun. She had acted for the good of the Kin, the good of humanity, and out of her own strong beliefs that revealing the Kin to the world would lead only to conflict, pain and death. Still troubled by her actions, each time they met she also tried to persuade Angela that she would never see Vince again.

Angela knew that they were both right. Vince was universes away, trapped in a whole new place and time created by the fairy Grace.

Sometimes she wished that he was dead. She hated herself for thinking this, but the constant not knowing was so much harder.

Hiding, living a lie, their lives on hold, she and Sammi had grown closer than they ever would have if none of this had happened. That at least was a silver lining. She knew that a time would come when they would have to re-evaluate their situation and face the future with a more solid plan, but she was good at persuading herself they should wait another few weeks.

Angela looked through the steam from her coffee mug, out the open front door and into the woods. She had always been a city person, but now she loved the wild, relished the wilderness. She went running most days, and she and Sammi often kayaked along the nearby river. The woods here were vast and beautiful, and she was discovering places where people might never have been before.

It was all a placeholder. She and Sammi both knew that their lives would have to move on one of these days.

Just another few weeks, she thought. *Just a little while longer.*

Sammi appeared in the doorway with several eggs in her hands. She smiled at Angela and went through to the kitchen, then glanced back into the living room.

"Someone's coming," she said.

"Huh?" Angela sat up and spilled coffee onto her T-shirt.

"Down the valley. They're walking, and they'll be here soon."

Angela didn't ask how Sammi knew this. There were things about the girl that didn't add up, and she did her best not to confront them. Since being struck by lightning twice and taken into the fairy's Fold, Sammi had displayed talents and tendencies that had not been evident before, as far as she knew. Angela was ready when she wanted to talk about it, but she would not bring it up herself. That felt like too delicate a barrier to break.

"Jay, do you think?"

"No. I think it's her."

Angela knew who she meant, and she felt a prickling of anger and resentment. She welcomed it because it was a real feeling, a true sensation, as if she really was still alive and back in the world. Lilou was the reason she and Vince had been pulled into the world of the Kin in the first place.

"Do you think she'll want some eggs as well?" Sammi asked.

"I'm sure she will." She smiled. After everything

Sammi had seen and endured, kindness shone through. Angela felt she could learn a lot from that.

Ten minutes later a figure appeared at the end of the lane leading into the woods. Angela recognised Lilou's walk, her natural grace stiffened with caution. The nymph had to be careful among humans so that her charms did not overwhelm them. She'd seen Lilou a few times since the closing of the Fold, and lately she seemed slower than before, weighed down. Perhaps she was growing old.

Angela had never asked her age, but knew it ran into centuries.

"Changed your hair," Lilou said as she approached the cabin.

"Again."

"I like it short."

"Thanks."

"Want some scrambled eggs, Lilou?" Sammi called from the kitchen window.

"Hello, Sammi! And yes please, that sounds great."

"What brings you here?" Angela asked.

Lilou stopped a dozen steps from her, perspiring lightly from the walk up through the wooded valley to the escarpment where the old cabin sat. The lane was steep in places, and rocky, and only navigable by car using a four-wheel drive. Jay had bought them the old Jeep that was parked beside the cabin. Angela only used it once a week to go into the nearest town seven miles away to buy groceries. They were isolated here, and that was how she liked it.

Lilou stared at her for a while, not replying. Sammi started singing in the kitchen, a modern pop song she'd picked up from the radio. It was something about love and dancing, things Sammi had not experienced and rarely done. *Just a few more weeks*, Angela thought again.

"I wanted to see you both," Lilou said. "It's been a while."

"Six months."

"You're keeping okay? Both of you?"

Angela looked around at their beautiful, wild surroundings. It wasn't really an answer.

"How about you?" Angela asked. "What have you been doing?" Lilou wiped a sheen of perspiration from her face, and Angela sighed. "Come and sit down." Her voice was softer, and Lilou's gratitude was obvious.

"Thank you."

They sat together on the wooden bench outside the front of the cabin, and moments later Sammi emerged and gave Lilou a friendly hug. It made Angela feel awkward, wondering whether she should have done the same. Sammi's good nature and kindness often put her to shame. Sometimes in a kid of her age such behaviour was born of innocence and naivety, but Sammi was neither. She'd seen and done more things before her mid teens than most people do in a lifetime.

"You smell," Sammi said.

"Thanks."

"Like you've been living wild."

Lilou shrugged and glanced at Angela.

"Coffee?" Sammi asked.

"I would fight and kill a grizzly bear for coffee," Lilou said.

"I'd watch that!" Sammi said, darting back inside. "Though my money wouldn't be on the bear."

"Great kid," Lilou said quietly as Sammi continued singing.

"She is."

"She can't stay here forever."

"She won't!"

"Neither can you."

"What do you expect me to do, Lilou? If I get arrested, what happens to Sammi? And is this really why you came here? Couldn't we just pass the time of day first?"

"No, no," Lilou said. "I came here to see you both, and to ask..." She trailed off. It wasn't like her to be uncertain, even vulnerable. Angela had seen that more in Lilou since the Fold, and especially since Frederick Meloy had sacrificed himself to help them escape. It had been obvious to anyone that Meloy was in love with Lilou. What hadn't been so clear was that perhaps she was also fond of him. He'd been big and brash, a brutal man who'd found his calling in the Kin, but he'd also possessed an almost childlike quality, an innocence that might have drawn Lilou to him.

Angela observed, but didn't care enough to ask. Vince had worked for Meloy as a relic hunter, and saving Lilou from brutal thugs and murderers had been the catalyst for everything that had happened since. It was unreasonable to blame them, but she had to direct her blame somewhere. Grief and anger were not a good combination to carry around.

"Ask what?" Angela said. Sammi emerged then with coffee and a bowl of scrambled eggs and some toast on a tray. She dashed back in to grab forks and plates, and the hot sauce she knew Angela liked.

"I'm asking something of you both," Lilou said, and they waited until Sammi pulled up a folding chair and joined them. "It's a favour. I want you to come to Massachusetts with me."

"Why would we do that?" Angela asked. "We're safe here, unknown and—"

"Are you?"

"Yes."

Sammi looked back and forth between them, eating her eggs. She was sharp. She'd pick up on Angela's anger, and Lilou's unusual vulnerability.

"You've been in the same place for too long," Lilou said. "I've been keeping watch, especially for the past couple of months."

"Keeping watch on us?"

"Partly, but also on people in the surrounding communities. There's a man who runs long distances through these hills sometimes, and he says he's seen lightning balls chasing him in the forest."

Angela glanced at Sammi, who was looking down at her eggs. A brief, tense silence was all she offered. She knew that Sammi was changing, and Sammi knew that she knew. *I have to talk to her about all this one day,* she thought.

"There's a place I need to go," Lilou said. "I think you should come too."

"You can't even drive," Sammi said.

Lilou shrugged. "Never was much need for it in London."

"Do any Kin drive?"

"Of course they do."

"Wow. Even if they can fly?"

"But why ask us?" Angela said. "It's not like you need us. We're only humans."

Lilou ignored the barbed comment. "You've shut yourself away up here. I'm spending my time wandering the wilds, hundreds of miles a month, after so long constrained in London. So in a way we're both aimless. It'll do you good, and I could... I need the company. It's a long way to travel alone. And you know I'm not at my best among people."

"What is this place?" Angela asked. Lilou's comments about watching out for them troubled her, but not as much as what she'd seen and heard. Whispers about her and Sammi would grow into rumours, and rumours stuck. Soon they might have people driving out to watch them from the woods.

After that, strangers knocking at their door. Clips on the internet. People seeing her face who knew how to see past cut and coloured hair and contact lenses—like the British police whose Most Wanted list she likely still topped.

"It's a valley," Lilou said. "There was a town there a long time ago called Longford. Something happened there, and the town was abandoned and the valley flooded. Now it's drained again. The dam ruptured, the water's lowered, the remains of the town have been revealed."

"Why does this interest you?" Sammi asked.

"Because there were Kin there," Angela said.

"There were. And I lost an old friend when the disaster happened," Lilou said.

"What was the disaster?" Angela asked.

"Contagion." Lilou shrugged. "The official story is that there was a disease outbreak that killed most of the townsfolk. They cleared the town and flooded the valley. But there are other tales about what happened."

"Your friend died there?" Sammi asked.

"What was he or she?" Angela asked, and it was the question that cut to the root of the conversation.

"Mohserran was a selkie," Lilou said. "I haven't seen him for over a hundred years, maybe more, and he hasn't been seen since the valley was flooded. Yes, he probably died there along with two other Kin, one of whom might even have been from the Time, but no one knows for sure. And I need to go, because there aren't so many of us left that we can ignore three who are missing and might not be dead."

Sammi left her aunt and Lilou talking outside the cabin and went for a walk into the woods. She liked going up to the waterfalls, and she loved pretending that she was the only human who had ever seen them. There was nothing to indicate that was not true. They were wild and untamed, and when she was there she felt in control of herself. Lately, it was one of the few places she did.

At the cabin with Angela and Lilou—and often when it was just her and Angela—she had to work harder and harder to control the pressures building inside. She smiled and joked, joined in the conversations, provided a light response to Angela's worried, dark tone, and all the while her mind pulsed with constrained possibilities, and her senses thrummed with things she should not see, sense, smell.

She knew that Angela perceived these changes in her, and that the fairy's interest in her had been the first warning sign. She also knew that her aunt respected her enough to let her discover her own self. That, or maybe she wished to deny her niece's growing strangeness.

When her mom was alive, Sammi had been a normal little girl. When it was just her and her father, surviving together had taken most of her strength, distracting her from the unusual feelings she had, the strange thoughts that affected her dreams and sometimes followed into her waking hours.

Now that she was an orphan, Sammi felt the full gravity of that secret she kept inside drawing her in. Being struck by the fairy's lightning had awoken it. Being touched by Grace, looking into her eyes and seeing a reflection of her own, had allowed it release.

Sometimes the pressure needed venting. That was why she liked walking in the woods on her own, and at the waterfalls she felt secluded enough to let herself go.

Today the pressures were greater than ever. Lilou's presence often brought them on, because she knew more about Sammi than Angela. The nymph had never been overt about it, but on those few occasions she had visited them in the cabin Sammi had caught Lilou glancing at her with a strange look in her eyes. It might have been curiosity, and sometimes it might have been fear.

The woods were peaceful today, and as Sammi approached the waterfalls she sensed that she was the only person for miles around. The sounds of the falls drew her in, a whisper in the distance, a grumble, and then a roar as she entered the narrow ravine and negotiated the wet rocky path along the side of the stream. The falls were maybe ten metres high, a series of tumbles and splashes rather than a straight drop. Sometimes she was lucky enough to catch a smear of rainbow colours in the mist, but today the sun had yet to penetrate the ravine. The water fell in shadow, and if she listened hard enough, she thought she could hear ancient voices of the wild whispering lost secrets beneath its roar.

Sammi sat on a rock she knew well, far enough above the stream and pool to avoid getting wet, close enough to feel the cool kiss of mist against her skin. She closed her eyes and breathed in deeply, smelling the innocent tang of forest water. Deeper down were scents of older things. She could not identify them, but she knew that they were secrets. She felt a tingle of excitement and fear at their smells, as if she'd been offered a brief glimpse behind the veil of reality.

They are reality, she thought. *As am I, whatever I'm becoming.*

Such thoughts frightened her. Becoming something more was drawing her away from the life she knew, even though that life had changed so much over the past couple of years. She feared the idea of her mom and dad fading in her memory, part of the story of someone so different from her that they became strangers. That frightened her so much. Yet she was also aware that she had little choice in the change, and the excitement was too much to ignore.

Sammi held out one hand and opened her eyes. Her fingers tingled, and the quicks of her fingernails sizzled and glowed. Arcs of electricity danced between her fingertips. Across her left forearm and bicep she saw the fernlike trail of subtle scars from the lightning strikes two years before begin to emerge once again. Back then they might have been a map, but now she knew that they were more a guide to her emerging self than a particular place.

As the electricity danced and spat, she raised her hand and urged it to form together. The resultant lightning ball fell from her hand and bounced from the rock at her feet, drifting slowly towards the pool, throwing up a hiss of steam as it struck the surface, and then disappearing below.

The sense of release was immense. The lightning ball was all her stresses combined—the effort of hiding herself behind a smiling mask; the fear at what she was becoming; the grief at what she might leave behind. Sitting by those roaring falls she became someone else for a little while, and her human concerns faded away as the sparking electricity diluted itself through the violent waters.

She became the Sammi she would one day be.

4

This might have been Vince's hundredth time walking around the edge of the Fold. It usually took him a whole day, with a few stops to pick berries and nuts or eat scraps of food he took with him. He tried to make every walk slightly different. Today, the sun beat at his back as he walked along what might have been the eastern ridge above the valley. Some days the same ridge appeared more like the northern extreme. The sun rose and fell, the dark skies were speckled with stars he did not know, and there seemed to be no patterns to any of it.

The only certainty was that there was no escape.

He strode along the hilltop with the Fold spread out across the valley to his left. From this high up he could make out familiar landscapes and features. The winding river was one of the constants, its path cast into the rock of the land, water always flowing in the same direction. Where it came from, where it went, he did not know. Trying to follow the river presented him with the same problems as attempting to leave the Fold in any other direction. Past the river towards the other side of the valley were the rocky slopes where he had made his home. There were several caves there, and he had taken the shallowest and smallest for his own. Deeper, darker caves were home to other things. He saw the woodland that smothered the head of the large valley, the sharp escarpment and cliffs that provided a distant boundary, and somewhere down on the valley floor lay Mallian.

He was too far away to see, and Vince was not interested in looking.

After so long, his clothes were beginning to fail. He washed them weekly in one of the small streams tumbling through the gnarly landscape around his cave, laying them out in the sun to dry, but the hard living and the rigours of foraging and fending for himself were taking their toll. His jeans had worn at the crotch, and several rips on the legs were fraying and growing worse. His T-shirt was weakening at the seams. His boots and socks were worn, underwear threadbare, and the light jacket he'd been wearing when he was trapped in the Fold had gone missing days after his arrival. He sometimes thought he saw a fleeting figure wearing the jacket—one of the Kin the fairy had brought here— but he had never managed to get close enough to see for sure.

He had made a coat of rabbit furs in anticipation of winter, but true winter never came.

He reached what he judged to be the highest point of the hill and took a good look around. It was a warm day and a refreshing breeze swept past him as he looked down into the valley that had become his home. The wind came from behind him, from beyond the valley, and carried scents he could not identify. He did not understand that. Like the river, it showed signs of starting and ending beyond the Fold. But that could not be.

Vince had lost count of how many times he'd attempted this, but he had to try again. Trying was what kept him moving, and alive. Not trying would be to give up.

Turning his back on the valley, he walked across the exposed hilltop and then started down with the breeze in his face, moving away from the Fold and the wide basin. He had never done this in this exact place, although he recognised some of his surroundings from previous attempts. *Maybe this is the time I find the chink in the Fold*, he thought, and despite his failure every previous time, his heart beat a little faster at the possibility. The landscape was vast and stretched for miles into the distance, with no visible barrier and no indication that his whole world now consisted of one large valley that it took a day to circumnavigate. He saw hills and rivers and lakes, all of them *beyond*, and he was careful not to take his eye off them.

I've seen them all before, I know they're not in the Fold.

There was no point at which he sensed a change. One moment he was descending a steep slope towards a landscape he did not know, the next he was heading back down into the Fold. He could see the river following its familiar twisting route, the rocky terrain where his cave waited for him, the woodlands in the north. He did not feel his direction alter, nor his perception of where he was heading. It would almost have been better if he had felt a dizziness, and a sense that his reality was being changed and distorted. Better than this. Better than knowing for sure there was no escape.

It wasn't at all like being turned around or misled. It was simply as if this was the whole world, and there was nowhere else to go.

Disappointed once again, he walked back down into the valley. It was there that his day changed. It had been some time since he'd witnessed Grace hunting, but now he saw the results of one of her attacks.

The Kin was cowering beneath a tree at the edge of a small pool in the woods. Vince had chosen to walk back towards his cave through the woods because he wanted to collect some berries, and to see if any of the small snares he'd set had caught something more substantial he might cook. The valley was home to rabbits and voles, as well as a species of flightless bird he had not been able to identify. So far it was only rabbits he had been able to catch. The other creatures seemed aware of him and his intentions, and he was worried that the rabbits would eventually grow more cautious too. There was fruit and some nuts, and a few of the roots he'd dug up were palatable, if not pleasant to eat. But he must already have lost thirty pounds since he'd become trapped in the Fold. If he started losing out on an occasional meat meal, he feared he would waste away.

He wasn't sure what the Kin was that sat hunkered and moaning beneath the tree. He thought he'd seen it before from a distance, although most of those in the Fold kept themselves to themselves. He sometimes spoke to a few, but never to this one. It was small, slight, and it might have been graceful if it wasn't twisted by pain. It was holding onto its shoulder and keening, rocking back and forth and pressing its hand to a terrible wound.

It would heal. They all healed, in time for Grace to make a meal of them again.

Vince moved out of the trees and started walking around the pond. The ground was marshy and his boots sank in, stinking water seeping inside. He kept his eye on the Kin, watching to check its reaction, ready to turn and run the other way if it seemed at all threatening. He didn't think it was. After a long time living in the Fold, he had only had cause to fear the Kin a couple of times, and he believed that both times were his fault.

Vince wasn't sure just how long he had been shut away in this place. No two days felt the same length, and there was little other way of marking the passage of time. His phone had ceased working a day after he was trapped here, and his watch followed thirty hours later, battery bleeding dry. He'd started trying to track the passing days by scratching marks on the cave wall, but he'd forgotten a day or two, then forgotten that he'd forgotten, and then one day had felt like six. After that he saw little point.

Months, for sure. Probably a year or two. Every single day of his confinement—a natural day or one extended by the Fold's strange physics—he thought of Angela, and he mourned for her because he was becoming more certain day by day that he would never see her again. The Fold was somewhere else.

All of which made trying to find his way back the only thing that kept him alive. He'd come to believe that communicating with the Kin might be the only chance he had.

As he approached the wounded creature he started whispering, as if talking in subdued tones to a wounded animal. "There, don't worry, I won't hurt you, just coming close to see if I can—"

The Kin hissed. Vince froze, still ten metres away, ready to turn and run. He thought it was female, her body wiry and strong. And covered in scars. He wondered how many times Grace had hunted her and taken her down, biting a chunk of meat from her body before letting her limp or crawl away. What would that do to a mind?

"I only want to help," he said, holding his hands out.

"Fuck off, human." Her voice was deeper than he'd anticipated, a heavy growl rattling like stones in a tin.

"Why can't she eat you? Huh? You got some sort of agreement with her? Some arrangement?"

Vince shook his head. *No agreement, no arrangement*, he thought, but he had often wondered the same thing. Why didn't Grace bite chunks out of him?

The only reason he could think of was that he would not heal.

"Let me have a look at—"

"Fuck *off*, human!" This time the Kin moved, shifting from vulnerable and wounded to vicious in the blink of an eye. She crouched on all fours and faced up to him like a wild dog, ready to leap and take a chunk out of him. The wound on her shoulder and upper arm was red-raw, still bleeding and horribly deep. Perhaps the wounds, old and new, had driven her mad.

Vince turned and ran away from the pond, into the woods and onto a path he had wandered before. Panting hard, running fast, he didn't look back until he burst from the forest and out onto the grassland across the valley floor. With the river to his left he glanced back and slowed to a jog. The Kin was not following him. He suspected she was still at the pond, content to see him gone and now nursing her wounds once more, keening in pain and grief at what the great fairy had done.

He looked around at the stunning landscape as his heart settled and perspiration cooled on his skin. Grace had certainly ensured that her eternal home was a beautiful one. He wished the injured Kin had allowed him closer. Few of those lured here by Grace ever did, as if the only human here was in part responsible for their predicament. Trying everything he could to escape, gathering as much information as possible, he thought it was only through them that he would finally make his way back to the world.

Lonely, craving company, Vince found himself heading towards the only Kin that he knew for sure would talk to him.

"She doesn't eat you because human flesh tastes like shit." It sounded like Mallian knew what he was talking about, but Vince chose not to pursue that line of conversation. He had merely mentioned the wounded Kin, and the Nephilim's comment made him suspect he could read his mind. After everything that had happened, something so mundane would not surprise him.

"Sometimes I'm not even sure she knows I'm here," Vince said.

"Of course she knows. She just wouldn't demean herself by acknowledging you."

"You do."

"Beggars can't be choosers."

"She hasn't bitten chunks out of you, either."

"She wouldn't dare," Mallian muttered.

"Really? You're not saying that very loud. Afraid she might hear?"

"Huh."

"Maybe she's waiting for you to mature."

They sat in silence for a while, Vince looking down towards the river, Mallian staring up at the sky. It was what the Kin did most days and nights. He had not been able to move since those first few moments in the Fold, when he'd tried casting the glamour that would take the fairy under his control, and she had turned it around and pinned him to the ground. Vince was responsible for that. He had stolen away one of the relics that Gregor, the old relic hunter, had taken half a lifetime to find, and which Mallian had needed for the spell to work.

The Nephilim didn't seem to blame Vince for what he had done. After the Fold closed, it had taken Vince a long time to approach the prone figure, and many days more until they had exchanged their first words. Vince took some comfort from their strained, strange conversations. He suspected that Mallian did too, though he would never admit it.

Lately, Vince had started to wonder how long their talks might continue.

Mallian could not move. His arms and legs were pressed down into the ground. At several places along each splayed arm and leg his patterned, leathery skin was compressed as if by an invisible binding. Vince had watched him attempting to move from a distance, and sometimes when they were talking or simply sharing company the Nephilim writhed and twisted against his unseen, unknowable constraints.

Over time, he was starting to wither away.

"I've got some berries for you," Vince said.

"Oh, wonderful. More berries. Can't you get me a rabbit?"

"None in the snares today."

"None that you're telling me about."

Vince stood and leaned over Mallian, dropping berries into his open mouth from high up. He never went too close. He didn't like the look of those teeth. Mallian always wanted meat, and Vince didn't for a second believe that he would not rip his arm off and chew flesh from bone, given the opportunity.

Mallian munched and swallowed. A quick glance at Vince as he did so was his only sign of gratitude.

"Never thought I'd become vegetarian."

"Lots has changed," Vince said.

"And yet everything remains the same."

Vince frowned and moved away to sit down. It wasn't the first time Mallian had made such a comment, and it troubled Vince. Perhaps it was the nature of the Fold, but he sometimes had a disquieting sense that time was motionless here, not moving on. The Kin lived, moved, ate, slept, and were hunted and feasted upon by Grace. Trees and grasses grew, small mammals, birds and insects lived and died. The river flowed, entering and leaving the Fold in ways he did not understand. Yet there was a stillness to the land. A stagnation, like a held breath or the space between heartbeats.

"I see her, sometimes..." he said, trailing off.

"I see her too."

"No, I mean I see her standing still. In a forest, or along the riverbank, or up on the hillsides. She has her head tilted, as if she's listening or sniffing for something."

"Looking for something else to eat," Mallian said.

"You really think she has to *hunt* for her meals?" Vince asked. "She reaches out and takes what she wants, when she wants."

"It's this place she's created," Mallian said. "There's no forward motion, no change. Nothing degenerates, but nothing grows different, either. Maybe she's searching for change she'll never find."

"You're changing," Vince said.

"I'm dying," Mallian said. The words hung in the air, heavy and loaded, ringing in the sudden silence. The Nephilim snorted and looked away, trying to distance himself from what he'd said.

Vince also looked away, but he wasn't sure why. He had never heard Mallian sound so vulnerable or defeated. He was embarrassed for the Kin, as well as feeling a surprising surge of pity. For a creature so strong and proud, being trapped here like this must be the ultimate nightmare. Vince couldn't kid himself into thinking that he was helping keep Mallian alive. The berries he dropped into his mouth, the occasional chunk of raw meat he caught and fed him, were nothing compared to the fuel he should be imbibing. It had been months or years, and the Nephilim was still alive.

If he was dying, it was because he was losing the will to live.

"Ascent seemed to work really well for you."

"Fuck off, human."

"I'm hearing that a lot today." Vince stood and smiled in Mallian's direction. He didn't expect a smile in return, and he didn't get one, but something about Mallian's expression had softened.

I have to remember who he is.

Vince remembered Mallian crushing people's heads in Mary Rock's house in London.

He wants to expose the Kin to the world.

He was the reason he and Angela were a universe apart.

And in doing so he's happy to risk war.

He might be trapped and withered, defeated and dying, but the Nephilim was still a monster.

"I'll bring meat next time."

"I'll be here."

Vince smiled again and walked away.

Sunset came late that day. The sun hung above the western hills for what seemed like hours, and Vince sat by the small stream just downhill from his cave to watch. He leaned against a fallen tree and dropped off a couple of times, startled awake by a fly landing on his nose, and a loud exuberant call from some indefinable distance. *At least not every Kin here is in pain*, he thought, but he wasn't sure how long that would last. He didn't think that every Kin had fallen prey to Grace yet, but most had. They carried the scars to prove it.

He still felt threatened almost every moment he was awake, and when he slept the dreams were often bad, haunting. In some ways he had learnt to live with the danger. The same had been the case in London when he was collecting relics for Fat Frederick Meloy, until danger had come looking for him. Here in the Fold it was part of every day, and as familiar as the air he breathed.

That didn't mean he did not try to avoid danger. It simply meant that he built his life around it.

As the sun finally touched the hills he contemplated the view for the hundredth time. For some reason the Fold enjoyed gorgeous sunsets most days, and Vince saw every one of them. They were all different. They were all impossible. The world beyond the ridge line around the valley did not exist. There were no distant lands being touched by this same sun. There was no dark and light in the Fold, only dark *or* light. It was as perplexing as trying to consider where the river began and ended.

Eyelids drooping again, Vince vowed to one day drop a stick into the river close to where it entered the Fold, then wait to see if it was swept out the other side and in again where he sat.

But what about the air? he thought. *What about the*

sky, if I were able to jump up and fly like a couple of the Kin? What about the ground if I decided to start digging down like Dastion the tunnelling dwarf?

His new home was as enigmatic as infinity.

With dusk falling at last he retreated to his cave and lit the fires. He had become adept at surviving in the wild, and it only took him a couple of minutes to spark an ember alight and coax it into flame. Every time he did so he experienced a thrill, because fire meant warmth and safety. It meant that he was surviving.

With the fires lit, he retreated into his small cave. It was cool in there, the heavy air always hidden from the sun and daylight. It smelled like air never stirred by life, and never felt against skin. He had found places like this in London, deep below ground or in buildings abandoned for years or decades. Back there, he'd always found a way home.

Near the rear of the cave he knelt down and uncovered the rucksack. It had travelled far in its lifetime, tracking back and forth across the globe on the shoulders of the Kin-killer Gregor. He in turn had been killed by Mallian, the master he had served. A fitting, gruesome end.

Sometimes when Vince looked through the contents of the rucksack, he wondered if he had saved the world.

Some of the items were recognisable, most were not. Some obviously belonged inside a body, not without. Whereas before he would have been excited about such a haul, now they chilled him to the core.

Along with the relic he had stolen away and left back in the world, these were the items that had so nearly given Mallian control over the fairy Grace.

Things would have been very different if that had happened.

I might still be with Angela, he thought, but he might also be in a world where humans and Kin were facing up to each other. He knew Mallian as well as any human being, perhaps as well as some Kin. The Nephilim would have never backed down from a fight.

He still could not quite work out why the fairy had allowed him to retain the relics. Perhaps she had been mixed up and confused by Mallian's attempts at control. Or maybe once the Fold had closed for good, she realised that she had won.

Mallian certainly seemed to accept that he had lost.

"I might have saved the world," Vince muttered as he looked down at the relics, and the whole idea felt ridiculous. He was so far away from the world that he would never know.

5

After almost half a century alive, Bone was presented with an opportunity he'd thought he would never have. He'd have to do his best to not fuck it up.

He found it whilst performing a regular search online. He made the search so often that he tapped in the name and hit the necessary links almost without thinking. Foo Fighters were playing through his speaker, he was into his second glass of wine of the evening, and within the next hour a woman called Jayne would arrive. They had been messaging each other for a few days, and the previous day it was her who'd cut out the bullshit and posed the question: So shall we meet for some fun?

It was the sort of interaction Bone liked. Some text flirting, a few photos, then meeting for a fuck. If it went well and they liked each other he might suggest another meeting or two, but then he'd cut it off. He didn't want a relationship. He'd been there and done that, and falling in love with someone hadn't suited him. Ten years ago he'd had his heart broken, and like any scar tissue, when it mended it was knotted and raw.

He entered "Longford" into the search, hit matches

from the past seven days, and then sipped at his glass of wine. He was looking forward to Jayne's arrival. She liked red wine, she said, and rock music, and she insisted they use protection. He was a careful person, and he respected such caution in other people.

Another place, another time, perhaps they might have become lovers.

She can never know me for real, he thought. *I hardly know myself.* The same went for all of the women he met through dating sites. Most were looking for the same as him—a bit of companionship for an evening, and then no-ties sex. Some sought a little more, but they quickly understood where his boundaries lay. It was a superficial life, a cheap way of meeting partners for sex, but he justified it to himself because it went both ways. The women he met were strong and confident, seeking their own way through life just like him.

He finished his wine and went to pour another glass. Distant though he was from the world of stable relationships, Bone still really liked sex, and he was looking forward to this evening. Even in their brief text exchanges he and Jayne had hit it off, and he was anticipating a fun, adventurous night.

Glass filled, he walked back to the computer and scanned the search results. Usually the search brought a series of old articles about Longford, and perhaps an occasional photo or two of the wide, still reservoir, its surface calm, its secrets long-forgotten by almost anyone.

Today, there was a hit.

"Old Town Revealed as Earth Dam Ruptures", the headline read. There was one photograph, grainy and from a distance as if taken with a poor camera phone. It showed a uniform grey landscape he did not recognise, surrounded by a border of wooded hillsides he knew only too well.

"Holy fuck," he muttered, and the wine glass slipped through his fingers. It smashed as it hit the wooden floor, splashing wine across his bare feet and jeans. He didn't notice. His mind was in the past, his perception drawn in and afraid, and the sense of threat that had accompanied him all through his life became even more heightened.

His phone pinged as a text came through. It was from Jayne, a promise about what she was going to do to him. He sent her a short apologetic response, then dialled another number.

"Jordan," the voice said, curt and cold.

"I need the Longford job," he said.

She fell silent for a while, and he imagined the security procedures she was initiating—phone tracing, call recording, voice analysis. He didn't care because he had nothing to hide. Or not much, at least, and the things he did hide were deep, deep down.

"Who the fuck is this?"

"Bone."

"How did you get my number, Bone?"

He smiled as he scanned more reports on the computer. "Really?"

"*I'm* supposed to call *you* if you're needed."

"Jordan, you think I've worked for you this long without wanting to know a little more about you than your name?"

More silence.

"I'm at home," Bone said. "I'll put you on camera phone if you want, just to make sure."

"No need," she said. "I can see where you are."

"So I'm getting this job?"

"What makes you think there *is* a job?"

"Come on," Bone said. "I'm looking at it now. It's all over the net." He had to keep his voice level, not let his eagerness take hold too much. Whenever he thought about Longford some of his caution lifted and emotions took hold. He had to be careful that didn't show through.

No one knew where he was from. Not even Jordan.

"Why are you so interested?" she asked.

"Our esteemed military ancestors infected the population with some weird virus called Kovo," he said. "It drove them mad. The authorities gassed them, buried the truth, flooded the valley. And there were rumours of 'strange creatures in the hills'."

He heard Jordan's slight intake of breath. Sometimes he felt almost sorry for her, because he knew how much she would love to get her hands on a live Kin. That's what her department was for, and why he worked for them. It was also why he kept his biggest secret to himself. The few times he'd found a real live Kin on an assignment, he had let it go. He sometimes fed a few old relics through to Jordan, just so that she didn't think he was totally useless, but by working for the government outfit committed to discovering the truth about the Kin, he was best placed to keep their existence a secret. He was their buffer between maintained secrecy and discovery.

He knew what their discovery would mean. Persecution. Vivisection. Annihilation.

He did this for himself and for his father, and now he had a chance to return home.

"You think they might really have been there?" she asked, as open and candid as he'd ever heard her. He didn't reply. Silence was the great prompter, even for someone like Jordan who played chess in every conversation she had. It took maybe thirty seconds.

"Okay," she said. "It's yours. I'll email you the details. I doubt there'll be much to find, but if there are any relics there, they'll need retrieving. Usual protocol— you're on point, and anything needs attending to, you report back to me through the usual channels."

"Why don't I just text you?" he said, smiling. He thought perhaps he heard a soft chuckle on the other end of the phone. He'd met Jordan a dozen times, had seen her dedication to her work, and he wondered whether she sometimes sat alone in a darkened hotel room surfing sites similar to those he looked at. It made him sad to think that was the case. He was lonely enough for everyone.

"Just keep your head down, Bone," she said, "and get there fast. The gawkers and treasure hunters will be there soon."

"I'll be there sooner."

"Okay, good. Stay in the shadows."

"Sure. Have a nice evening."

"Nice? I've got to get a new fucking phone and number." She disconnected and Bone dropped his own phone onto the desk.

He breathed in deeply and let his breath out slowly. Longford. He had spent so much of his life travelling that he'd long-since stopped believing that he would ever return home.

A Grey carried everything he needed with him. The tools of his trade were varied, but the heart of Bone's talent lay within him. He used and nurtured the talent he had been born with to be the best that he could be.

Over the past twenty years he had only met two other Greys. The nature of their work meant that meetings were rare, and secrecy was as much a part of their daily lives as eating or breathing. The old man had crossed trails with him on an assignment in Canada fourteen years before, when both of them had been sent to pursue a woman who could allegedly read minds. Nile, the old man, believed she was the result of an accident, a brain trauma that might have left her damaged and different. Bone knew better. He'd let

Nile take the lead, because the older man believed he was wiser, and doing so would mean he was not so wary. It was Bone who found her. She was so obviously in distress, and he'd had only minutes to try and define exactly who or what she was before Nile arrived. In that short time, he managed to establish that she carried blood similar to his own, and did not know.

He told her and sent her on her way. He hoped it would help her understand.

The other Grey he met was called Jodine. At first he'd suspected that they were alike, and he had spent some time on their assignment trying to discern whether she knew as well. Once they'd tracked down their quarry—he was simply a madman, so not significant in Bone's eyes—he'd decided that Jodine was merely someone with an exceptional IQ and physical aptitude. If he'd approached her about his own origins, he would have compromised himself, turning from Grey into a target of the Greys. So they parted ways without him saying anything.

Bone was grey amongst the Greys, inhabiting a deeper level of secrecy than the most secret government organisation. While his peers sought the legendary Kin because they might be dangerous, damaging or potentially viable as weapons for the military or security services, Bone worked with his own secret intact—that he was not entirely human.

His purpose was to find more like him, make sure they knew who or what they were, and let them go.

Bone himself was not sure what he was. He hoped that finding others similar to him might help him to discover himself. All he knew was that Mohserran had not been human, and that non-human blood ran in his own veins. His abilities to slip through shadows, his Greyness—the talent or affliction that his dear lost mother had called his sleek—was something to do with Mohserran.

If only he'd had a chance to ask questions of that strange creature.

Once or twice when he'd tracked down troubled, dangerous Kin, he'd had the feeling that they knew so much more about themselves than they let on. Once, he'd caught and bound a man responsible for several deaths in rural communities across the north-east, his teeth sharp, his eyes strange. Before letting him go, Bone had taken those few quiet minutes to talk to him about what he might be.

The man had not spoken a word, but he smiled as Bone spoke, like an adult listening to a child's innocent, naive take on the world.

Whoever, whatever, wherever the Kin were, if they knew of Bone and his mission, they seemed content to leave him alone. He was helping them, after all.

At the forefront of the government's attempts to find living Kin, he was best placed to ensure they were never found.

He left his current home and headed towards Longford without a single regret. He would probably never return to this place, and even though he had lived here for three years, he had amassed little. Material wealth meant nothing to him. He had money in the bank, and sometimes he used it for his own pleasure. On occasion he worried that he was not really living, but drifting through and past life, letting reality pass him by while he reached for errant shadows. Sometimes he grabbed on, more often he did not.

Out on the street, he felt as apart from things as ever. A few people smiled or nodded at him, and he returned the gesture, but most passed by without a glance, as if they didn't see him at all.

6

Lilou wanted Sammi to sit up front while Angela drove, but the girl insisted she take the back seat. Lilou thought it was because she wanted her and Angela to talk, but less than an hour away from the cabin she looked back and saw Sammi stretched out asleep.

"Is that all they do?" Lilou asked.

"All who do?"

"Teenagers. Sleep. Is that it?"

"Long time since you were a teenager," Angela said.

Lilou sighed. She'd once feared that she would spend a lifetime chipping away at the barrier between her and Angela, but a familiarity had grown between them. They sat in silence for a while, and at least it was comfortable. They weren't like strangers looking for something in common, but more like friends who no longer had anything to say.

"Sorry," Angela muttered a few minutes later.

"Don't worry," Lilou said. "You have every cause to hate me."

"I don't hate you. Not at all. I hate everything that happened, but you and Vince..."

"We were close," Lilou said. "Nothing more."

"I'm not even sure I care about whatever might have happened anymore," Angela said. "If something did happen, it was your fault not his. And not even your fault really because of what you are. I can't hate you, Lilou, because you're the nearest thing to Vince left to me."

Lilou felt tears threatening. It was a while since she had cried, and it surprised her.

"We both lost so much," she said.

"Like you said, you wander hundreds of miles, I sit on my cabin porch. We're both adrift."

Lilou was slouched down in the seat and she tapped her foot against the dashboard. "Fuck it," she said, sitting up and reaching for the stereo. "Let's have some music."

Angela laughed out loud, startling Sammi awake behind them.

"We there yet?" the girl asked, befuddled with sleep.

"Yeah, a proper teenager," Angela said, still laughing.

A tension seemed to have been broken, and though they travelled for a while without talking, Lilou felt happier than she had in a while. Having some sort of direction gave her life a purpose she had been lacking since the Fold closed. And she believed that taking Angela out of the rut she and Sammi had fallen into had moved them both on as well. They would never get over what had happened, but they could all try to take control of their lives again.

When she betrayed Mallian, Lilou lost the best friend she'd ever had, the creature who had been the centre around which her whole life orbited. He was brusque and cruel, and sometimes so embittered that even those close to him suffered the fallout of his fury and rage. She loved him. He terrified her.

She had not realised how much she relied on him until he was gone.

Even as she fought against him and his ambitions for Ascent, he was still there, still the focal point of all her thoughts, efforts and life. Now he was a universe away, and whether dead or still alive in Grace's Fold, he was gone from her life forever. She had felt control slipping as she'd fought against him, and the moment the Fold closed, the world around her had become deeper, darker, and more inimical than ever before. She hoped that what they were doing now might give her an opportunity to establish some sort of direction once again. Mohserran had not been a close friend, but she had known him since she was a young nymph many centuries before. The chance of him having survived whatever had befallen Longford, and then decades buried and submerged behind the dam, was slight. But nothing was impossible with the Kin. It gave her purpose, and the concept of trying to track him and the other two missing Kin had seeded an idea about what her life could be from now on.

She hoped that Angela and Sammi might take some comfort from this journey as well, and would perhaps see that hiding didn't necessarily mean standing still.

"Wish we could share the driving," Angela said.

"I'll give it a go."

"I want to get there alive."

"Okay, I'll be in charge of the radio."

"So what's the favoured music of the Kin?" Angela asked.

"Spooky mythological creature rap." Lilou chuckled and sat back in her seat, watching the world flash by outside. It was the human world, but her world as well, a place where she drifted through shadows and deserted places. It was also somewhere that was starting to feel less and less like home.

Late that afternoon they stopped for food. The roadside diner might have been out of a movie, with a truck park to one side, cars slewed across the forecourt, and a neon sign proclaiming State's Best Chili above the entrance. Lilou had enjoyed watching films when she lived in the safe places back in London, because she said it gave her an insight into the world that she could not experience for herself. Mallian had considered them pointless human inanities. It was something else they had disagreed upon.

"Haven't been somewhere with so many people for quite a while," she said.

"Put your mask on," Angela said. "You know."

Lilou nodded. She'd been used to doing that in London, but these past couple of years spent wandering the hills and woods—back in a landscape that reminded her so much of her early days—she'd been able to let her guard slip for long periods of time, and it had felt good. But now she was worried that she was out of practice. Angela and Sammi couldn't afford attention being drawn to them, so it was Lilou's responsibility to be as careful as she could.

They took a nook by the window and when the waitress came they ordered coffee and sandwiches. She glanced at Lilou several times as she scratched on her pad, even looking back over her shoulder as she returned to the counter.

"I'm trying," Lilou said, looking down at her hands. She clutched them before her on the table, concentrating on her white knuckles. Over the decades and centuries it had become second nature to draw in her nymph's allure and conceal it from the human world around her.

She glanced around the diner, and no one was looking her way, no eyes were widening at her natural beauty. For now, it would do.

"It's good to be away from home," Sammi said. "But do you really believe your friend might still be alive? After all that time buried at the bottom of a reservoir?"

"I doubt it," Lilou said.

Their coffees came, and this time the waitress only gave Lilou a couple of glances before going to another table.

"But you said...?" Angela began.

"If there's any slight, remote chance, then I have to see." She stirred her coffee and breathed in the warm aroma. It smelled good. It brought memories of times near and far, and places as well. Some of them settled her, a few troubled her even more. The longer she lived, the more the structure of her life consisted of memories rather than new experiences.

"And you wanted to get us away from the cabin," Sammi said.

"Of course I did. I care about both of you."

"Company for you," Angela said, but there was no bitterness to her voice.

"I don't have much," Lilou said. "Even the couple of Kin I've come across here are private, unsociable creatures."

"It's good for us," Sammi said.

"Sure." Angela sipped her coffee.

"And it'll be a harmless adventure," Lilou said. "A road trip to an old valley full of muddy ruins. It'll take your mind off things."

Neither Angela nor Sammi replied, and Lilou knew what that meant because she was thinking the same thing. *No it won't be harmless.*

It was something to do, a place to go, that was all. If all she found when they arrived there were the buried bones of Mohserran and the other two Kin, then they would return to the cabin and the woods. She was not putting them in danger. After everything that had happened, she would never do that.

7

It took him some time to decide what had been missing from the final glamour. It took him a little while longer to see if he could find it in the Fold. Now he knows, and he has spent a long time luring the creature to him. Putting in the groundwork. Gaining trust. The Kin knows what he is, and *who* he is, and that, it seems, might be a help.

The pombero has heard of Ascent, and it has become its greatest passion.

"She's eaten from you again," Mallian says.

"A while ago, but the wound still hurts." He turns his leg this way and that, revealing the dried gash on his thigh. It is an indentation, an ugly scoop of missing flesh. "This is the third time, and it's taken longer to heal than before."

"Maybe our great and wise fairy isn't so great and wise."

"What do you mean?"

"Perhaps you, her victims, will rot away and die after all."

The pombero makes a sound somewhere between a purr and a groan. He is a small creature, more man than Kin, his mixed heritage giving him the appearance of a short, stocky human, but with the mind of something other. Mallian first saw him on his twelfth long night in the Fold, stalking along the river close to where he was trapped against the ground by Grace's glamour. He was only a shadow then, one of many that Mallian had seen and was still trying to put a name to, a face, a history.

He dislikes and looks down upon humans, but he *hates* mongrels. They are a taint on the purity of the Kin. But just as he spends time talking with the human Vince—and is even starting to enjoy some of their conversations—he has to hold his hatred deep in order to achieve his aims.

"You really think she'd have made such a mistake?" the pombero asks.

"What's your name, creature?"

The man looks troubled. Mallian has asked three times before, and each time the pombero has scampered away and remained absent for many days. *There's power in a name*, Mallian thinks. *He knows that. Not as stupid as his human face seems, perhaps.*

This time he does not run away.

"I don't seek to own you," Mallian says, lying. "Only to know you."

"My name's..." The small man looks away, frowning.

"I'm your friend. I'm not here to eat you."

"Markus."

"Markus. Very human."

"As was I, until she brought me here."

"You were never fully human."

"I know that now," Markus says. "I didn't know it back then. Back in the real world."

"Not even an inkling?"

The pombero shrugs. "Always knew I was different, of course. But mostly that's just taken as madness."

"Do you feel mad now?"

"Only at her." He looks off into the distance, even though any distance here is finite.

I have to be careful, Mallian thinks. *I have to lure him in, because I'm in no position to grab.* His friend Jilaria Bran had sacrificed herself for his cause, but they had been close for many decades. This part-human, part-Kin mongrel creature might be far less likely to accede to his request. The time to ask is not yet, but it will be soon.

First, there are other ways to build Markus's confidence in him and get him on his side.

"Why are you mad?" Mallian asks. He doesn't really care, but letting the creature vent will give him more cause to listen to what Mallian has to say next.

"She took me away from everything I love," Markus says. "The first time lightning struck me my wife was there when I surfaced, nursing me back to health. My daughter, too, back from university to help. Days later, maybe three, maybe four, we were sitting on the deck in our garden. Clear blue sky. No clouds. I was feeling better for the first time, and Sarah was tracing those strange patterns on my calf and foot. The bolt came from nowhere."

I don't care, Mallian thinks. "Go on," he says.

"This time they were close," Markus says. "When I woke, they were dead, both of them. Burned. Scorched and melted. And a creature, a fleeting thing, took my hand and guided me from that place as if it were saving me."

"But it wasn't saving you," Mallian says. "It was taking you from your dead wife and daughter and bringing you here, to this place."

"Yes. Bringing me here."

"Just so that Grace can eat you, watch you heal, eat you again."

The pombero looks down at his scarred leg. Around the wound radiate the old lightning scars, like fine fronds or a satellite image of a complex river tributary.

"If you wish to hit back, there's something you can do for me," Mallian says.

"Does it have to do with Ascent?"

"Quiet, quiet," he says. "I'm not sure how far her senses reach, and if she hears that word on the breeze she might come back to feed on you sooner than you'd wish."

A visible shiver passes through the pombero. That's good. It draws it more onto Mallian's side.

"But yes," he says, "it has something to do with that."

Markus's eyes light up. He nods.

Mallian tells him what he wants.

"That's all?"

"For now." *There'll be more*, he thinks. *Much more. When the time comes for you to suffer for me, then we'll see just how much you've embraced your Kin blood.*

He watches the pombero dash away along the riverbank, back towards where the human has made his home in the small cave. Markus runs with an animal gait, and exudes a strength that no man can project on his own. Mallian thinks, *Perhaps this mongrel is not so unnatural after all.*

8

Not long after he arrived, Vince began mapping the Fold. He had no pens or pencils, and nothing to draw on even if he had, but his memory had always been good. It gave him some small sense of purpose. Rather than moving on through the days and weeks with little to occupy him other than striving to survive, it became a project. He didn't walk its hills and forests every single day, but most days he went some way from the cave he used as home. Whether foraging for fruit and nuts, or simply trying to get to know the Fold better, he tracked his routes and remembered what he could of the landscape's contours, twists and turns.

In doing so, he had come to understand a little of how the Kin brought there by Grace existed. Though some of them were humanoid—and several could have easily passed as completely human—others had fully adopted their Kin heritage and adapted accordingly. He'd witnessed from afar several strange metamorphoses as the deniers no longer denied, and the people they had been living as in the real world melted away to allow their true natures to the fore.

It was a disturbing process to witness. Every week

that passed left Vince feeling more and more alone. The Fold grew stranger, not more familiar. Even though he was not averse to strangeness—he had spent some time as a relic hunter in London, seeking out peculiar objects wherever and whenever he could, and as such becoming au fait with many of London's most obscure locations—he felt any semblance of his old life being steadily wiped away.

For the first few weeks he had seen other humans who often appeared just as lost as him. Now, he was the only human left. Even the shapeshifter Fer had not projected as human for a long time, instead choosing to live its life as creatures known or less familiar. To Vince, it felt as if the Fold was growing, expanding and moving on, and he was the single point keeping it locked into the past. He was becoming rare.

He was also learning where some of the Kin lived. Many of them were elusive, and whether shy or simply secretive they kept away from him, ensuring that he knew as little about them as possible. Others were quite open about their movements through the irregular days and nights, and a couple were happy to converse with him, telling him their names and the names of the others.

Fer lived in a small shack it had built high up on one valley side, close to the ridge but not so close that it could look over the ridge and beyond. Perhaps that meant it had accepted its lot living in the Fold. The shack was a beautiful affair, built from fallen logs and twigs, mud and leaves, flowers that still bloomed and shrubs that formed hanging curtains over the doorway and glassless windows. There were heavy blocks as cornerstones, silt from the riverbed formed into strange, haunting gargoyles around the walls' upper reaches, and a slab of slate was used as the main door, hung on heavy bone hinges that came from no animal Vince recognised. It was a fascinating building, reflecting Fer's wide and varying range of appearances in its diverse materials and construction. It seemed to grow up out of the ground, and Vince was certain some of the walls were still expanding, the roof still sprouting ferns.

Shashahanna was a mermaid, her name almost as musical as the songs she sang as she bathed in the river, and the pools and ponds that it fed close to where it entered the Fold. She seemed unafraid of Vince, and unconcerned when he sat at a distance and watched her swimming. She was distinctly alien and entirely beautiful, and she lived in a clump of fallen trees washed up on one shore of the river. He sometimes saw her climbing in and swimming out of the pile, like some exotic otter, but he never ventured close, and neither did she invite him in. Theirs was a comfortable relationship, silent and maintained at a distance.

High up on the opposite side of the valley from Fer's home, Dastion the dwarf had his mines. He had only spoken with Vince once, soon after the Fold was closed and Vince took to wandering day and night looking for a way out. Dastion had already started digging then, using his big strong hands to haul at rock and soil, and fashioning levers and props from tree branches he tore down. Vince found him sitting on a rock one day, a powerful short soul who seemed to bear a heavy weight on his shoulders and in his sad, deep eyes. Back then he still looked like a swarthy, strong human, not the hairy tunnel dweller he had become. For a second Vince had convinced himself that another human soul had become trapped with him.

Dastion swayed where he sat, and Vince saw the almost empty bottle in his hand. It must have been the dregs of a drink he'd brought with him. They exchanged names and some of their histories, spoke of what had happened and what might come, and although Dastion was quite welcoming, Vince quickly came to realise that he was just like the other deniers. Kin, although he had not yet accepted the fact.

His acceptance came quickly.

Dastion's underground explorations had progressed rapidly, and the refuse piles from his excavations grew across the hillside, forming a new landscape that looked moonlike and alien. For a while the large swaths of detritus were home to nothing alive, but then grasses quickly spread, and plants made this new fertile soil their home. Vince hadn't seen Dastion for a long time. Perhaps the dwarf now preferred to spend his time deep down below the surface.

Maybe he was hiding from Grace down there. Maybe he was digging towards the boundary, only to find his direction reversed, much like when Vince walked up over the hilltops.

Grace was the Kin who remained most elusive. Vince had no idea where she made her home—if indeed she lived in any single place—and although he sometimes saw her from a distance, she always ensured that they never drew close. She often travelled back and forth across her domain, and after all this time if they were destined to simply bump into each other it would have happened by now. He might have welcomed a chance to confront her. She kept apart from Vince on purpose.

With a map growing in detail in his mind every day, the one place that still disturbed him most was the clearing by the river where he had last seen Angela.

It wasn't only the memories that plagued him when he went and sat at that place. It was as if it did not belong inside the Fold at all.

His walks often veered that way, and he'd given up pretending to himself that it was not on purpose. There, he was as far away from Angela as anywhere else, but he felt close. *She* felt closer. The ground was twisted into swirls, grass stripped from the surface and mud turned fluid and hardened again into patterns that might tell a tale, if viewed from the correct angle. It reminded him of the trace-work of burn scars that had bloomed on Sammi's arm and shoulder. He had not been able to translate them, either. Rocks were scorched, plants withered, and even the air seemed to carry an uncertain tinge, like heat haze where there was little heat.

Whatever strange magical violence had forged a path from this contained world and into another still hung there, echoes held in the land and remembered in the air. He wished he could read the signs and understand those echoes. He wished so much that he could replicate the fairy's power and open the doorway one more time. But he was only a human being. In this world, he was a little less than nothing.

As he stood to leave the site of the vanished doorway, he spied something from the corner of his eye. A shape moved in the shadow of trees, then grew still again when he turned to look. It was large, too big to be one of the smaller mammals that the Fold supported. Somewhere beneath those trees, a Kin was watching him.

He stared, glancing left and right in case he could catch that movement again. Leaves fluttered on the trees, stirred by a gentle breeze. Nothing else moved.

"Come on out," Vince said. Whatever was there, he would be less afraid if it was ready to reveal itself. He'd seen a lot in his short life. He much preferred to confront dangers head-on than to have them haunting him, unseen and ready to pounce.

Nothing emerged.

He started back along the river, staying close to the bank where a path was slowly being worn into the landscape. He was partly responsible, but he also saw footprints there he did not recognise, especially after one of the regular afternoon storms.

He glanced back every few seconds, but there was

nothing behind him. Neither was there anything ahead. Yet still he felt eyes upon him, the attention of some inhuman thing that set his skin afire with dreadful anticipation.

Vince had often wondered whether some of the Kin trapped here with him might eventually see him as food, much like Grace saw them. Could he fight off Dastion if he chose to attack? Or Fer, if it came at him in the guise of a bear? He thought not. He doubted he'd even be able to run very far.

He walked faster, then started running. One thing he'd noticed since being here was that his fitness had improved. There was no alcohol, no processed foods or refined sugars. He walked miles every day. He ran sometimes, too, enjoying the sense of freedom it gave him.

He heard nothing matching his footsteps, so he sped up and veered away from the river. The forest swallowed him up. As far as he was aware nothing lived nearby. Some birds were startled from bushes to his left, though he didn't know whether they'd been frightened by him or something else.

Switching to the right, he ducked down and glanced back.

The creature paused, looking around in confusion. Then he locked eyes with Vince.

It was not the first time Vince had seen this Kin close up: very man-like, small and stocky with no particularly animalistic attributes. He'd spoken with the pombero before; the creature was open about what he was, and although he did not claim some of the more unsavoury aspects of the traditional myth—the sexual predator, the sullied outlook--he admitted that accepting his blood and birthright had given him a sense of freedom that he'd never previously experienced.

Vince suspected the pombero had endured deep loss, but he would not discuss it. Both times they had spoken, Vince's probing questions about who he'd left behind had sent the man fleeing.

This time it was Vince who was running, and he didn't know why.

"What?" Vince asked.

The pombero stared at him. Something about his bearing set Vince on edge. There was threat there, violence coiled in his stance, a promise of something in his eyes.

"What?" Vince repeated, voice weaker than before. Fear could do that.

He stood and started running again, flitting between trees and heading back towards the river. He heard the Kin chasing him. This time he did nothing to mask the fact that he sought to capture Vince, though his intentions were still unclear. Vince didn't imagine they could be benign.

The trees didn't grow so thick there, and the path worn into the riverbank meant he'd be able to run faster. A few hundred metres ahead was a small gulley where a tributary joined the river. It was overgrown, but Vince knew exactly where it was. He could leap it if he really stretched, and perhaps the pombero would tumble in behind him.

If he reached it without being caught.

He had been hunted before, by humans as well as Kin, but his terror was as rich, his fear cutting. With very little left to live for, he wanted nothing more than to survive. He still wanted to find his way home.

He leapt a fallen tree, skirted around a rocky outcropping, sprinted through a wide swath of long grasses and brambles that scratched his legs through his jeans, then as he approached the river, he risked a look back.

The pombero was less than a dozen steps behind him and closing fast.

Gasping in shock, Vince cut left and went for a rise in the landscape. There were tumbled rocks on the other side, and perhaps he could lose himself in there, or at least confuse his pursuer long enough to—

The hand grasped the back of his shirt and pulled, jerking him backwards so hard that his feet went from under him and kicked upwards. He landed hard on his back, the wind knocked from him. The blue sky blurred and grew darker, and he feared he was about to lose consciousness.

Then the pombero's face appeared above his, and Vince bit his own lip, hard. If he was about to die, he wanted to stare death in the face.

The pombero panted, sweat beading his face.

"Er..." he said.

"What do you want?"

"I didn't mean to..." Vince's attacker drew back, allowing Vince to sit up.

It was ridiculous, and Vince almost laughed. He'd run fearing attack, terrified that the pursuing Kin wanted to run him down and eat him to refuel and recharge itself after having been feasted upon by Grace. The scars were obvious, the more recent wound on his calf still weeping and wet.

"What do you want?"

"The backpack," the pombero said.

"What backpack?" Vince risked the ruse, emboldened by his would-be attacker's apparent reticence. Maybe he had run because Vince had run. But he needed the backpack for something—or someone—and that could only be Mallian. Vince was surprised it had taken the Nephilim this long.

"I'm not what you think I am," the pombero said.

Vince stood. The pombero allowed it, but it was also very clear that this pursuit was over. If Vince made to flee, he'd be brought down again, and harder this time. Any doubts in his attacker's words were not reflected in his appearance. He was strong, solid, and ready.

"I don't think you're anything," Vince said. "And I'm no threat to you. Not like her." He nodded down at the man's leg.

"The backpack."

"I don't know—"

The punch was so fast that Vince didn't see it coming. A powerhouse blow to the face, it crunched his nose and sent him reeling, tripping over his own feet to fall onto his back. His eyes watered, nose cold and filled with white-hot pain.

"I'll torture you," the man said.

Vince could only gasp.

"I'll peel you. Hands first, then arms. I'll wear your skin as a coat."

"You don't know what you're—"

"Human," the pombero growled, and in that sound Vince heard no trace of humanity. This was a Kin through and through, whether he'd once been a denier or not.

"Even if Mallian gets that rucksack, it's no use to him."

"Where is it?"

"I don't know. I lost it when I was first shut in here. I've been looking for it ever since."

"I don't believe you," the pombero said. "I always know when a human is lying."

"How?"

"Their lips move. Now take me to it, or I start peeling."

Vince considered his options. It didn't take very long, because there were none. "This way," he said. They'd reach his cave in ten minutes. In that time, he had to come up with a plan.

* * *

Close to the cave, Vince ran. He put on a sprint, skidded past the narrow cave entrance, and snapped up one of the sharpened sticks he kept tucked against the rock. He'd known the time would come when he had to defend himself, but still it shocked him.

He spun on his heels and crouched down, spear held before him. The pombero—he'd refused to tell Vince his name, whether human or Kin—had come to a standstill on the other side of the cave entrance. He looked angry, his forehead wrinkled into a scowl, his jaw hanging open. His teeth seemed larger than before, sharper, or perhaps it was just that they were on show.

He glanced at the spear, then at the cave.

"Stay away from what's mine," Vince said. He tried to sound confident and threatening, but the edge of fear in his voice was obvious.

"Nothing here is yours." That voice, those words, sent a chill through Vince, and he gripped the spear harder. He'd taken hours sharpening this and several other weapons, rubbing them against a chunk of rough stone to wear down the tips, hardening them in his fire, smoothing a couple of hand grips along the lengths. He'd hoped he would never have to use them. He remembered the feel of a blade in his hand parting skin and flesh, grating against bone, and he was desperate not to experience the same sensation ever again.

The pombero came at him. Vince drew in a sharp

breath and held it, bracing his feet and jabbing forward with the spear.

At the last second the man dodged sideways and ran into the cave.

"It's not in there!" Vince shouted, but he heard the man scrabbling around in the shadows, and he knew that he'd find it. *I should have hidden it better. I should have buried the relics, destroyed them.*

As he took his first step towards the cave, the pombero emerged carrying the rucksack. It was Gregor the Kin-killer's, and it had travelled the world growing heavier with parts of the Kin he had murdered and cut apart.

Now this man-Kin had it, and Vince knew who had sent him here, and he wasn't sure there was anything he could do about it.

"That's mine!" Vince said, gesturing with the spear.

The man moved faster than he'd ever thought possible. He took a couple of steps and leapt, landing inside the spear's arc, lashing out with his left fist and connecting with Vince's cheek.

Vince grunted and staggered back, feeling the spear ripped from his hands as he did so. He stumbled over a rock, pinwheeled his arms—

—if I fall I'll be a sitting duck, spear through my stomach, pinned to the floor just as surely as Mallian and bleeding into the dust of this fucking place—

—and then fell. He went to roll aside to avoid the inevitable strike from the spear, but then he saw the pombero standing still, staring down at him.

"They're no use to him," Vince said.

The pombero shrugged his big shoulders. He wasn't even breathing hard. Vince looked at the spear in his hand, ready to roll, kick out, fight if it came down towards him.

"You don't know what he is," Vince said. "You don't know— "

"Shut up, human." The man threw the spear away, looked down at Vince again, then turned and ran. In seconds he was out of sight, and moments later his footfalls echoed away to nothing.

Silence hung over the clearing, and then birdsong came in again, and the scratching of insects and the buzzing of flies filled the air. It was as if the Fold had seen nothing amiss.

Vince stood and retrieved the spear. His heart beat fast, his nose smarted, eyes watered. He was confused. He'd had the thirteen relics since Mallian had attempted to control Grace, and the fourteenth required for the spell—the one that Vince had stolen and hidden away back in the real world—meant the other thirteen were useless.

He had not been able to identify what it was. A small, dark, knotted lump of petrified flesh, it could have been any body part from any dead Kin. He'd buried it deep in the woods, and even if he could get back to his own world he would never, ever find the relic again. It was lost to the world, and lost to Mallian.

Vince shivered. A cool breeze came from nowhere. He imagined he could hear Mallian's sarcastic laughter on the wind, smell his rotting breath. He'd believed the Nephilim was dying, trapped against the earth of this place by the fairy's own powerful glamours. He thought the Kin had given up and was resigned to fade away.

But all this time he had been scheming.

As he approached the glade where Mallian was imprisoned by invisible bonds, a small part of Vince hoped he would see the Nephilim back on his feet. He'd be weak, unsettled, and needing to feed, but a Mallian that had escaped the fairy's bonds might be a Mallian who could get him home.

It was a terrifying notion. If the Nephilim took control of the fairy, his long-held desires would come to fruition. A return to the real world, exposure of the Kin, Ascent. Myth against military might, Lilou had once said, and her words had seared themselves onto Vince's mind. He could hardly imagine such a conflict, and the misery and death it could cause.

Yet a selfish part of him—one he could not control, but which he knew was a foolish dream—only wanted to see and hold Angela again. To hell with the rest of the world.

When he reached the glade, Mallian was where he always was. Arms outstretched, legs splayed, he seemed to be asleep. Yet as Vince approached the Nephilim opened his eyes.

"Hunting rabbit for me after all," he said.

"This is for protection." Vince carried the spear in one hand, ready to swing it up and forward if anything threatened him. He hadn't been fast enough back at the cave, but he was more ready now. He stayed back from Mallian, watching for any tricks. The big Nephilim's limbs had not moved, and he could see the indentations in flesh and skin where the fairy's invisible bonds still held him tight to the land.

"Protection from me?"

"Or from anything you'd send against me."

"Me? Send? Why would I do that?"

"Because I foiled your plans for total world domination."

"You're the only one who'll talk to me."

"Don't try to make me believe you care about having someone to chat with."

Mallian sighed, a deep rattling sound that Vince felt through the ground. He looked around, cautious. He'd have to keep his wits about him. *Mallian doesn't care about me. I'm a human, and he hates humans.*

"Anyway, it failed," Vince said.

"What failed?"

"The pombero you sent to steal from me. I saw it off."

Mallian's expression did not change.

"You're desperate," Vince said. "Flailing in the dark. Can't you accept that you've lost?"

"I accept nothing," Mallian said.

Vince froze, then took a couple of steps closer. Mallian's eyes flickered his way, but he still did not move his head. He looked so weak, so old. Vince had no idea how the Nephilim was even still alive, nor how long Grace would allow him to remain so.

"So you did send—"

"Talk if you want to talk. I'll admit I enjoy our occasional exchanges. But don't challenge me, and don't assume anything about what might or might not have happened to you. Your mind's too small to understand."

Vince thought of saying more, but instead he took four steps forward until he was standing close to Mallian's right shoulder. It was from this position that he sometimes dropped food into the Nephilim's mouth, always from a height so that he could avoid those teeth should Mallian manage to lift his head from the ground. This time he offered no food.

He pressed the point of the stick against Mallian's throat and leaned against it.

"I'm not afraid of you," he said.

"Of course you are," Mallian growled, and he projected every dark, terrifying aspect of himself into those words. His teeth clacked, his eyes narrowed and reflected all the dreadful things he had done, and his voice might have scared both angels and demons.

Vince stared right back. "I'm really not," he said. "Not anymore. Even if you were up and walking around, I wouldn't fear you. Every bad thing that can happen to me has already happened. Pain, torture, death, that would be a mercy."

"Perhaps I just won't take you when I return to the world," Mallian said.

Vince leaned on the spear. It puckered the Nephilim's skin and he drew in a sharp breath, and held it.

"I could kill you now."

"It'll take a lot more than a sliver of wood to kill me."

Vince eased back and stepped away. Mallian smiled.

"Whatever you're trying to do won't work," Vince said.

"I'm looking at the sky. Relaxing here. Waiting for the darkness to fall. That's work enough for now."

Vince left the Nephilim and returned along the river to his cave. Since his first day trapped in the Fold it had felt progressively more alien to him, that he was the odd one here, the being that didn't belong. The whole landscape was observing him, and hidden away across the meadows and hillsides, and in the forests, were Kin watching his every move.

9

In the darkness he returns, and Mallian welcomes him with a smile.

"It's a good thing you've done," Mallian says. He can see the rucksack slung over Markus's left shoulder. "And there's plenty more to do. I knew you wouldn't fail me."

"I've had it for a while," Markus says, dropping the rucksack beside the Nephilim. "I've looked in there. I know what some of these things are. Others, I'm not so sure."

"They're tools," Mallian says. "They're a way out of here."

"How can bits and pieces of dead things offer a way out of this place?" The pombero sounds like a human, his mind closed and admitting no entry to wonder. Mallian feels the urge to reach out and snap his neck, tear it from his head, and feel the weak mongrel blood spatter across his hand. If he could have, he would have. But if he could do that, he would not have required the half-Kin's help in the first place.

"There's so much you don't know," Mallian says. "How old are you?"

"Fifty-seven."

"Just a child. You came here as a denier, and you've grown since then, but there's still so much you don't understand about the Kin. And for someone like you, so much you'll never know."

"I want to learn!" he says. "I'm one of you now, I always have been, and coming here opened my eyes."

Mallian closes his own eyes in response and breathes in deeply to compose himself. His anger is rising. It is simmering just below the surface—it always has been, because that is the nature of who he was— but he is in no position to submit to his anger now. He has to rule it, rather than the other way around.

"Tell me!" Markus says. "Teach me!"

"I'll teach you what you need," Mallian says, opening his eyes again. He sees the same skies, the same view. He is striving to change that, and to do so he has to maintain self-control. Fury has its place, but that is not here, not now.

Soon, though.

"It's a glamour, both ancient and powerful. I'd do it myself but..." Mallian tenses his arms and legs for the ten thousandth time since being trapped in the Fold.

"Anything to get away from here," Markus says. "I never thought it would be like this. When I arrived here I was angry and scared. But when the Fold closed I experienced such a sense of... *freedom*. As if the bonds that had held me to the world—home and wife, children and work, my friends and dreams and aspirations—had all been snipped, and for a while I was flying, and alone. I was soaring. And then she... the first time she..."

"She started eating you."

"Yes."

"She's a monster," Mallian says.

"A monster."

Mallian nods, gesturing the pombero closer. "I can put her down."

"I'm here to help. Only to help."

"I know. But can you help enough?"

"What do you mean?" Markus kneels by his side, so close that Mallian could lunge and grab his arm or leg in his mouth, if he so desired. But that would be the last resort.

"I need your tongue."

Markus blinks, then smiles. "Anything. Tell me what to say, where and when to say it. Do I speak it over these?" He picks up the rucksack again, and Mallian is struck with a sudden, rich memory. It's been happening more and more lately, as if his mind is retreating to better times—memories sharp in sense and sound, so clear and precise that he could almost be there.

Gregor the Kin-killer holds the rucksack, proud of what he has achieved through his long years of hunting and mutilating, and ready to claim his reward. Though growing old in human terms he also retains a childlike innocence, a belief that everything he has been doing has been to elevate himself and make something new.

Mallian experiences a brief but surprising pang of guilt, even regret, because he lied to Gregor. All that awaited him was a quick, bloody death at the Nephilim's hands.

Mallian shakes his head slowly.

"The words of the glamour are ancient and very particular, spoken in a language long lost to the world. It could be that I am the only Kin sane enough to still speak these words. Your human mouth wouldn't wrap around them."

The pombero looks surprised, then offended.

"Your young Kin mouth," Mallian says, correcting himself, outside at least.

"Then... my tongue."

"Your tongue," Mallian says.

Markus holds up the rucksack and looks back and forth between it and Mallian.

"Most of them had to die to give what was required," Mallian says.

"You're saying I'm lucky."

"I'm saying you're honoured. You'll become legend," Mallian says.

The pombero drops the rucksack close to Mallian's side, but not too close. Wide-eyed, he stares the Nephilim up and down, gaze lingering on his arms and legs where they are held close to the ground by the fairy's invisible glamours.

Then he turns and runs, not once looking back.

Mallian sighs. The long haul, then. He closes his eyes and considers what he might do next.

* * *

He's surprised that he fell asleep.

When he wakes the pombero is sitting a few metres away. Close enough to smell, but not so close that Mallian can clasp him, or bite him. The mongrel is cautious, afraid. Yet Mallian hopes that his presence is a good sign, because it could mean that he is thinking things over.

Mallian does not speak. He's said all that needs to be said. He will not beg. Instead he lies there and looks up at the sky. He wonders whether, if he could extend his vision and travel along its lines, he would eventually meet the gaze of some unknowable alien creature staring back at him. Such a thought would make any human and most Kin feel small and insignificant, but not Mallian. He feels more in charge, more in control. He is at the centre of everything.

"What will I get in return?" Markus asks at last. The pombero has sat in silence for so long that the sun has moved partway across the sky, and the light has changed towards dusk. Mallian can feel a chill on the air. There are no real seasons here, but he senses a cooler spell approaching.

"I've told you," Mallian replies, "you will become legend. Songs will be written about you. Everyone will know your name as the Kin who enabled Ascent to commence."

"I don't mean in the future when I'm dead. What

fucking use is being talked about when I won't be there to hear? I mean here and now. I mean today and tomorrow, if your plan works and you get the fairy to open the Fold again. What's my payment? What's my reward?"

Fucking humans, Mallian thinks. He blinks slowly, keeping his eyes closed for a few seconds as he reins in the rage. *Such selfish thoughts reveal him. He'll never be Kin.*

"My commander," Mallian says. "My right hand."

"But I'll be unable to issue orders."

"You think a Kin only speaks with its tongue?" It's a strange question with no real answer, but the pombero does not wish to appear ignorant. He does not question what Mallian has said. His doubts are still obvious, but so is his thirst for reward, and now his desire for power.

"The armies of the Kin."

"Yours to control," Mallian says. "Under my overall command, of course."

"Of course," Markus says, glancing aside, and Mallian thinks, *Already there's scheming going on inside his tiny mind.*

"You'll tell everyone what I did?" Markus asks.

"Everyone will know."

The mongrel nods once. Then he pushes his long, sharp tongue out beneath his teeth, stares Mallian in the eye, and bites down hard.

10

Next morning, after a restless night in a cheap motel, they stood looking out across a desolate landscape.

Angela had never seen anything like it. It took her breath away. It looked as if an artist had swept a broad grey brush across the valley. Both apocalyptic and strangely beautiful, the landscape before her was almost leached of colour, tinted only with light and dark greys and varying shades of beige. Where they stood, high on the hillside—above the level of the old reservoir—they were surrounded by lush trees, shrubs and grasses, colourful blooms speckled the view, and even the dawn sky above them seemed deeper and bluer than it was above the grey valley. Such vibrant colours made the contrast all the more striking. Even more startling was the stark dividing line between normal landscape and colourless valley, reality and bland, unreal monotone. The reservoir levels must have been consistent over the years, and now the water was gone its bed was revealed, drying and cracking in the sun. Lower down near the valley floor some dirty brown pools remained, reflecting nothing of the clear blue sky. A winding river flowed through the basin, a dark band of filthy water that continued until it met and flowed through the ruin of the dam further down the valley.

The blasted landscape, and the river, pools and puddles, bereft of colour and sun, might have been part of another world.

"It looks like the moon," Sammi said.

"Sort of beautiful," Lilou said.

"It's like we're looking back in time," Angela said. Sammi raised a questioning eyebrow. "Like old black and white TV pictures."

"I'm too young to remember." Sammi smirked.

"Sort of beautiful, but frightening as well." Lilou took a few steps forward, and seeing the nymph set against the vast greyness, Angela thought the whole scene looked even more alien. The view made her dizzy. The revealed reservoir bed was two miles across, and stretched maybe four miles from the ruptured dam and back into the foothills. Somewhere down there, buried beneath decades of silt, lay the remains of the small town of Longford. The scope was staggering.

It was so far apart from the world she knew that it made her think of Vince.

Often over the past two years she had wondered about where he was. Lilou could offer no clue as to what the fairy's Folded Land might look like. All she said was that it was her own world. Angela had glimpsed the place, but at the time she'd been fighting for her own life and Sammi's, and had not had a chance to take it in. It had looked like a valley—possibly a little like this place before the dam was built and the reservoir grew to wash it away—but any more than that was subject only to her imagination.

The fairy Grace was a creature beyond her level of understanding. She remembered her as a victim of Mary Rock, trapped and tortured. No one—not Lilou or Mallian, or any other Kin she'd questioned about it—could guess how Mary Rock had managed to capture and imprison such a powerful Kin. Perhaps the fairy had grown weary of hiding, and become careless. Perhaps Mary Rock had tricked her into believing that she had some benign aim in mind, rather than the terrible tortures she'd put the fairy through. She and her sick clients had been trying to *eat* her. Her deep age had already set Grace apart, but Mary Rock's treatment might have driven her mad. And in madness, what worlds might she conjure?

Perhaps the Fold looked much like this place, a blasted and bland landscape where life was forced to struggle and scratch its existence from the ashes, mud and bare sun-bleached rock. Maybe it was a lush place, a forest or jungle with exotic wildlife singing a constant natural jazz, day and night filled with different sights, sounds and smells. Vince might spend his time hiding from the cruel sun and struggling to keep warm at night, or he could pass every hour avoiding inimical wildlife intent on stinging, biting or poisoning him.

A flooded world, a parched place, a landscape of sharp rock or smothering trees. He could be anywhere like that, or nowhere at all, and sometimes what she imagined for him made her feel sick.

Was he missing her? Did he remember her at all? Was he alive or dead? He was so far away in space, time and understanding that sometimes these distinctions didn't seem to matter. Like Schrödinger's cat he could remain alive and dead in her mind forever, because he was so unreachable that she would never know otherwise.

That didn't stop her from talking to him, in her mind and sometimes out loud.

"There's something wrong with this place," she muttered, and she closed her hand by her side, imagining Vince's fingers entwined in hers.

"You feel it too," Sammi said.

Lilou glanced back at them. "It's just a flooded valley," she said. "Longford's down there somewhere, or what's left of it. Just down past that hump in the land, towards the river, I think I can see the remains of a building?"

Angela couldn't see it, but she did not care. Vocalising the wrongness of this place seemed to amplify its effect on her. Its greyness and blandness gave it the appearance of being unfinished, yet perhaps that sense was misleading. In truth, it looked and felt like somewhere that had been finished long ago, and which had since shed itself of humankind. This place had moved on.

"Other people have come," Angela said. She could

see signs across the valley—the glint of early morning sunlight from vehicle windscreens, a couple of columns of smoke that might have been from camp fires.

"The curious," Lilou said. "It's not often a dead town is revealed to the world again."

"Nice way of putting it."

Lilou smiled. "It's fine. It's an adventure."

"I've had enough adventure to last a lifetime," Angela said, and for a moment she felt Vince squeeze her hand, and she knew what his response would be.

Maybe just one more.

To their right, and further down the valley, was the dam. It was a vast structure stretching from one valley slope to the other, its side facing them the same grey colour, the deep fault in its centre obvious, a wound on the land. It looked like a huge cleaver had come down and smashed the dam in two. Angela guessed that a minor leak could progress over time into something more substantial, rocks undermined, concrete cracked and swept away, until one tumbling rock led to a chain reaction. There had been no cataclysmic failure, but downriver beyond the dam the landscape was still flooded in places. It had been a slow disaster.

As they descended through the forest towards the shore of the old reservoir, Lilou called a halt.

"There's security ahead," she said. "I can hear them."

"Security for what?" Sammi asked.

"They don't want people getting to Longford," Angela said.

Sammi shrugged. "Maybe it's just 'cause the ground's dangerous. If this has only just happened there'll be quicksand and stuff, and the river's flowing pretty quick."

"Maybe that's it," Lilou said.

Angela was unconvinced. "Lilou?" she asked.

Lilou glanced back and forth between them.

"What else could it be?" Sammi asked.

"Plenty more," Angela said. Her heart sank. She shouldn't have been surprised that Lilou had lied to them, but now they were here she needed to know why, and how much.

"It's pretty much like I told you," Lilou said.

"Pretty much?"

"My friend might have died here. I want to know how and why."

"So do I," Angela said. "Before Sammi and I go a step further."

"Angela, it's an adventure!" Sammi said. But Angela held up a hand, saying nothing.

The silence hung heavy.

"There's nothing dangerous left, Angela," Lilou said at last. "Everything bad happened years ago. A military experiment that the government tried to cover up, a mistake."

"Military experiment?" Angela asked.

"I've only heard rumours, and most of those are from Jay."

"You talk to Jay?"

"Of course I do. We're both doing our best to look out for the two of you."

"I don't need babysitting!" Angela snapped.

"What experiment?" Sammi asked.

"They used some sort of drug or virus on the townspeople," Lilou said. "It drove the residents mad. They died horrible deaths. So the army used a suppressant on the population to negate the virus, made sure everyone was dead, then flooded the valley. Wiped the whole place from memory."

"They knew about the Kin here?" Sammi asked.

Lilou shrugged.

"They infected the town. Gassed it. Then made sure everyone was dead," Angela said. "What the *fuck* are you bringing us into?"

"That was forty years ago," Lilou said. "It's just a place now, hardly even a memory. It's not dangerous here anymore, Angela. We're here to tell the end of the story."

They continued downhill, skirting around a couple of casual police officers who were sitting on the bonnet of their cruiser. One was smoking, the other surfing on his phone. They didn't seem at all concerned about the exposed valley before them.

That didn't make Angela feel even slightly better.

11

Bone found it hard looking down into the valley and seeing it so changed. He walked along the ridge instead, looking left across beautiful open countryside whilst also painfully aware of the greyness to his right. There lay home, in a sea of almost featureless silt and water, a ruin that threatened to overwhelm him if he dared look at it for too long. His heart beat harder than usual, his tongue was dry and stale. He'd never believed that he would feel so sad coming back home.

Last time he'd returned he had seen the peaceful, rippling waters of the reservoir and found some affinity with them, hiding the truth beneath the surface just like him. Perhaps with the water flooding the valley there had still been a possibility that Longford persisted as it once had, a town beneath the surface, preserved and continuing on through life and death set apart from the world above. Now, he knew that it was a ruin. Longford was no more. He had spent his life adrift, and seeing the emptied, drying valley snipped the last thread that had kept him pinned to the world.

There were other people here. That was inevitable, but it set him on edge. Sightseers were to be expected, and he could slip past and around them easily enough, silent and sleek as ever. They wouldn't know what to look for, and would not understand even if they had any inkling of what he sought.

What troubled him more was the police presence. They stayed high in the hills and seemed casual and laid back—there simply to ensure the safety of those visiting, rather than anything else—but he had no desire to tangle with the authorities. He sleeked past them as well. He came so close to one officer that she frowned and glanced around, rubbing at her eyes as if she had dust in them, or the itch of a painful memory.

Soon he found himself in a place that he recognised from long ago. The hillside had changed—trees had fallen, others had grown—but the contours were the same, and if he stood facing uphill it might almost be forty years before. But he could smell death in the valley. The scent of silt and reservoir bed was on the air, the decayed remains of countless fish and plant life, like time itself had slowed and sunk to the bottom of this valley that was once home.

Bone closed his eyes and breathed out slowly, then looked again.

He saw his tree. He'd known it was close, but hadn't realised how close. It was up to his right, past a small rise in the valley side, and even though it was changed so much he knew it was the place from which he'd once watched his life change. Nestled inside that tree he had observed his childhood ending, and felt the cruel coolness of the world closing around him, indifferent to his struggle and loss. Such coolness had remained with him ever since. His search for those like him was a way of insulating himself against it.

He went to the tree and looked inside. It was dead now, and over the years it had been reduced by time and rot. One whole side of the trunk had fallen away, offering the inside to view. No one could have hidden in the old tree anymore, even if they were small enough. He tried to imagine it as it was back then, but it had changed too much. Instead he reached out and plucked a shard of soft timber from the trunk. It was damp and slick. He dropped it.

It was time to move on. In his life, and in his purpose for that day. Time to go down into the dead valley to ensure that the past remained the past. He turned his back on the tree and started downhill.

Across the hillside and to his left he saw three people looking down into the valley. He didn't know them, but something about them seemed familiar. He'd had this feeling before, and nine times out of ten he was wrong. But when that one-in-ten time occurred, he found someone else like him.

Kin.

He froze and dropped down, hiding behind a corrugation in the land. His heart fluttered like a nervous bird in his chest. He'd come here looking for a dead Kin—his father—and to discover more of the story of his life. He had never expected to find some living. They were so scarce, like the rarest of treasures, that he never grew used to finding them.

From this distance it was hard to make out any details about the three figures, only that they were women. Their eye colours were unknown, their shapes hidden, the shades and textures of their skin uncertain. Yet two of the three seemed to radiate an inhuman aura.

Perhaps it was simply that one Kin was always able to recognise another.

He guessed they must be here for the same reason as him, but he didn't want to mix with them right now. He concentrated, gathering the sleek around himself, then started downhill. When he reached the junction between the living world and the dead he paused. He looked down at his boots where they still stood on green grass and damp soil, with ants crawling around them and a small spider exploring the thread of one lace. Then he took three steps and he was standing on the dried mud of the reservoir bed. He was a grey man in a grey world, and he started down the featureless slope towards whatever might be left.

Everything had changed, but he still found his way to the cave on the hillside, as if he was drawn there by something, a thread still connecting him to whatever might be inside after all this time. As a child he had never been allowed to visit the caves, but he and his friends from the town had often crept close. Others in town had dared each other to knock on the door of Old Man Parsons' house, because Parsons had died when he was one-hundred-and-four and everyone said he would haunt that house forever. For Bone, Emily and Jake, the cave was the equivalent of their haunted house.

In truth, Bone had never been afraid. With him it was more fascination, and a subtle rebellion at going close to a place that was forbidden to him.

He was surprised to see the cave entrance still visible. It had been submerged for decades only a handful of metres beneath the reservoir's highest level, and though silt had built up and swallowed part of the opening, some water flow or current must have persisted to prevent the cavern from becoming totally filled with silt. He recalled a stream trickling from the cave mouth all those years ago from higher up, singing from the darkness and throwing occasional rainbows if he crept up to spy on it at just the right time in the afternoon. Maybe the stream still poured in from high up on the hillside, finding its way down between rock strata and through cracks to provide a gentle current to clear some of the persistent sediment.

He also feared that once he was into the cave mouth, all he'd find would be a wall of mud.

With the sun on his back, and keeping low and quiet so as not to attract attention, he approached the cave where his father had once lived. Then, for the first time in his life, he entered.

It was cooler inside. His boots sank into the mud.

Muck clung to the walls, caked hard, forming features that almost looked like a giant creature's insides. Stalactites of mud hung down, dripping muddy water. The floor of the cave mouth sloped towards the opening, so much of the water had drained when the reservoir flowed out through the damaged dam. Still the silt was fluid around his feet, sloppy mud that grew deeper the further in he went, until it flowed over the top of his boots. He didn't mind.

As it grew darker, the lifelessness of the place struck him. There was no plant life here, as there should be this close to the mouth of a cave—moss on rocks, ferns, creeping plants probing in from outside. There were no insects or flies. Nothing crawled, nothing buzzed. When he breathed he could taste only dampness and mud. There were no memories of this cave carried on the air, because until recently there had been no air in here at all. Any echoes of his father and the other Kin that had lived here had been dissolved in the reservoir waters, spread through the whole lake and then let out in the constant flow that had taken it all away.

"There's nothing alive here," Bone said, because he felt the need to fill this place with sound. His voice was muffled, swallowed by the land and forgotten. He felt that there was a danger of it doing the same to him.

Plucking a torch from his belt he flicked it on and started deeper into the cave. Daylight still penetrated past him, casting his shadow ahead, and the yellow torchlight flickered from pools of water and slick mud. Shadows danced and glimmered. As the darkness grew, and the torch was his only light, his shadow filtered away to nothing.

He slopped through mud that was almost knee-deep, trying his best to make out the shape and size of the caverns. Bone so wanted to see the place as it had been before, but it was changed just as surely as the rest of the valley. Perhaps given the right equipment, he might be able to clear out the cave and restore it to something resembling the place where his father, the selkie Mohserran, had once lived with two other Kin. But he did not have the time.

As the cave opened out into a wider cavern, the stream flowing through it became more obvious. It cut through several feet of silt on the floor, running a twisting course through the cave and back down towards the entrance. There, it must disperse into the mud he'd waded through, or perhaps disappear into cracks in the land to re-emerge further down the valley side. It formed a distinct barrier through the cave, and if he wanted to reach the other side he would have to jump.

Bone scanned the light around the larger cavern. Rock protruded through the caked silt in places, mostly high up on the ceiling, where a narrow fault chimneyed up so high that the torch could not penetrate that far. Maybe it even emerged onto the valley side above the reach of the old reservoir.

They might have escaped, Bone thought. *If they*

knew these caves so well, maybe they retreated here from those hunting them, then burrowed and crawled their way to freedom?

It seemed an unlikely idea. Though he remembered the chaos of that night, the violence, the fear in his father's eyes and the blood on his face, he also recalled the sense that his father gave him his last breath to save his life.

But what if I was wrong?

If they had escaped, infected with whatever the military had exposed the town to, they would not have gone to ground. They'd have stalked, hunted and killed, many times over. He would have heard about them. The world would have known. He was here to ensure there was not even the smallest possibility of that happening now.

As he prepared to leap across the dip carved into the solidifying silt by the stream, Bone shone his torch down and saw something beneath him. A hand. It protruded from the mud, and seemed to claw at it, as if still seeking a way out even after all this time.

He froze and changed position slightly, shifting the torch so that its beam landed on the object from a different direction. He jumped into the pit and landed with both feet in the stream. The cold was a shock, but seeing his boots washed clean was somehow satisfying.

The hand was thin, skin leathery and hard, and still attached to an arm which disappeared into the soil. He reached out to touch it, then held back. He didn't think it was his father's hand. He wasn't sure why, but there would have been a familiarity if this was his father, a sense of closeness after so long apart.

Bone reached out again and touched the hand. Cold. Hard. It might have been a stone sculpture, not the remains of a living thing.

He drew a knife from his belt, flicked it open, and started digging around the arm. The silt fell away and disintegrated into the stream. Great clumps dropped aside, and Bone was worried that the whole bank might collapse and crush him down into the water.

He dug, scraped, and realised how hard his heart was beating, how sweaty he was even though it was cool in the cave.

No, not cool. It was cold. Maybe the stream sucked in any warmth and swept it away.

The arm was connected to a torso. It appeared to be naked, covered in a fine down which was not caked and stuck to the skin. He worked upwards from the shoulder towards where the head should be.

No, this was not Mohserran. This was one of those two other creatures who had shared the cave with him, and shared their time in Longford, too. Francine the werewolf, perhaps, or the other creature. Both vaguely human, they were also utterly different from any normal person in ways his child's mind had found difficult to understand. They kept to themselves, and to the families they had attached to—in the same way, he had come to understand, that Mohserran had fallen in close with his mother—so he'd never had much cause to speak to either of them, nor to ask who or what they were.

Now he was looking at the remains of one, and he saw its pelt, the curve of its head, the teeth almost too large for its mouth, and one closed eye. Burial had darkened its skin and fur, hardening it almost to the consistency of a fossil. The werewolf.

The gentle movement of torchlight across its skin gave the body a strange semblance of life.

"It's not you," Bone said. The reason he'd asked to come to Longford was somewhere else in these caves, and he knew that on the way back out he'd bury this body again. It had spent its life living cautiously amongst humans, and avoiding most of them. He would ensure it had a restful death.

As he turned to climb from the stream he flicked the torch away from the exposed arm, and the hand closed into a claw.

Bone gasped and fell back, stumbling across the stream until his back was pressed against the opposite wall. Sand tumbled across his shoulders, head, and the back of his neck, like fingers playing across his skin, as he aimed the light directly at the corpse.

The hand was mostly closed. Unmoving. It must have been like that before. Hadn't it?

"Fuck's sake," he muttered, and this time he kept the light directed onto the buried body as he edged up the stream until he could climb out.

He moved deeper into the cavern, heading towards a darker space at the rear which appeared to be a low route into further caves. He had no idea how deep or extensive this cave system was, but it was constantly edging upwards, the levels of silt thinning the further inside he went.

Pausing to adjust his belt and jacket, Bone heard movement behind him.

He spun around and cast the light back the way he'd come. Shadows dashed for corners, crevasses, and behind rocks. Nothing else moved, no more sounds echoed from the walls.

"Fuck's *sake!*" He was spooking himself.

He ducked down and started crawling through the narrow gap towards the next cavern. He remained alert for any sign that the gap was growing too narrow to navigate, and was conscious that he didn't know what lay ahead. If this was just a crack that led nowhere he did not want to trap himself, or become wedged, or find himself slipping down a slope into a narrowing space, unable to turn around, stuck forever until—

He heard something ahead of him. He paused, head tilted as he listened. The sound came again. It sounded like something moving against stone, scraping and shushing.

Having come so far, he wanted nothing more than to flee.

He carried on, and soon the light disappeared into a larger chamber ahead of him. He crawled out into it, kneeling up and stretching the stiffness from his back.

As he stretched, the light landed on a corpse.

It was propped against one wall. Shreds of material hanging from its bony form were moving, swinging, although the body was motionless. Still, and staring right at him.

It was little more than a skeleton, head wrapped in loose skin, teeth exposed. Long, sharp teeth. Its arms were fixed out to either side, but other limbs hung free. Wings. They were leathery and thin, tipped with claws that opened and closed, opened and closed, clasping at the air as if trying to gain purchase on nothing.

Bone stared at the creature's dead, dark eyes, and it started to scream.

The sound was shocking, and horrible. Bone screamed back. The creature thrashed its wings and they stirred up clouds of dust, flicking wet silt across the cavern. It was buried up to its waist, and must have been there for decades since the valley was flooded, hibernating in this dark cave and submerged beneath mud and water.

Decades.

It screeched again, twisting against the confining mud, its shrivelled body displaying amazing strength.

Not my father, Bone thought, and he turned and started pushing his way back through to the first cavern. The screeching followed him. The noise carried a promise of pain. The corpse looked hungry.

One of those others Mohserran shared its space with had wings, always kept tight to its body, almost as if it was ashamed of them. *I never asked the gargoyle's name.*

The gargoyle was here, and the werewolf was buried down by the stream. So where was his father?

He burst back into the first cavern and slipped, tumbling down into the channel worn by the stream, the thing's screaming following him down as if sound itself could clasp hold of him and squeeze, claw through his flesh, crunch his bones.

Sometimes he was afraid of the Kin, but mostly he saw them as the gentle, frightened creatures most of them were.

He had never been this terrified.

As he crawled, trying to stand, something grabbed hold of his left leg. He shouted out in surprise and aimed the torch down. The buried corpse had its hand around his ankle. It was shaking, shivering where it was buried, and silt was falling away from it, uncovering more of its body and face as it turned its head—a creak, a crumple—to look at him with black, oily eyes.

Bone screamed, long and loud, and tugged his leg out of its grasp. He ran along the stream, climbing from the channel and following the footsteps he'd left on his way in. He wished more than ever before to be out in the sunlight, a Grey Man seeking the colour of the world.

As he ran, he saw a shape slip away from deeper shadows ahead of him. It moved in a jerky, uncertain fashion, an ambiguous form given sharp edges.

Just before its pained, mad growls joined the screaming coming from behind him, Bone thought, *Father*.

12

It was the first dead Kin Vince had seen since being trapped in the Fold. He'd witnessed plenty before, and the memories of them would stay with him always. Ballus the mad satyr had murdered so many, and Vince still had nightmares about the old enclosed swimming pool where he'd kept their rotting bodies. His legs were scarred from where Ballus had attacked him with the broken parts of dead creatures, their exotic, unknowable corpses broken down into sad remnants, relics of things that should not be.

The pombero sat propped against a tree, head tilted to one shoulder, his arms splayed to either side with hands on the ground and palms facing upward. He looked more human in death, not less. His eyes were open and staring past Vince at the sky, as if seeking some sort of saviour from the heavens, or perhaps a form of escape. Vince suspected he had found it.

His mouth hung open and his tongue was missing, bitten clean through. The stump was a bloodied, clotted thing, and blood had dried in globules against his teeth and around the outside of his mouth. Deep purple bruising stained his neck and throat. His hands were also covered in dried blood, and his fingers were thick with it.

It looked like he had bitten out his tongue, and then worked at the wound to prevent the blood from clotting. He had either bled to death or drowned in his own blood. Whichever, he had been determined to die.

There was no sign of the missing tongue.

Vince crouched before the pombero's sad corpse, waving away the flies, flicking off beetles and ants that had gone to work on the drying blood. The small woodland was almost silent, as if in respect, or perhaps in shock at the death. The older wounds on his body were obvious, places where Grace's fairy teeth had bitten in and taken chunks out of his flesh. Perhaps that was the reason he had chosen to end things.

But where's his tongue?

It seemed like a difficult way to commit suicide. There were several places in the Fold where a drop from a cliff would be enough to kill yourself, a river to drown in, sharpened quartz shale to slice skin and vein. Biting out your own tongue and ensuring the blood kept flowing must have been an incredibly painful, wretched way to die.

"And where is the tongue?" Vince muttered. He looked around the corpse, stretched to see behind him, lifted his hands to make sure it wasn't hidden beneath them. A carrion creature could have made away with it, he supposed, snatching a free warm meal moments after the poor creature had bitten it off and spat it out. Maybe he'd performed the bite somewhere else and stumbled here, choosing this peaceful glade as a good place to die.

Vince froze. It was so obvious. He muttered a curse and stood, staring down at the dead man and wondering who he had left behind. He'd spat the word *human* at Vince like it was something dirty, but until recently the pombero had lived as a human, perhaps aware of his strangeness, perhaps not. There might be a partner, children, friends, all missing him now that he had been struck by lightning and vanished. They would never see him again, and never know what had happened to him.

But if what Vince suspected was true, the terrible results of his sacrifice might become known to them all.

He started walking down towards the river, turning things over in his mind. The pombero had stolen the rucksack for Mallian, of that much he was sure. He also knew that the Nephilim still did not have every relic required to perform the spell that might give him a hold over Grace. That was because Vince had stolen one of them back in the world and buried it where no one would ever find it again.

A small relic, like a knot of dried flesh.

Like a tongue.

"Your slave is dead," Vince said.

"I have no slaves. Come here, scratch my nose, would you?"

"And have you bite my hand off?"

"I told you. Human flesh tastes of shit."

It was growing dark, one of the Fold's intermittent nights drawing close. It had been some time since the last one. Vince slept when he was tired, not according to the time of day or night it might be. He did not feel tired now. He felt afraid.

"You killed him," Vince said.

"Me?" Mallian sounded almost convincing. "I haven't moved from here in many months, maybe years. How do you think I could kill someone?"

"You talked him into it. Told him what you wanted."

"Are you on about that rucksack again?"

Vince didn't answer. The more information he gave, the less chance he'd have of easing the truth out of the Nephilim.

"You're dangerous," he said instead. "You always have been, and I'd be a fool if I thought otherwise."

"Then be a fool, Vince. I'm finished. Look at me. Have you really looked at me, since you've been coming here to talk with me? I'm weakening, fading. I'm nothing like I was. My age is catching up with me."

"And everything you've done."

"Yes, everything I've done. It all comes home to roost. I've led a life longer than you can possibly comprehend, seen things you could never understand. Done things that would make you rejoice, and other things that would make you vomit and faint. But I'm close to the end. Near enough that I can sense the darkness when I close my eyes. It's gathering around me, ready to close in and take me when I'm tired enough, or starving enough. Or when I give in."

"You'll never give in," Vince said. "Don't try to persuade me otherwise."

"And don't pretend to know my mind," Mallian said, his voice low and quiet. Vince shivered. It was like hearing a rumble through the ground, the threat of doom approaching. Of all the Kin he had met, he must never pretend that Mallian was anything approaching human.

"What do you want?" Mallian asked. His tone gave the question added weight. He wasn't asking why Vince had returned to him now, as dusk fell and a Kin lay dead against a tree. This was something deeper.

"I want to see Angela again," he said. "I don't want to carry on living without her."

"I can take care of that."

"What, so you'll kill me too?"

"No. I can ensure you'll see her again."

"By taking control of Grace." The words hung heavy in the air. Mallian did not respond, and Vince went a little closer so that he could see him in the failing light. Night always fell quickly here, as if Grace made the decision to welcome in darkness for a spell, and the land obeyed her will. Vince wondered where she was, who she was hunting, what she would be eating that night.

Mallian was staring up at the sky. A spread of new stars was reflected in his eyes, and Vince wished he knew the stars and constellations better, so that he could tell whether these were familiar or unknown. Mallian probably knew. He seemed to know everything.

"I can't allow that," Vince said. "Angela and me, that's nothing compared to Ascent."

"You really think I can still do that?" Mallian asked.

Yes, Vince thought, but he said nothing.

"Look at me. I'm weak. I'm dying, Vince. If you can't see that, then you're a fool."

I'm no fool and I don't see that at all. Still he said nothing. Vince knew that sometimes silence was the greatest weapon.

"I'll die here soon. Or I'll die elsewhere if I manage to escape. And that's all I want. To die on my own terms, not hers. If I use the spell and have Grace open a way back into the world, that's good enough. I'll go through, find somewhere quiet that means something to me, and live out my days."

"Where?" Vince asked.

Mallian managed the semblance of a shrug. "Perhaps Istanbul. I met a succubus there once, and she fell in love with me. For a while she was happy. Maybe I'll walk the night-time streets until I feel some echo of her. Or the Scottish Highlands. The witch Jilaria Bran and I fought there together for a while. We won great victories. Maybe I'll find the cave where we went to lick our wounds, bury myself deep."

"She sacrificed herself for you," Vince said.

"She loved me."

"She loved your cause. Would you betray her

sacrifice now and give up Ascent?"

"I gave it up many moons ago," Mallian said quietly, and Vince was shocked to see a tear escape the corner of his eye. The Nephilim would never show such weakness. Not on purpose. This was an unconscious tear, and perhaps the only way he knew he was crying was a blurring of the stars. "Even if I hadn't, I'm too weak to make it work now. I need to be a figurehead for Kin to follow, not a... a *walking corpse.*"

For just a few seconds Vince had doubts. Only a few. He could not afford them. He only hoped he had judged Mallian's opinion of him correctly.

"What do you need?" he asked. He glanced around at the shadows. He didn't have to feign concern that they were being watched. Darkness brought new fears to the Fold.

"I have what I need," Mallian said. "I simply need you... I don't have the strength. I need you to arrange them for me, and perhaps to say the words."

"What words?"

"I'll tell you. You can repeat them, louder. Loud enough to work."

He believes me, Vince thought, and he breathed deeply to still his racing heart.

"Come closer," Mallian said.

Vince took a few steps towards the Nephilim. He had never been this close in the dark. Mallian's animal smell seemed amplified in the shadows, exuded from his naked body in warm waves. He appeared larger, his teeth glimmering with borrowed moonlight, his breathing slow and heavy.

"A little closer," he said. "It's under me."

"The rucksack," Vince said.

"I'm as desperate as you."

Vince knelt, and only at the last second did he realise his mistake.

Mallian twisted and clasped Vince's left ankle with one powerful hand. Wrist still secured to the ground by Grace's spell, his fingers bit in deep, crunching muscle against bone.

Vince gritted his teeth and grunted. There was no point trying to escape. And his ploy depended on him taking whatever came next.

"If you fail me, I'll make sure you suffer forever," Mallian said. "The pombero wasn't the only mongrel I have under my control. As the fairy eats them, so I'll have them eat you. Small chunks, just enough to hurt, not enough to kill you. A finger, an ear, your cock. I'll have them eat you alive over a long, long time. If you fail me, human."

"Why would I want to do *anything* that means I'm trapped here?" Vince said, and he injected every ounce of love he had for Angela into his voice. For a moment he believed it himself. He believed he was capable of helping Mallian, if it meant he and Angela would be together again.

If he dwelled on Angela long enough, he thought that belief could become fact.

"Under me," Mallian said, and he had to let Vince go and arch upwards so that the human could reach the rucksack hidden beneath the Nephilim's back.

Vince could feel Mallian's heat, smell his rank odour, and as he reached beneath his back he felt the hardened nubs and ridges where there had once been wings. He wondered at Mallian's real, deep story, the true tale of his time on Earth and elsewhere, and he feared that to know would drive him mad.

Then he felt the rough material of the rucksack. He curled his forefinger through one strap and pulled, slowly, not wishing to startle the Nephilim with any sudden movements.

Even then he worried that he was being played with, a mouse to Mallian's ferocious cat.

"I have it," Vince said. "You can lie back down. You won't be there for much longer."

That final untruth gave him the couple of seconds he needed. He rolled back, stood, stumbled backwards some more, and only then did he allow himself to look at Mallian.

Mallian glared back at Vince with murder in his eyes. "No," he said.

"I'm sorry," Vince said, though he really was not.

"No," Mallian said again.

"You know I can't let you do it. Maybe you are fading away, losing touch. You'd have never believed me before."

Mallian was shaking. There was no more talk in

him, no pleading, not even any threats. As Vince turned around and ran, the fallen angel roared so loud that he feared the Fold might fall apart beneath the scream.

Vince ran, and ran, losing himself so that he lost anyone or anything else coming after him. Then he started hiding the relics from the rucksack. There were thirteen in total, the ones gathered by Gregor—he assumed that Mallian held onto the fresh pombero's tongue in one of his hands—and Vince dropped them at random, kicking them beneath rocks, wedging them down cracks in the ground, lobbing one into a pond and another into the flowing river. In his fear, there was no way he'd be able to remember where each one was, even if Mallian managed to escape, capture him, and torture him for their whereabouts. With each relic he hid away, he felt the reality of Angela becoming less and less solid, until the woman he loved was as faded and obscured as the landscape around him.

He'd never really held any hope of ever seeing her again.

Now, he had made sure.

Perhaps the human is right. Maybe he is fading away and growing vague. There is no way he would have been fooled like that if he possessed all his faculties.

But inside, Mallian is on fire. His fury is a furnace that scorches every part of him. He is shaking with hatred and rage, so much that he wonders whether he will shake himself free from the fairy's invisible bonds. Wouldn't that be a blessed irony? The Nephilim whose wings had been ripped away, confronting and defeating the fairy whose wings remained folded and furled. He wonders if she has flown in the past thousand years, or whether she has grown so old that she's forgotten how to.

He will throw her from the highest cliff to find out. But only when he's finished with her. That will be her payment for the power she will bring to him—a fall to her death, just as he once fell to this long, frustrating life.

Ascent remains everything to Mallian. His heart might beat weaker than it ever has before, but his purpose is his true life, his real heart, and that is as white-hot as ever. Even hotter. He's had a long, long time to dwell on the implications of Ascent, lying here with grass dead and rotted beneath him and his subtle movements having scraped and worn his impression into the ground. He is the junction between land and sky, and when he escapes—not if, but when, because he cannot consider any other possibility—he will be the bridge between past and future. The past, a place where the Kin slink through quiet places and hide in shadows. The future, during and after Ascent, when those Kin who choose to stand with him will rise triumphant. Even those who do not side with him will be allowed to persist, and they will thank him for that. He will be their hero and their king.

The human fooled and betrayed him, which is what

humans do. He will be dealt with. If Mallian's anger were an energy, Vince would be a simmering husk in whatever cave or hole he is hiding in right now.

He looks up at the stars and feels them staring back down at him. They see him, and mark him, and none of the other Kin in this place are seen by the stars. They pass their time running and hiding and being eaten, existing rather than living, and they will live and die without making their mark on this world, or the wider world where they all came from.

He shifts his shoulders and feels the damp soil compressing and shifting beneath him. He has made his mark. Until the moment he fades away, or the fairy finally comes to kill him herself, he remains determined to make Ascent work. Every cell in his body strives for that. It's all he needs and wants. It's all that is left for him.

He cannot believe that he will fail. It's not about fairness, because Mallian more than most Kin understands that life is not fair. Life is what you make it, and he will make life triumphant.

13

Sammi thought that Lilou was right and this would be an adventure. She also suspected that the valley was more dangerous than it seemed. It was a feeling, an inkling, like static raising the hairs on her arms, even though on her left arm she hardly had any hairs since being struck twice by lightning. The markings she'd had for a while after the second strike had risen again, like a memory of sheet lightning scorched into her vision. They reminded her of the terrible man Gregor, the Kin-killer. She did not like those memories, but they would always be a part of her.

She had come to trust such feelings. They were part of the change taking place within her, linked to the sparkling lightning she could conjure from her fingertips, and the returned markings on her arm, and other, deeper changes that she had yet to make sense of. She wished her dad were alive so she could ask him about it. She wished her mom was here. She had Angela, and she was doing her best. But sometimes Sammi felt so alone.

She was certain that the Kin blood came from her mother's side. She had been convinced for almost two years that she was different, ever since she faced the fairy and saw something of herself reflected in that unknowable being's eyes. She remembered the feeling of Grace's hand around her upper arm, the gentle urging as she tugged her through from this world and into her own Fold. Sammi would never forget that momentary sense of belonging nowhere as she balanced between worlds. Just for an instant she had been part of neither, and the nightmare potential of slipping into the spaces in between was horrible.

It continued to give her nightmares. She quite liked silence and solitude, but in those spaces between worlds she had experienced true nothingness. She never wanted to see or feel that again.

She thought that her aunt Angela was aware of the changes taking place within her, even though Angela had no Kin blood—she and her mother had been sisters, though her mother was adopted. Lilou definitely knew. Neither of them talked about it much, and that suited Sammi. She wanted to discover it for herself before discussing it with other people.

Walking down towards the remains of Longford, she was alert for the indefinable danger she felt from this place. Maybe it was because it looked and felt so different from anywhere she had ever been before.

It could also be because Lilou was certainly hiding something from both of them.

The summer sun was low and already hot as they passed from green to grey and started down the gentle slope of the old reservoir bed towards the valley floor. Lilou took the lead, while Sammi and Angela followed close behind.

"We should have brought more water," Angela said.

"We're walking through a reservoir."

"Ha! Yes. Maybe a couple of weeks ago, fish were swimming around our heads."

"The ground's hardening under the sun," Sammi said, "but there are still lots of damp areas, puddles and pools. You can see the sun shining from them down in the valley."

"No way I'm drinking from them," Angela said. She didn't elaborate on why, but Sammi silently agreed. *They'll be contaminated*, she thought, *with whatever makes this place so strange. And there are all those bodies buried down there.*

Lilou was a woman of mysteries. She came to see them now and then, but she rarely told them much about where she'd been or what she had been doing. Angela knew her from London, and just sometimes a tension formed between the two of them that Sammi could cut with a knife. Neither had said, but she was pretty sure it was to do with Vince. Lilou was a nymph, and Sammi had sometimes felt the effect—a deep attraction, a beguiling allure. Maybe she'd had the same effect on Vince in London. Maybe something had happened.

Sammi didn't ask and didn't wish to know. The more she felt the change within herself growing, the more attractive Lilou's exotic origins became to her. She told Angela she was fine living isolated in the cabin in the woods, but there would come a time soon when that was not enough. At least now she could escape into the trees and explore her new talents, the bright shining potential she felt blooming deep inside.

Coming here was another escape. She could see that Lilou believed it too, because the nymph moved with a cautious enthusiasm, eyes wide and her usual defences slipping now and then so that she exuded that naked animal magnetism that seemed to set the air around her aflame. Sammi only wished Angela could welcome the chance to escape.

She's only human, Sammi thought, and she let out an unconscious giggle.

"What's up?" Angela asked.

"Just enjoying being out doing something different," Sammi said, and it wasn't a lie. Angela smiled and it touched her eyes. Maybe somewhere beneath her fears for the future and bad memories of the past remained a sense of adventure.

The drying reservoir bed was not as smooth as Sammi might have expected, and they followed several shallow depressions that led down towards the remains of the settlement. As the slope decreased and they neared the outskirts of what had once been a thriving small town, Sammi began to pick out more details of what the flooding of the valley had left behind.

To the eyes of Sammi more than two years ago,

before everything in her life had changed, this might have been a desolate, forbidding, unwelcoming landscape. But Sammi today saw it as something amazing. No efforts appeared to have been made to prepare the valley for flooding, other than the construction of the dam. Many trees remained standing, stripped of all branches and bark and remaining now as pale, sodden fingers pointing skyward. Old woodland that had once been lush and rich now consisted of acres of these peculiar sculptures to the past, many of them already darkening as they dried, dead wood flesh growing brittle beneath the sunlight they had not seen for decades. In weeks or months they would probably degrade and crumble, falling if touched, blowing down and away in the slightest breeze. Countless other trees had already fallen beneath the water, roots undermined and their trunks driven over by the softest of currents. There were piles of broken wood and tattered trunks spread across the valley floor close to Longford, carried there by the last of the water as it had found its own level and drifted towards the broken earth dam.

Everything was covered in silt, a fine coating as if a light grey mist had descended across the world. Where the sun had baked it dry it had crumbled from many of the landscape's features or fallen away beneath the slightest breeze. Elsewhere it remained, making ghosts of whatever it touched. These were memories of trees, echoes of rocks, recollections of old tumbled walls known only to those spirits that remained.

Because there were remnants. Sammi felt them deep in her bones, in places where she had never felt anything before. That was another aspect of the change settling over her, as the grey dust of ages had descended across this valley. She sensed a presence there in the dead old town, something old, like the echo of a breath exhaled many years before. Deep inside, she heard that breath.

It was pained, and that was troubling.

She glanced at Angela and Lilou, wondering if they felt the same. Angela wore her normal frown, an expression Sammi had come to know but which she believed hadn't been there a couple of years before. Her aunt had told her the story of how she and Vince had become involved with the Kin, and with the gangster Fat Frederick Meloy, and she made no secret of the fact that she resented what it had done to their happiness. Amazing though they were, the Kin were also responsible for the destruction of the comfortable, happy life she'd been leading. So much that she'd planned had changed. So many ambitions had been trodden beneath the feet, hooves and claws of creatures that mostly did not care. Whether or not Angela sensed the sadness that Sammi felt here, she knew that her aunt would be expecting trouble.

Lilou was unreadable. She felt Sammi looking at her—her stance changed, the way she held herself—but she didn't acknowledge it. *I think I could make her tell us what she's hiding*, Sammi thought. *But not yet. I'll give her the chance to come clean on her own.*

How she could make her, Sammi didn't know for sure. The change didn't tell her that much.

"Longford," Lilou said, pointing past a tumble of trees and rocks to a more regular-shaped mound.

"Is that a building?" Angela asked.

"What's left of one," Lilou said.

Much of what had once made this building a home was gone. If it had once been two storeys, there was no evidence of that now, with the walls reaching barely to shoulder height. Patches had been scoured clear of silt by wind or had simply fallen away once revealed to sunlight, and the old brick peered through. Tired, crumbled, still it held on even after decades submerged beneath the reservoir. Walls stood straight, holed here and there where windows and doors had fallen or rotted away. The ground level was at least two feet higher than it had been pre-flood, giving the house the look of a shrunken thing, or a dwelling for little people. But the floor plan was quite clear, and the structure close by could only have been a garage.

"Anyone home?" Lilou said, but she didn't call too loudly, and her chuckle sounded nervous.

"Let's look," Angela said.

"It might be dangerous," Lilou said.

Angela glanced at her. "You wanted us to come." She approached the old home and Sammi went with her.

There was nothing within the walls that might have

identified it as a house. No furniture or belongings, no internal structures. Just the outside walls, encasing a layer of flat silt that was cracking beneath the sunlight.

"Maybe they moved all the people and furniture out," Sammi said.

"It looks... sad," Angela said. "Like it's been forgotten."

"Mostly." Lilou was beside them now, and she leaned through an opening in the wall to peer closer. "Wow. Look at that."

At first glance Sammi thought it was the body of an unknown animal, strange ribs exposed in a twisting ribbon. *Kin!* she thought, and her breath quickened, her heart beat faster. Then she saw that it was not the remains of anything that had lived. It was a keyboard, warped and with many keys missing, but still settled into the shell of a decayed wooden piano. It was slumped in one corner of the room on broken legs, half buried, a useless thing.

"Look over there," Angela said. "Is that...?" She didn't finish her sentence, but walked around the old house rather than through it and approached the garage. Sammi jogged after her. Her footfalls on the silty ground felt strange, and it reminded her of how it sometimes felt walking through the pine woods close to their cabin, like there was a hollowness to her footsteps, as if the forest floor was settled on hidden spaces underneath, caves or tunnels, unknown shadows. She thought perhaps the tree roots were so interlocked that they formed a canopy over the space beneath, leaves and pine needles gathered over the decades to form a false ground. Or perhaps there were caves down there, inhabited by pale blind things that listened to her footsteps and made up stories about what could make such a sound.

"They left their car," Angela said. "Ford?"

"Don't know," Lilou said. "They all look the same to me."

"Oh yeah. You don't drive."

"Weird," Sammi said. The garage had mostly rotted away, the skeleton of heavy timber walls sagged and holed and fallen onto the vehicle. The car was rusted and deformed, but the windows were still in place, obscured by a slick plant growth on the inside surfaces. It was another sad sight, another forgotten thing.

Then Sammi saw some objects that definitely were bones. Through the lowered rear windows, she could make out a shape nestled on the back seat.

"Something's in there," she said. She approached the car, stepping carefully past the fallen walls, and leaned in closer.

Sediment had settled inside the car as well, but the skull protruded above its level on the back seat, empty eyes staring back at her. Its curved spine arched up and down again, and stretched up behind it was a twisted, broken leg.

"Dog," Angela said behind her. "Big one. Me and Vince wanted one, but our place was too small. We were going to wait 'til we got somewhere bigger."

They walked through the remains of the old town, and it began to take shape in Sammi's mind. They saw more homes, a line of larger buildings that might have been shops on a main street. The simple two-road layout provided four distinct districts of ruined buildings. The northern corner was on higher ground, and there were more old trees protruding from the mud, the house outlines larger and more opulent. There stood the largest ruin they had found, and Lilou led them that way.

It was a church, stone walls supporting the bare remains of a tumbled structure that had once been the spire. *Maybe there's still a bell in there*, Sammi thought, and she imagined its lonesome ring echoing unheard through the depths of the reservoir for four decades. The spread of silt around the church was wide and flat, spiked here and there with the tops of what could only have been headstones. They were walking across a hundred bodies.

Then she looked past the church and saw the footprints.

"Someone's been here," she said, pointing.

"Security?" Angela asked.

"Maybe," Lilou said. "They're going the way we're going."

"Out of the town?" Sammi asked. She looked uphill past the church, towards where the line of green began several hundred feet higher.

"Not that far," Lilou said. "There are caves."

"Is that where your friend Mohserran would have been?" Angela asked.

"Maybe."

They passed the church, and this time it was Lilou who saw the skeleton. And this time, it was not a dog.

Somehow the body had become entangled with a tree. The trunk was short and stunted, but it retained the stumps of several low branches, pale and bleached by water. Sammi found it difficult to make out where bone began and wood ended, but it was obvious that this was the remains of a human. Or at least, a humanoid.

"They didn't even remove the bodies," Angela said.

"Been just hanging there," Sammi said. She was the first to approach the body, and Lilou called her back, just as she'd expected. *Hidden things*, she thought, because she was more certain than ever that Lilou wasn't telling them everything.

"Sammi!" Angela said, and Sammi turned around.

"What? You think it's going to bite me?" She spoke to her aunt, but looked at Lilou. The nymph said nothing.

Closer to the skeleton, it was easier to see what had happened. The tree was close to crumbling, the skeleton fragmented and with parts missing, but the chain that bound the two together was still obvious.

As was the hole in the skeleton's skull.

"One of yours?" Sammi asked Lilou.

"What do you mean?"

"I mean there's more to this than you've told us. They never even tried to evacuate the town."

"Of course they did," Angela said, and she looked at Lilou, waiting for her to confirm it.

Lilou opened her mouth.

"No lies," Sammi said, "only the truth," and she *forced* herself when she spoke, shoving herself forward, gathering all the change she felt inside—the ache in her bones, the bright sparks of potential blooming and expanding like stars being born—and making it her own. She shocked herself with how different she felt, and the surprise on Lilou's face was a manifestation of her own feelings. She'd never seen the nymph looking so defenceless and open. Sammi was shocked and a little disgusted to feel a sliver of wicked delight at Lilou's discomfort. She didn't enjoy feeling like that. Sickness rose in her throat and she swallowed it down, and Lilou cringed as if she was tasting the same.

"The truth..." Lilou said. "They infected the town. Some sort of nerve agent or biological warfare that went wrong. People went mad, the government tried to solve it and cover it up. They put it down to a contagion, closed off the town from the outside world. Then they went about systematically tracking down and killing everyone in the town. After that they flooded the valley and erased Longford from history forever."

"Or until the dam broke," Sammi said.

"Right. Thing is, there were three Kin living in the town and integrating with the community. One of them was Mohserran."

"Your selkie friend," Angela said.

"Such a gentle soul. I'm not sure what he was doing this far inland, but it could be he used the river to swim back and forth to the sea when he was in his seal form. Or it could be he found love."

"They'd have been killed too though, right?" Sammi asked.

"That's what we're here to find out."

"It's what *you're* here to find out," Angela said. "We're just here because you dragged us. And I don't like anything about this place, or what it might be doing to Sammi."

"You always knew there was something," Sammi said.

"I knew you were different," Angela said, tears in her eyes. "I guess I've been trying to ignore it. Hope it went away."

There was silence for a while, awkward and loaded.

"I didn't mean to lie," Lilou said.

"Doesn't matter," Sammi said. "You did it for a reason, right?"

"A good reason," Lilou said. She was quieter than usual, and wouldn't catch Sammi's gaze.

"What reason?" Angela asked.

"To make sure they're dead," Lilou said. "The three Kin who were here when the town was gassed and then flooded. Including Mohserran, who really is an old friend. I have to make sure they're all dead."

"Why?" Sammi asked, but she thought she knew.

"Because after what was done to them, they're too dangerous to live."

"How do you know all this?" Sammi asked. "If they came and killed everyone, how do you know what happened?"

"A human escaped," Lilou said. "I've never met him, but he became something of a friend to the Kin. He protects them, hides them, helps them flee if that's what's required. He told the story to an uldra, a sort of fairy, way north of here, in Alaska. That story spread. We don't trust anything a human tells us, of course, but together with everything we know about this place, it makes some sort of sick sense." She swept her hand around, indicating their surroundings. "And no one has seen Mohserran or the other two in forty years."

Lilou finally telling the truth made the tension between them darker. The weight of her lie could not be diluted by its revelation. That would take more time, and a rebuilding of whatever trust had been there to begin with.

They headed out of town, all of them silent. Sammi was simmering with the remnants of the power, exhausted, as if she'd just run a marathon. She was also scared of what was happening to her. She knew it was a good thing, something she could use to help people if she used it in the right way. But she didn't want it.

Many little girls grew up dreaming of becoming fairies, but she knew that fairies weren't always good.

They left the strange ruins of Longford, and all the way Sammi was looking for more remains that showed how the town's residents had been murdered. She felt sick to the soul at the events of several decades before, and also at Lilou's lie. She didn't believe the nymph had brought them into danger—after so long, nothing could remain alive under the water and buried in mud—but she had lied to them, probably because she'd known that Angela would have said no.

As they passed the outermost remains, Lilou stopped and shielded her eyes to look up at the hillside. "There. See those rocks? The caves are there."

Sammi looked, and she saw a man hauling himself over a pile of boulders, dropping to the ground, rolling, and then standing and running downhill. When he caught sight of Sammi, Angela and Lilou he changed direction until he was aiming right at them.

"One of the Kin?" Angela asked, and there was a trace of fear in her voice.

"No," Sammi said, although she thought, *There is something about him... the way he runs... the way he looks.*

"Run," the man shouted as he drew closer. He waved at them, eyes wide, not slowing down. "Run!"

14

And there I was almost trusting Lilou for a moment, Angela thought. It was a sad betrayal, but one that hadn't surprised her. She'd always believed that the nymph was out for herself, and this only went to prove it.

And now her lie had put them all in peril.

Angela's first thought was for Sammi. Most of what she worried about lately was to do with her niece, apart from those long lonely moments she spent thinking of Vince, and now more than ever she wanted to do everything she could to look after her dead sister's girl.

Even though Sammi was changing, she still needed protecting.

"Who's that?" she asked as the man ran towards them, waving and shouting.

"No idea," Lilou said, "but he's been in the caves."

As the man approached, Angela saw movement past him in the ridge of large rocks from where he'd emerged. A grey shape was coming up into the sunlight, moving slowly and with a strange, staccato gait. It was like watching a film with one in every five frames removed.

"What the hell is that?" Angela asked as the shape emerged fully into sunlight. "Does it have *wings*?" It was pale grey and fragmented like a statue cracked in the heat. She thought of Mallian with the scars where his wings had been ripped off, and the fairy Grace who, if she even had wings, never appeared to use them.

"Can't see," Lilou said.

"Mohserran?" Sammi asked.

It was the man who answered. He stopped a few steps from them, looking back and forth and panting hard. Older than her, he was fit, and otherwise nondescript. He looked startled, worried, but not outright terrified.

"Mohserran's still down there," he said. "This is one of the others."

"Who the hell are you?" Lilou demanded.

The man focused on her, and in that unguarded moment he saw her for what she was. "Who are *you?*" he replied. Angela suspected that just for a second, any thought of danger and fear was purged from his mind.

"We can do this when we're somewhere safer," Sammi said. "We should run?"

"We should run," the man said, glancing back at the figure. It was standing still by the pile of rocks, swaying back and forth as it looked around with one hand raised to shield the sun from its face.

When it turned towards them, Angela felt the full weight of its glare. She had been stared at with strange, alien eyes before, but this felt different. She felt the mass of its intelligence, and the burn of its madness.

They hurried back towards Longford. Angela ran

close to Sammi, resisting the temptation to grasp her hand, and made sure that Lilou was between them and the man. Whatever had happened here was mixed up in her mind, and the appearance of the man, and the creature he was fleeing, made it even more confused.

"Holy fuck!" the man said. He was looking behind them, and Angela and the others skidded to a stop to follow his gaze.

Another figure had emerged close to the first. It was down on all fours and shaking its head as if something inside was loose. It was snorting, and dust seemed to be spurting from its nose every time it did so.

"Come on!" Lilou said. "We have to hurry."

"Hurry where?" Angela asked.

"Anywhere but here."

When they reached the half-buried remains of the first building Sammi glanced behind them and said, "They're coming."

The words chilled Angela. To see Lilou's fear scared her more, and she found it was Sammi she turned to, the poor girl who had lost her parents, been kidnapped by a spirit and then hauled into an alternate world by a mad fairy. Sammi, who she knew had been changing since that moment.

"Here," the man said, looking around. "We can defend ourselves here."

"Against them?" Lilou asked. The two of them swapped confused glances, as if sizing each other up.

"And with what?" Angela asked. "You got weapons?"

"Nothing that'll be effective," he said. "They've just woken up. They'll be confused."

"And hungry," Lilou said.

Angela could see the two shapes now, coming down the hillside after them. The first was staggering from left to right, its wings hanging loose behind it as if heavy and broken. An old tree trunk crumbled beneath its impact, tipping slowly to the left and smashing across the hardening ground. A haze of dust rose around it and the figure stopped, staring at the spreading cloud as if searching for something within its expanse.

The second shape remained on all fours, zig-zagging down the hillside towards the town with its nose to the ground. It continued snorting and sneezing dust. Its front limbs were bent, elbows arching almost above its back and tipped with pale white points like bare bone. Its rear limbs were thicker, and stronger. It was gaunt, and she was amazed it had any strength at all.

"They've been down there all this time?" she asked.

"Yes," Lilou said.

"But why aren't they dead?"

"We don't have long," the man said.

"Just who the fuck are you?" Angela asked him. His arrival angered her. If he wasn't here, if he hadn't gone down into the caves and perhaps woken them, maybe they would still be asleep down there. Or in hibernation. Or whatever it was insane Kin infected by human fucking biological warfare fucking shit did.

"He's Bone," Lilou said. "You're him, aren't you? The one who escaped."

His eyes went wide and he blinked at the nymph.

"You can help us," Lilou said. "We need to find somewhere to trap them and barricade them in. One of these old buildings, maybe a basement, or we could see if there's somewhere more solid beneath the church where we can—"

"We can't ever let them leave here," Sammi said, staring past Angela. The Kin were advancing, but slowly. The dog-creature sniffed at the ground, drifting left and right and picking up their trail. The winged Kin looked at its feet as it walked, glancing up occasionally to look for them, shielding its eyes against the midday sun. Now that they were closer, they frightened Angela even more. Even the cruellest Kin she had seen displayed a level of intelligence in its features, signs of consciousness and self-awareness that often belied its appearance. These two Kin were skeletal and denuded, slavering and grunting, like rabid animals resurrected to seek a fresh kill.

"What do you mean?" Angela asked.

"Look at them. If they get out into the valley or beyond, what do you think will happen?"

"She's right," Bone said. "They might still be infectious."

"After all this time submerged in water and muck?" Angela asked.

"In their bodies," he said. "Blood, saliva, piss, other fluids."

"Oh, great," Angela said. "Thanks for this, Lilou."

"So we have to trap them," Sammi said. She nudged Lilou. "You're bait."

"Me?" Lilou said, but she smiled at Sammi, as if proud.

"Trust me." It was obvious from Sammi's voice that she did not trust herself.

"They're closer," Bone said. "They know we're here."

Angela felt a rush of emotions. Sorrow for what Sammi had been through, losing her parents so young and plunged into a strange, dangerous world. Sadness at her own predicament, her comfortable life torn apart forever, the love of her life a universe away. Most of all fear for this young girl who was changing in ways none of them yet understood.

And fear *of* her.

"I trust you to try," Angela said.

"What about Mohserran?" Lilou asked.

"Still down there," Bone said. "He... I think he let me pass."

"Let you? Why?"

"Later," Bone said, nodding past her. "Look."

The dog-Kin had reached the first ruined building and was sniffing at it, digging its nose hard into the dried, cracked surface and emerging with damp mud on its tip. It looked something like a dog, but no dog Angela had ever seen.

"What is it?" she asked.

"Werewolf," Bone said, sounding sad. "Stuck in its

change. Francine only ever used to hunt rabbits."

"Back this way," Sammi said. "We need to lure them into Longford and find somewhere to trap them."

"You're sure you can do that?" Lilou asked, but Sammi did not reply.

They followed Bone back between the grey mounds of fallen buildings. The landscape of the old town offered more places to hide, and they moved quickly and quietly.

Behind them, one of the Kin howled. It was a broken, gargled scream, the first noise from the throat and mouth of something that had been put down almost four decades before. But it was not a feeble sound. It sang of fury.

"Oh fucking hell," Angela said. When Lilou glanced at her she felt a surge of anger towards her for bringing them into this. She'd taken them from the safe, boring cabin in the woods and put them in danger once again. If they got out of this, she would make her pay.

Bone led them as if he knew the layout of the drowned town, glancing around as he ran, moving confidently left and right until he signalled them to stop.

"There," he said, pointing at a low mass from which a brick wall protruded.

"What's that?"

"Convenience store. It had a big walk-in fridge out back."

"There's no way that'll still be in one piece," Lilou said.

"We can see."

They slipped past the wall and into what had once been a large store. Like all the remains in the town it was open to the elements now—roof gone, walls fallen, nothing recognisable inside. The uneven surface of cracked, dried mud hid anything that might have survived, but Bone led them towards a higher mound near the back, to one side of which a tall thick wall still stood solid.

"This way," he said. "I think."

"Sammi," Angela said, and she hated that she was asking anything like this of the girl. Sammi grabbed her hand. It felt hot. Her skin was burning, and Angela noticed for the first time that the trace-work of fern-like scars had emerged once again on her forearm. The memory of the lightning strikes had come to the fore.

"I'm still not sure," Sammi said, and she sounded so lost.

"Get sure," Bone said. "Francine's here."

The ragged werewolf had mounted a small hillock close to the store's remains, and now it stood looking down upon them, breathing hard, mucus and dust dribbling from its nose. It displayed no human attributes that Angela could make out. The sounds it made, the way it stood, indicated that its greatest desire right then was to eat them.

"Look at its eyes," Lilou said, and Angela looked closer. The werewolf's eyes seemed to glow a gentle yellow, as if backlit with a flashlight. The yellow dripped, a discharge that left twin sticky trails down either side of its long, thin snout.

It looked sick and old, furious and hungry.

"That's the infection," Bone said. "*Don't* let her bite you. *Don't* let her scratch you."

"You've seen this before," Angela said.

"She's going to jump," Bone said. "You have to keep her occupied."

"It'll be occupied eating my face off."

Bone went for the thick wall, picking up something that might have been an old metal chair leg. He started scraping and hacking at the mound of silt washed up and hardened against the facade, and within a few seconds Angela heard a sharp rapping sound.

"It's still here!" he said. Lilou went and helped, leaving Angela and Sammi standing side by side.

"Whatever you're going to do..." Angela said.

"I'm working on it." Sammi's voice was deeper and more level than before, quieter, and when Angela glanced at her sidelong, she saw the concentration in her expression.

Angela looked around for a weapon. She found a rock the size of her fist and picked it up, hefted it, knew that it was all but useless against one of the risen Kin.

The werewolf lowered its head into an attack position. It was thin and wasted, but that detracted nothing from the threat it presented.

Bone and Lilou were frantically digging in front of the wall, and part of an old metal doorway was already exposed. *They'll never uncover it in time*, Angela thought. *And even if they do, it'll never open.*

"Don't you have a gun?" she asked Bone, but he either didn't hear or chose to ignore her. *Need a silver bullet against that anyway*, she thought, wondering if that were even true.

The werewolf stopped growling, relaxed, and eased back, and Angela stood taller beside Sammi and wielded the rock. She felt a momentary sense of hope—was the creature in two minds? Were there too many of them?

"Get down!" Sammi said, looking over her left shoulder. Angela dropped to her knees and rolled onto her side. She kept hold of the rock and brought it up before her face as she landed on her back, ready to smash it into anything that might be jumping or charging at them.

The figure she saw must have been the third Kin, Mohserran. He was running towards them, his steps unsteady but his intentions clear. His sunken, shrivelled face was moulded into a visage of pure rage. He was naked, skin folded and hardened into a leathery hide over the decades of his burial or submersion. His limbs were thin, but they seemed strong. Long hair flowed behind his head as he ran, like seaweed caught in a current. His eyes flamed yellow, much brighter than the werewolf Francine's.

Hopeless, Angela thought, and then the world caught fire. Bright white light filled her eyes. She was blinded, and although she felt a pulse of heat it only caressed and stretched her skin rather than scorching flesh from bones. A boom thundered through the ground and air, compressing her eardrums and driving pain into her skull. The impact lifted her and slammed her back down, winding her. She felt a wave of dust and other debris drive across her, stinging exposed skin and scouring her face and upper arms. She clenched the rock in her hand even harder, and when she squinted she saw sparks leaping across her whitened fingernails, jumping from one to the next and dancing on the exposed stone in between.

The sparks were everywhere.

She rolled into a crouch and brought the rock up over one shoulder, ready to swing it forward.

Mohserran was down on his knees close to her, almost close enough to touch. His yellowed eyes were wide, his mouth drooped open, his long hair was splayed over his shoulders, heavy with dried mud. He reached for her with one clawed hand. His neck and left arm were coated with a smooth, dry fur, and here and there it was singed and smoking. Lightning danced back and forth across his bared teeth.

Though he reached for her, he was looking at Sammi. He was frozen to the spot, knotted muscles quivering but not obeying his silent commands. He was a sculpture of fury.

Sammi was on one knee beside Angela, left hand resting on the ground, right hand still held out before her. She held onto white fire. It rolled across her palm and back and forth between her fingers, a pet eager to do its master's bidding.

"Francine!" Bone shouted.

Sammi knelt up and swung her hand around, and Angela felt the bolt of white fire—

Lightning, that's lightning coming from my niece's hand!

—surge past her on the right. She rolled to the left and turned just in time to see it striking the werewolf as it leapt. The creature was knocked from the sky, writhing in the dust as sparks coursed across its withered body. It set its denuded fur on end.

"Oh, no," Sammi said, swaying where she knelt. Her eyes were wide and she drooled. The arm supporting her against the ground shook, and Angela went for her just as she fell. She dropped the rock and caught her niece in her arms, but her skin was so hot that Angela gasped and let her go. Sammi fell to the dusty ground, breath knocked from her with a gentle sigh. Angela reached for the girl again, but she could feel the heat radiating from her, and she didn't know how Sammi wasn't burning up, her brain and organs shrivelling and melting beneath the ferocious onslaught.

Maybe she will die, maybe she's not ready for this and doesn't even know what it is. The Kin have screwed with my family and this is the end result, this sweet innocent girl burning to death from the inside out before my eyes while I can't do a fucking thing about it.

"Sammi!"

"Grab her!" Lilou said.

"I can't, she's burning hot and she's in pain, can't you just—?"

"We're not out of trouble yet," Bone said. "The gargoyle's coming. You look after her, we'll look after you." He was wielding the metal chair leg, and Lilou had found a heavy spiked branch somewhere. They stood between Angela and the third Kin.

It was stalking them. Moving left and right, it glanced between its downed kin and them. Its face was twisted and contorted, its body squat and wasted. Time had only made it uglier.

"And we don't know how long they'll stay down," Angela said. She scooped Sammi up, surprised at how easily she lifted the girl in both arms. Her skin was still hot, but no longer too hot to touch. Angela had heard urban myths about parents lifting crashed cars from their trapped children. Maybe her strength now came from love.

Her eyes watered at the heat. Sammi's eyes flickered, sightless.

"I've got you," she said.

"You sure that's a gargoyle?" Lilou asked.

"Yes," Bone said. "And he's strong."

"He's been under water for forty years," Lilou said. "He'll be weak and confused. When he comes, take him from two directions."

The gargoyle saw his chance and came at them. He stumbled, wings rising up for the first time as a form of balance, and Angela saw how tattered and ripped they were. Even if he wanted to fly, she doubted he ever could.

She readied herself to drop Sammi and protect her however she could —fists, feet, nails and teeth, she'd fight to the last so that her niece might have a chance at survival.

Bone feinted left and then jumped right, swinging the chair leg in his left hand. It connected with the gargoyle's right arm. The gargoyle cried out and fell, and Bone landed beside it and rolled quickly away, eager not to make contact. Lilou came in from the other direction and jumped on the fallen Kin, bringing the branch down across the back of the creature's head. Its face was driven into the ground, muffling its cries. Careful to avoid the teeth, Lilou raised the branch to strike again.

The gargoyle rolled and kicked out, both clawed feet just missing Lilou's thighs as she staggered back.

Lilou revealed herself, arms held out, smiling.

Angela had never experienced the full effect of Lilou's alluring nymph power. Lilou spent most of her time keeping it close and tight, concealed from the world even though her true instincts urged her to be herself. Fighting against instinct was the way most Kin had survived this long, Lilou had once told her, and Angela had often been aware of the nymph's struggle.

Now, Lilou allowed herself to flow, to be herself in the face of this danger, and the rapture in her expression was wonderful to behold. Angela felt her knees weaken. Warmth bloomed at her core, and at that moment she loved Lilou and desired her, more than she'd ever believed she would desire a woman.

She took a step forward, and Sammi groaned in her arms.

"Ang..."

"I'm here!" Angela said, tearing her eyes from the nymph. "I've got you."

"I feel sick."

The gargoyle halted its attack. It stared at Lilou in confusion, then when she turned and walked towards the half-uncovered walk-in fridge it followed. Lilou glanced at Angela and frowned, and even in that glance Angela flushed with desire.

Then she recognised the look. Lilou needed help.

"Bone," she said.

"Yeah... yeah..." he said from away to one side. He too was caught in Lilou's thrall, but he was also aware of the delicacy of their situation.

Angela put Sammi down. The girl sat up, one hand braced against the ground.

"I'm okay," she said. "Go and help."

Angela hated leaving Sammi in this state even for a second. Seeing her like that, feeling her burning up, only confused her love/hate relationship with the Kin even more.

"We have to get the door open," she said.

"And we don't have long." Bone nodded behind them. Mohserran was still shaking where he stood, but there seemed more sense to his movements now, as if he was trying to extricate himself from some constraining fluid sticking him to the air. The werewolf that Bone had named Francine was still down, but no longer writhing in pain. It moved back and forth, feet slapping the ground, legs lengthening with each movement, hands propped beneath its shoulders once more. It pushed with every roll and came closer to rising up.

They didn't have long at all, and Angela didn't think Sammi had any more fight left in her.

They skirted around the gargoyle, both of them doing their best to avoid looking at Lilou. But it wasn't only the sight of her that made her so alluring. Angela could smell her, like early morning blossoms, ripe fruit, smooth rich coffee. Everything she loved. She could almost taste her on the air, and she experienced a rush of sexual images that surprised and excited her in equal measures.

"Oh hell," Bone said. "I've never known..."

"Nor me. But she's not doing it for us."

They climbed the low wall and dropped down the other side, landing in front of the entrance to the old walk-in fridge. From this close it didn't look very large, but Angela guessed it extended back into the ground behind the wall, the rear half of the building smothered by decades of silt.

The door was largely exposed, but the handle was a rusted mess. Bone worked on it with the chair leg, but the metal merely bent and then cracked.

"Better hurry," Lilou said. She drew a small knife from her belt and held it hidden by her hand.

"We're trying."

"I mean it."

The gargoyle now stood directly in front of Lilou. Its face was more monstrous than before, its body resembling cracked stone, and its erection swung before it as if steering the way. Its yellow eyes burned brighter, and Angela realised the terrible danger Lilou had placed herself in. The small knife she held would be all but useless once this creature pounced.

Angela snatched the chair leg from Bone and stepped up beside Lilou, raising the bent metal back over her shoulder.

"Handle's stuck!" Bone said behind them.

"You better stop," Angela said to the nymph.

"If I stop—"

There was another bright flash, an explosion that turned the gargoyle's eyes from yellow to white. A heavy impact thudded through her feet from behind, and Angela already knew what she would see when she turned around.

Sammi was slumped across the head of the wall, dregs of white fire dripping from her hand, falling slowly to the ground as if made from feathers.

The handle to the big fridge glowed, and Bone winced as he grabbed it and worked it back and forth. With a creak it clicked back into its housing.

"We're in!" he said, and he swung the door open two feet before it stuck on the uneven ground.

Angela took a deep breath against the stink she

expected to emerge, but whatever might have been inside forty years ago had rotted down to nothing. There was only darkness.

Lilou backed up against the door, and when the gargoyle followed Bone stepped around it and shoved it through the opening.

"What about the others?" Lilou asked.

"You stay and keep watch here," Bone said. He shoved the door closed and waited until Lilou added her weight to its outer surface. "Me and your friend here will get them. Right?"

Angela nodded. She caught Sammi's eye and, exhausted and drained, the girl still managed a smile.

In her eyes Angela saw a sort of madness, and she had the terrible feeling that she should fear her niece more than these mad, recently woken Kin.

Taking care to avoid tooth and claw, they dragged Mohserran and the spitting, shivering werewolf across the dusty ground and managed to force them through the doorway into the metal structure. There was a damp, forgotten smell to the fridge. It was larger than Angela had thought, but still barely big enough for the three Kin to be contained.

Every second they pulled and pushed, she expected the werewolf or the strange man Mohserran to shake off their fugue and bite back. Burning yellow, their eyes displayed a depth of madness that terrified her more than their teeth and claws.

With the door shut behind them, lock braced with

the metal chair leg and loose soil shoved back in and compacted against the structure, her attention turned to her niece. She was sitting up on the wall now, and she looked shrunken by what had happened.

"I did it," Sammi said.

"You did," Angela agreed. "But *what* did you do?"

Sammi's smile slipped. "Just for a bit I felt..."

"Powerful," Lilou said. She was panting hard, sweating, and grey dust was stuck to her skin in dark streaks.

"I never realised," Angela said.

"I didn't know how much I could do," Sammi said. "I knew I had something, felt it growing and changing. But I didn't know how much I had until now."

"You still don't," Lilou said.

"We can talk later," Bone said. "Right now, we've got to figure out a way of permanently containing them."

"That wasn't Mohserran," Lilou said. "That wasn't my friend. I haven't seen him for over a century, but I remember so much about him. How proud he was, how amusing, how he loved life and loved to love. That... thing wasn't him. Whatever the army or whoever did to him, he'd never want to be like that. We don't need to contain them. We need to kill them."

Bone's eyes went wide. His stance became harder, readied for more violence. *He knows them,* she thought. *If he has a personal link, we need to watch out.*

A deep and regular banging began from the half-buried structure. The exposed metal door shimmered, and with each impact it seemed to blur as dust fell from its surface. The bent chair leg wedging the handle closed seemed solid, and the impacts settled the silt piled back against the door.

Even so, she wouldn't put a bet on how long the three Kin could be contained.

"How the hell are they even still alive?" she asked.

"The Kovo," Bone said.

"What's that?"

"The infection. It's kept them alive, somehow. Didn't you see their eyes?"

"You know them," Sammi said.

"I know them," he said, but he offered no more. Angela saw a level of control in him, as if he was accustomed to situations similar to this. He reminded her of the Kin-killer Gregor, but Bone seemed to have a link with the Kin, something close and personal, not simply a desire to kill.

"We need to figure this out," Lilou said. "But there's something else."

Angela raised an eyebrow.

"That was fairy stuff," Lilou said, nodding at Sammi. "I'm sorry, kid, but it can't be denied. You've got fairy blood somewhere in your past, and everything you've been through is bringing it to the fore. I've suspected for some time, but didn't want to say anything in case it confused you or... hurt you. But I've been keeping watch."

Angela glared at her. Lilou shrugged in response.

"I never believed she'd have anything like this much power."

"So what happens to her now?" Angela asked, terrified for her niece, sad for herself. *I'm losing the one thing left pinning me to the world I know.*

"Now, if Grace senses what just happened, she might show renewed interest in Sammi. She wanted her before. Now she'll crave her company for eternity."

"*If* she sensed what happened," Sammi said.

"It's a big if," Lilou agreed.

Angela heard no doubt in the nymph's voice, but it inspired hope, not fear.

Hope that Grace's Fold, and Vince, might not be closed away forever after all.

15

The Fold is in darkness, and there is lightning in the east.

She is crouched on a rock high on the western valley slopes when she sees it illuminating the sky. She has a rabbit clenched in one hand, its neck broken, throat ripped out and chest and body half-skinned, but she is not happy with its meat. The blood is too thin and young, and it tastes of the human world. The flesh is weak. She has chewed and swallowed two mouthfuls, and already she craves something richer. It is not long since she ate properly. She should control her hunger, learn to manage with wild animals some of the time. Her Kin need time to heal between meals.

She drops the dead rabbit and stands, looking across her valley at the lightning sheeting across the opposite hilltop. The sound that rolls in is subdued, but she can smell it on the air, ozone and the memory of old times.

That is not me. That is not from my world. She knows everything about the Fold, and if she sits and concentrates for some time she can feel its ebb and flow through her insides—the drift of its river along her veins, the breeze in the valley stroking down her spine, creatures large and small stepping through her flesh. She can become the Fold, and in those moments she knows everything that is happening within its confines.

She knows that the lightning is not a product of the Fold's ebb and flow. This is something else.

It's *her*.

Her nostrils flare as she breathes in new scents. Her eyes widen as she thinks of the girl, in her hands for such a short time but in her memory forever.

It's her, and she has found herself.

Another flash arcs above the hills, and this time the crack of thunder reverberates across the Fold. Startled creatures flap and flee. Closer to the river, a larger creature—one of the Kin, though she's distracted and cannot tell which one in the darkness—takes hoof, afraid that she is preparing to feed once more.

She is done feeding for a while. She wipes the rabbit's blood from her chin and starts down the hillside. The wings folded against her back, unused for so long that she is not even sure she can part them from her skin, itch and twitch.

The itch also exists in her mind. The Fold has not felt complete since the moment she first closed it off and made this place her new whole world. The girl would make it complete.

And now she has made herself known.

As she runs, the fairy opens her mind to the weight

and geography of the Fold, she gives it her power, and she readies to create a chink that will enable her to slip through.

When Vince heard the lightning, he thought that his time had come to die.

He'd been waiting for days for Mallian to take his revenge. Whenever he saw, heard, or smelled a Kin he hid, terrified that it had been sent by Mallian to murder him, and even more terrified that it had been sent to disable him and drag him back to the Nephilim. He could barely imagine the tortures Mallian might be intending for him. Maybe he'd be fed to the fallen angel, held to his mouth by a strong Kin while Mallian bit, chewed, and bit again. He'd eat him alive, just as Grace was eating the Kin she'd lured to her Fold.

Maybe he'd be pinned to the ground close to Mallian, thick sticks driven through his hands and feet to hold him there. Then Mallian would talk to him as he slowly died from hunger, thirst or exposure, telling him what he would do to the ones Vince loved if and when he finally escaped Grace's bonds.

The potential for agonies to come was huge. The chance of escaping Mallian's wrath, even though right now he was unable to move, was slight. The Nephilim held weight, not only in his frightening size but his personality and aura, his hold on other Kin. What he had done to the pombero proved that.

Vince had changed his long, lonely, hopeless future into something short and filled with dread.

He considered taking his own life. It was an awful, shameful thought, but one which lingered. It had crossed his mind before during the time he'd been in the Fold, but had vanished again, like a bird flying into his view and then disappearing once more. Since stealing the rucksack back from Mallian, the idea had returned once again and settled on his mind. He never believed he was serious—never found himself on the edge of a long fall or with a sharp rock pressed to his wrist—but considering the most efficient methods to leave the place that was no longer his world played on his mind. If he knew more about plants perhaps he could find something poisonous. There were fungi growing in the forests, but he worried about picking something that would cause him intense pain and a long, lingering death. The hills were very high in places, and there were a couple of locations where steep cliffs would provide him a long enough fall to almost certainly kill himself. But almost was not enough. He had no wish to lie broken and bleeding into the soil at the bottom of a cliff, watching the uneven days and nights pass him by with painful indifference.

Most of all, he thought about the river. He was a good swimmer, but if he weighed himself down with rocks he'd sink and drown. The problem with that was the nature of the river. He thought perhaps his corpse would wash against one end of the Fold and enter at the other, swept down the same stretch of river again and again over weeks and months while rot and impact against the riverbed slowly broke him down. He would become part of the Fold.

But he never got any further than thinking about it. He was too strong for that. And somewhere out there, a wrinkle in time or a universe away, was Angela. His love for her meant the idea of making any of his life-ending speculations real made him feel sick.

By the time the second burst of lightning sheeted across the sky he was deep in his cave, a heavy sharpened stick in his hand. The night outside lit up and he expected to see an unknown-shaped silhouette in the cave entrance. Something with hooves or wings, long teeth and fur. Vince loved the Kin, but he had never feared them more than he did right then.

The lightning could have been Grace in combat with Mallian, the great Nephilim somehow having broken his bonds. Even after two years or so in the Fold, Vince knew little more about Grace than he had when he entered, other than that her power was degrees more advanced than any other Kin he had ever met. Her power was magic.

He didn't think Mallian could counter that with anything approaching her capabilities—not now Vince had stolen away his ability to do so—but he did not know for sure.

There was no more lightning, but something about the Fold had changed. The air was charged with potential. The land held its breath. Even Vince found himself breathing lighter and quieter, in case a heavy breath jarred the place from its condition of anticipation.

He edged towards the cave entrance, stick held out before him, ready to jump back and defend himself if anything should enter. As the seconds and minutes ticked by, he became less inclined to believe the lightning had been anything to do with him. It felt too significant, too impactful to have involved a mere human.

When he moved out of the cave it began to rain. It felt like the Fold crying. Something passed by to the south, moving quickly through the woods and across the grassland, and though Vince could not make it out, he tracked its motion as its surroundings were stirred. Trees waved and shook, rainfall was disrupted, creatures took flight away from the moving object, and he knew at once what it was.

Grace was rushing towards the site of the lightning, across the valley floor and up the hillside towards where the raging sheets had illuminated the sky.

Something gone wrong? Vince wondered. *The Fold failing?* He didn't know and could not guess, but it provided something of interest to occupy his mind. Wielding the stick and grabbing a skin of water from his cave, he started off in the direction Grace had taken.

After three steps, the ground began to shake.

After another three steps, the sky to the east turned from night into day, and sunlight streamed in from somewhere beyond.

* * *

Mallian has been alive long enough to know what the lightning signifies. A fairy is casting her spells. This, however, is not Grace.

Held tight to the ground, he has to twist his head to the side and strain his neck to look up towards the eastern hilltops. There is no more lightning, but he understands that a change has occurred, a change that he never expected.

What he feared was permanent has now become temporary. The Fold suddenly feels paper-thin, like the painting of an idea rather than the idea itself. He is still trapped against the most solid part of this painting, but he can already feel something beginning to change. He senses a weakness settling around him, and as if in reaction his own strength begins to build.

His heart, old as the hills and witness to so much love and hate that he sometimes feels as if he has drowned a hundred times over, starts to beat faster.

I still see you, he thinks, imagining Vince running away with the rucksack in his hand. *Whatever is happening now, whatever it leads to, I still see you, you human piece of shit.* He has spent the past day and night imagining what he will do to Vince once he catches him. It has given him some bloody comfort following the apparent end of his scheme to escape.

Now, something else has happened to give him hope. The ground shakes. One impact, two, then several more, all thumping up through his head, shoulder blades and hips. It hurts, but he welcomes the pain because it means he is still alive. He draws it in and relishes it.

In the east, the sky bursts alight with the power of a blazing sun. Somewhere else it is not midnight and the sun is shining. Grace has made a way through from here to there.

It must have taken a huge amount of energy. Her whole mind, body and soul were put into the forging of this new doorway, and Mallian can feel the pressure it put upon her. He feels it because the bonds holding him down have grown weaker. He squirms his body left and right and it moves further than it has in a long time. He flexes his legs and tries to lift them, but they are still heavy and held down against the ground.

He tenses and twists his left arm. It moves slightly, then drops back down.

Gathering his strength, focusing all his attention on his right arm, he lifts it up, pushing all his concentration through his shoulder and into his wasted muscles.

His arm rises from the ground. It's heavier than it has ever been before, but his determination is stronger, and there is no way he will not grasp this unexpected chance.

Raising his hand directly above his face, he stretches his fingers wide to obliterate the stars.

16

Two years ago she'd been struck by lightning, twice, but even then she hadn't felt as bad as she did now.

Sammi rolled onto her side and puked again. Angela was there to hold her hair out of the way, but Lilou seemed distracted, pacing back and forth and looking away from them, as if she could not bear to watch. Bone stood even further away. *Strange man*, Sammi thought. *Like he's living in a dream*. She wasn't sure where the idea came from. Her stomach clenched again but there wasn't anything left to come up. Angela stroked her hair back from her forehead and over her ear, and Sammi had a flash memory of her mom doing that years ago when she was just a little girl.

Even then her mom must have known what she was destined to become. She wondered if she'd ever told her dad, and thought not.

"I feel like shit," Sammi said. Her head pulsed, eyes throbbed as if they'd been removed and boiled and rolled back in, her throat was dry, and her stomach rolled. She was covered in thick, cloying mud. The sick taste in her mouth brought memories of yesterday, and fears for tomorrow.

Each throb in her head was echoed by the *bang, bang, bang* coming in from the distance.

"I'm sorry," Sammi said.

"It's okay," Angela said. "I'm not stupid, you know. I knew something was different. It was so obvious. You think I thought you were disappearing into the woods to meet boys?"

Sammi laughed, and groaned. "I wish." And she did. Secretly meeting boys in the woods would have been much less dangerous than what she had been doing. She had never been out with a boy. She was sixteen and had never been kissed. Hiding out in the wilderness with an aunt obsessed about keeping you safe wasn't conducive to making new friends, let alone finding romance.

Lilou was still pacing back and forth. Bone was closer to the place where they'd trapped the three Kin. The sun beat down on the metal door.

"What about *them*?" she asked.

"Don't worry about them, worry about yourself."

She brushed off Angela's soft touch and sat up. Though in pain her senses felt heightened. The smell of the old reservoir hung in the air, the memory of dead fish and water, reeds rotting across the banks and dirty pools slowly being absorbed back into the land. Deeper in that memory was the town of Longford. She drew in a long breath and she could smell that place, as if it was still there and not just the ghost of a town. She was in the belly of the ghost, but she could sense its true, original size and shape. She felt the soil beneath her parting, her hand sinking down into the damp ground, fingers spreading and closing around silt and mud that had once floated in the great reservoir. When she breathed in she could taste the fear and confusion as the town's life had effectively ended. She heard people shouting, and crying, and then raging as they writhed in agony on the ground, or had their insides blown out by bullets.

Sammi gasped and shook her head, closed her eyes, and when she opened them again she was back where she had been.

"What is it?" Lilou asked.

"I can't control it," Sammi said.

"Of course you can." The nymph knelt beside her and held her hand. Sammi caught an expression in Angela's eye that almost broke her heart. *Lilou's looking after me like she can't,* she thought, and an immense sadness closed over and around her.

"It's not fair," she said.

"What *is*?" Lilou asked.

"Is the kid okay?" Bone asked. "That was something."

"She's fine," Angela said. "You need to stay away."

"And we need to kill those things before they get out," Lilou said.

"You're not killing them," he said.

"So what's your story?" Angela stood and walked over to the man. He didn't back down, but neither did he face up to her. Sammi sensed no real threat in him, but he was someone still filled with mysteries.

"I could ask the same," he said.

"Yeah, but I asked first, and we outnumber you."

Bone glanced at them all, as if sizing them up.

"And I can fire lightning from my hand," Sammi said, holding up her right hand. The skin of her palm was tight and shiny, but other than that there was no sign of what she had so recently done. It was so far beyond what she had believed herself capable of that it should have been surreal, unbelievable. And yet the power nestling within her felt so at home. The sickness was abating, although she still felt weak and woozy. *I'm someone I never thought I would be.* She smiled at Bone, and he offered an uncertain smile in return.

"Mohserran is my father," Bone said.

"I did wonder," Lilou said. "And you're the one who escaped from here, though you must have been a kid when it happened."

"Oh shit," Angela said. "Am I the only human left in the world?"

Sammi laughed. It was loud and strong, considering how weak and crappy she felt, and Angela's look of surprise at her outburst only made her laugh some more.

Bang-bang-bang came from the old cooler room, as if in response to the revelation. Bone looked that way and Sammi could not read his expression. *No wonder he doesn't want them killed*, she thought.

"He might have been your father once, but not anymore," Lilou said. "He's been under the water for forty years. And you've seen what they've become."

"He's still alive," Bone said.

"No."

"Yes! I came here to find out once and for all what happened to him, and the last thing I expected was to find him walking."

"You warned us about them," Angela said.

"They scared me."

"They scared *me*. If it hadn't been for Sammi..." She turned and smiled at the girl.

Bang-bang-bang.

"You know they're still infected," Lilou said. "You came here to find out what happened, I came here to make sure they're all dead."

"He saved me," Bone said.

"How come you weren't infected?" Sammi asked.

"I was. We all were, but it just made the humans sick. The Kin—the pure Kin—it drove into a frenzy."

"And you?"

"He fought against it for me. Gave me his last breath to escape. He's a good Kin. He wouldn't hurt anyone."

Sammi and the others looked at the metal door. It showed no signs of moving or bowing, but it was now mostly free of silt where the impacts had shaken it away. With the sun beating down on the metal surface, what had once been a walk-in fridge would quickly become an oven.

Sammi tried to extend her senses to feel the three Kin trapped inside. There was nothing there. She could close her eyes and sense Lilou and Bone, both of them in slightly different ways. Lilou, who was full Kin, was like a glowing red brand in her mind, seared onto her perception. Bone was more of a smudge, like heat haze in darkness, still there but very difficult to see.

The three Kin were blank spaces. Not even hollows, but pure absences. As if they were dead.

"They're not coming back," she said, and the adults all turned to her. "I'm sorry, Bone, or whatever your name is. Your father's not there anymore."

Bone blinked, then dashed to the door. He didn't quite touch it.

"I won't let you kill them. I've spent my life working to protect Kin. The agency I work for thinks I hunt them, and it's the best cover to ensure they're hidden away, kept secret. But this is personal, and I *won't* let you kill them."

"We might have more than them to worry about soon."

"What do you mean?" Bone asked. "Who? What?"

Lilou looked around them at the valley, as if seeking something in the sunlight. There was nothing out of place, nothing abnormal, and yet Sammi could feel a change on the air.

"You really think she'll come?" she asked quietly.

"I think she'll try, if she knows what happened here," Lilou said.

"You have to scare her like that?" Angela asked Lilou.

"Would you rather I just not say anything?" Lilou

asked. "She's over being treated like a kid, Angela. Sorry, Sammi, I know it's not your choice, but I'm just telling it like it is. You have fairy blood in you from somewhere down the line, and however diluted, its power is glowing through. That thing you just did might only be the start of it. Magic like that leaves a mark, a scar, like those lightning strikes left patterns on your arm. And Grace might see and feel those scars. If she does there's no telling..."

Lilou's voice started to fade. Sammi blinked, her vision blurring, as a distance grew between her own solid core and everything else. Reality seemed to be drifting away. She reached for it but could not lift her hands. She cried out, but did not even hear her own voice, and could not be certain that she had spoken at all.

Even the intermittent banging of the trapped Kin trying to escape quietened to less than an echo.

Where is everything going? she wondered. And then a more terrifying thought came. *Where am I going?*

In the distance, past the blurred place where Angela and the others stood, something very clear began to coalesce. It was another solid core, something with a weight and heft that fixed it to the world—past, present and future—but which was very different from Sammi's own mass. This core was much, much older than her, and much more powerful. It was a black hole to her moon, and as soon as it appeared, she began to fear she would never be able to escape its pull.

She's here, she thought, and the idea made the fine

trace-work of scars across her arm and shoulder sizzle and spit, as if Grace was once again casting down lightning to find her.

Sammi tried to cry out, but her voice was silent. She attempted to roll out of the way, but her muscles were locked in place, and however far she might move the alien presence would track her. It saw and marked her, and soon it would come for her.

With a supreme effort, Sammi ripped herself away from its gaze.

Before she stopped breathing and passed out she managed to say, "She's coming."

Lilou had confronted many dangers in her life, and many monsters—more recently of the human kind. Gregor the Kin-killer had been driven mad in his quest, and Mary Rock's cool purpose had been even more chilling. The murderous satyr Ballus bore his own insanity.

Grace was a whole new world, and now she was coming.

"What can we do?" Angela asked desperately. She was kneeling next to her unconscious niece, her eyes wide and pleading, and Lilou had no words of comfort for her.

"Nothing," she said. "You've seen what Grace can do. She wants something, she'll take it."

Angela's expression didn't change for a few seconds.

Then her eyes narrowed and she stood to face Lilou. "Fuck you."

"Huh?"

"For bringing us here, putting Sammi in danger, and then for giving up hope. I never have! She might come for Sammi, but I'll fight back. I'm not just going to lie down and give in."

Lilou laughed out loud. She couldn't help it.

"Don't mock me."

"I'm not mocking you, Angela. It's just... you have no idea what she is. She's a god to you and your kind. She's a god to *my* kind."

"So in that case what is Sammi?"

Lilou didn't answer. She shook her head.

"Anyway, I don't care." Angela looked down at Sammi. "I don't care."

"He might still be alive," Lilou said, more quietly. She meant Vince, but she also thought of Mallian. It was still rare that she *didn't* think of him.

"I know."

"Who might?" Bone asked.

"And she'll kill those things, at least," Lilou said, nodding at the metal door. The banging was slightly less insistent.

"Can you feel that?" Angela asked. She was looking up and away from Sammi, towards nowhere in particular.

"Yeah," Lilou said.

"What the actual fuck *is* that?" Bone was backing away from them, looking around, and he started waving his hands as if under assault from invisible flies.

Lilou felt her surroundings changing, filling with potential, as the world took in and held a huge breath. She was nervous of what was to come, but also felt a surge of excitement. She'd been adrift for two years, spending most of her time in vast forests, avoiding human contact and meeting only the occasional lone Kin. She had felt adrift in this vast country, and with Mallian gone it was, strangely, Angela to whom she felt closest. A human.

The return of Grace would mean some excitement entering her life once more.

An explosion rang out across the valley, a sonic boom, reverberating through the ground and setting Lilou's bones singing. She gasped and saw Angela drop to her knees. Bone became motionless, as if turned to stone by the blast.

Stirring, Sammi started to cry.

The boom was closely followed by a silent shockwave passing through the air and ground. Lilou's vision blurred as the dust shimmered, throwing up a haze that rose around her lower legs, knocking chunks of drying mud from the few standing walls, and instigating a resounding, hollow thud from the buried cooler room.

Lilou staggered, her sense of balance upset by the boom and the shifting ground and rising dust. Explosions echoed back and forth across the valley like giants calling to each other, and then finally faded away with a sigh.

"She's here," Sammi said. She was the only one not looking around, Lilou noticed, instead she knelt, staring at the ground between her legs. Perhaps it was resignation.

"Sammi, we should run," Angela said. "Get out of the valley and away from here, as quickly as possible."

"She won't let you," Lilou said.

"She'll have to catch us first. Sammi, *now*!"

"No point," Sammi said. She looked up, past Bone and the cooler, past the remains of the building, and out across what used to be the town of Longford.

"Sammi!"

"No point, Angela." She pointed at a shape in the distance, and Lilou saw an uncertain shimmer across the valley floor, like heat haze or a cloud of dust. A hole in the world. "She's *here*."

17

Hope reignited would be the hardest to lose again. He thought that as he ran towards the light. He was a child in this place, he knew nothing, and yet the first moment he'd seen sunlight bursting out from nowhere to light the darkness, Vince had hoped it was a way back to the world.

It's a crack in the Fold, somewhere she didn't enclose quite well enough. It's a secret route to and from the world, which she's kept open for her own reasons. It's someone or something entering from outside, and that's why she's rushing towards it, ready to defend or maybe greet them.

It's someone escaping.

He considered diverting from his course to make sure Mallian was still secure in his holding place on the ground by the river, but that would take too long. His memory of the doorway from the world into the Fold was confused, but he could recall how quickly it had slammed shut when Grace decided the time was right.

One second to the next might mean the difference between escape, and eternal damnation. Hope kept him going and gave him speed, and the potential of hope being snatched away once more gave him strength.

He loped uphill, spear in one hand and water skin over his shoulder, and though he felt better than he had in years, he still hated the place with a passion.

The effect of sunlight blazing through a rip in the world was strange, casting countless spears of light across the night-time landscape. He thought Grace must have reached the portal by now and gone through, so the fact that it was still open meant that she wanted it open. That was good for him.

No way she'd want the Kin to escape, he thought, and that slowed his forward motion. He didn't believe the fairy hadn't thought through whatever she was doing, but the fact that the doorway out of this world and into another was still open seemed strange.

"Fuck it," he said, and he accelerated again.

The shape came out of nowhere. He sensed the weight of it first as the shadow parted from behind a pile of rocks and came at him. He brought the spear up to defend himself and it was plucked from his hand. He heard the wood snap as it was discarded. He fell and rolled, hoping to jump up again and run, but the shadow came with him, mirroring his movement, filling his field of vision even though he could not see what it was.

But he could smell it. The air was filled with the rancid sweet tang, and as he pushed himself away and tried to stand he puked, warm vomit running down his chin and splashing on his hands braced against the ground.

Something big slammed against his back and drove

him into the ground. Winded, he tried to draw a breath
in past the puke filling his mouth, inhaling it, choking,
coughing and hacking as he attempted to draw in air
once again. He kicked and crawled, because he knew
that this was the moment when he was destined to
die, and he would not go without a fight.

Mallian! he thought, and confusion swallowed him
up, just as a different sun was swallowing the night of
the Fold.

His leg was grabbed, squeezed so tight he cried out
at the pain. He was lifted from the ground, hung upside
down, and then he saw the face, distorted, the wrong
way up.

Mallian, free from his bonds and upright once again.
He looked even worse now than he had when tied to
the ground, his face drawn and thin, skin and flesh
hanging down. He was smaller, his bulk less defined,
reduced by months of poor food and inactivity. But his
eyes were wide and bright, shimmering with madness
and filled with delight at being free.

"Vince," Mallian spat. Vince had never heard his
name uttered with such contempt.

He writhed and struggled but Mallian held him
fast, arm up, his dangling head level with the Nephilim's
stomach. Mallian had been crushed down wearing his
usual short skirt and shorts, but they had soon
disintegrated when his body functions rotted them,
and he'd convinced one of the roving Kin to rip the
remainder away. Now he was naked, and the terrible

sores across his body from malnutrition and being kept in the same position for so long were obvious. Wounds wept, and Vince could smell rot as well as filth.

Mallian lifted him higher, so their faces were almost level. Upside down he looked more monstrous and furious than ever before.

"Hi," Vince said. "Nice to see you up and around."

Mallian roared. The blast of sick, moisture-laden breath in his face almost made Vince pass out, and then he was moving, the world spinning around him, and he knew for sure that he was being swung down onto a rock. He hoped he would not feel his head coming apart. *One second I'm Vince, the next I'm nothing—my history and thoughts, my loves and hates, and every single precious memory of Angela gone.*

Then Mallian stopped swinging and let go.

Vince tucked into a ball just as he hit the ground. The breath was knocked from him, and his left arm struck a rock so hard that he heard the bone snap. He cried out loud, and Mallian kicked him with such force that bones ground. He rolled onto his back, doing his best not to scream again and failing.

Mallian leapt and landed astride him, then lowered himself so that his naked groin and behind were pressed against Vince's chest and stomach. He pushed down a little more, and more, until it was hard to breathe.

"Just fucking kill me, you vicious bastard!" Vince gasped.

"Why would I want to kill you?" Mallian said. His

teeth were gritted, one of his incisors rotten and black. Vince wondered why he hadn't noticed such deterioration in the Nephilim before. "If I wanted to just kill you I'd have done it long ago. I've always had uses for you, human."

"Dropping berries and nuts into your mouth."

"That, and more."

Mallian's head and torso were silhouetted by the brash sunlight bursting into the Fold from somewhere else. Vince felt a terrible desperation to get to that doorway and launch himself through, whatever might be on the other side. Even if he died doing so, at least then he'd die taking action, doing what he could to escape. He didn't want to die like this, with Mallian's naked sex organs resting on his chest, the giant's arse crushing his stomach down.

He supposed in Mallian's eyes he deserved much worse than this.

"How did you get free?" he asked.

"Where are my relics?"

"I don't know. Did she let you go?"

"You do know. You stole them, and you're a fool, so you'll have kept them close. You're a weak fucking human, you wouldn't have been able to resist keeping them somewhere you can peek at them from time to time. Things more amazing than you'll ever be."

"Things a human killed and stole to acquire."

"Your kind occasionally serves a purpose. Now where are they?"

Vince closed his eyes.

The punch around the face was like being hit by a train. His teeth crunched, his neck jarred, and his head pounded. At least it smothered the pain of his left arm, if only for a while.

"Look at me," Mallian hissed. Vince looked. Mallian didn't even have his hand fisted. He'd barely tapped Vince. If he truly punched, Vince would lose his head. He'd seen Mallian kill people with his bare hands—crushing, ripping, tearing. The Nephilim was as furious now as he'd ever seen him. Vince was a heartbeat from death, and any wrong move, any wrong answer, would be his last.

"I don't know where they are," he said.

Mallian growled.

"Really. You're right, they do fascinate me, but I've changed since I've been in here. Angela is my be-all, end-all, and any way back to her I'll take. I took those things from you to protect the world from you and your insane plans. But no, I didn't keep them. I'm way beyond that now. I threw them away as I ran from you, and I'll never be able to find them again."

Mallian bore down more heavily on Vince until he could no longer breathe and he was afraid his ribs would give way. He tried to move and struggle, but all Mallian had to do was use his weight and Vince was helpless.

"I need those pieces!"

"Why... I threw them... away."

"You *will* remember," Mallian said. "Somewhere in that rudimentary jelly you call a brain you'll remember. Let me show you how."

This is not going to be good, Vince thought. Mallian shifted and he saw past him, up the hillside towards where the sunlight flowed in. Mallian saw him looking, paused, smiled.

"That's right," the Nephilim said. "Grace has opened a portal. There's no reason it might be back to the world we came from, and not some other variation of it. But I think she's going back for something, or someone, close to you. I saw the way she coveted the girl. Maybe she's spent all her time here planning how to take her."

"Angela's not stupid," Vince said. "They'll be hiding away."

"From a fairy?" Mallian laughed, and Vince felt hopeless. He knew how powerful Grace was. Hiding wouldn't be enough.

"I need to follow her," Mallian said. "You'll help me."

"I won't."

"I'm not asking." Mallian reached down and closed his huge right hand around Vince's left shoulder. With a shrug he flipped Vince onto his side. Vince cried out in agony, feeling his arm flop unnaturally under his body, trapped there by his own weight. The pain came in wave after terrible wave, and then Mallian pressed down on his other shoulder, crushing his wounded arm beneath him.

Vince shouted again and again. The agony and inability to escape made him desperate.

"I don't know where they are!"

"Then remember." Mallian eased away and allowed Vince to roll onto his back. His fractured arm remained trapped beneath him, and he took a breath and shifted further. He felt sick and distant, and he feared he might faint. He bit his lip and winced at the fresh taste of blood. The pain was beyond anything he'd ever experienced before, even when Ballus the mad satyr had strapped him to a chair and slashed and gouged him with the bones of decayed Kin.

"Even if I did know, you need them to control her. I'd never allow that."

"Then I'll follow her back without them," Mallian said.

"And kill me first."

"I thought so, for a while. I've had a long time to myself. And since you took the relics, I've been thinking up some very creative ways to make you pay."

"I thought you probably would." Vince was looking for any way to escape, a momentary distraction he could use to flee into the shadows across the hillside. But the shadows were shrunk by the sun he was so desperate to reach.

"I think killing you would be too kind. I'll cripple you first. Maybe rip off both legs, or just one, so you can at least crawl. I'll take your cock and balls and feed them to one of the hungry Kin. I'll peel your limbs, but leave you alive, and then I'll follow Grace back into our world. Leaving you here with the knowledge of what I'll spend the next weeks, months or years doing. Tracking down the people you love. I'll begin with Angela and Sammi. I'll kill them slowly, terribly, in front of each other. Probably the girl first. I have all the time in the world, you know that. Then it will be the turn of my old friend Lilou, because I know you love her too."

"Only Angela," Vince said, and Mallian laughed.

"Everyone loves Lilou," he said. "That's why it'll be harder for me to kill her. After that, who knows? You have extended family, yes? I'll be their nightmare. I'll be the shadow following them in the night, the shape glimpsed from the corner of their eye. For the children, I'll be the monster under the bed." He leaned in close and looked Vince in the eye. "And I really will be under the bed."

"Fuck you," Vince said. "You're full of shit."

Mallian frowned.

Vince saw movement from the corner of his eye, maybe the distraction he needed. Mallian hadn't walked properly for two years. He was twice the size of Vince, stronger, more vicious and brutal, but right then Vince thought that even with a fractured arm he was probably faster.

"I see everything, human," Mallian said. "You think I've been lying there in the dirt doing nothing all this time? I've been planning and making friends. You might think you're the hero of the hour, but you're nothing more than an annoying hindrance."

"You think I'll help you when you make threats like that?"

"You'll help because I make promises like that."

More movement to his left, and Vince forced himself not to look.

"Sammi is innocent."

"Innocent fairy flesh tastes the best."

The shape came closer. It seemed to be circling, edging in behind Mallian, and perhaps that meant it was there to help. He'd tried to help injured Kin several times, tried to make contact with them, as much for himself as for them. Success had been limited, but perhaps whichever Kin this was, it would repay in kind.

All I need is a distraction.

"Maybe..." Vince said, and then the Kin came close, manifesting in strange sunlight and approaching from Mallian's left.

"Ah, Bah'Lia," Mallian said, and Vince felt hope shrivelling to nothing.

The short, slight Kin, humanoid and covered with a fine down, looked daunted and intimidated by Mallian's size and appearance, but also awed.

"I know where they are," Bah'Lia said.

"Where what are?" Mallian asked.

"The relics you want. I was following him when he discarded them."

"You're sure?"

Bah'Lia nodded, and Vince knew this was his only and final chance. If this Kin was telling the truth, Mallian had no more use for him, and with the portal still standing open, Vince did not want to die.

He wanted to live, and escape, and find his old life once again.

"Thanks, Bah'Lia," Vince whispered, and when he saw Mallian's confused frown—when the Nephilim looked at the Kin with growing suspicion in his eyes— Vince rolled onto his side, stood, and ran. As he accelerated he reached down and snatched up the sharp half of his snapped spear.

Every part of his concentration wanted to drag itself to the unbelievable agony of his broken left arm pressed across his stomach, but he pulled back, focusing on the ground before him, a dark land in the midst of night broken by the sun he sought.

He hoped that Bah'Lia had lied, and that it had not been following him as he'd cast those sad remnants aside, losing them so well in the long grasses and waters of the Fold that he would never remember where they were. If it had seen, then Mallian might still be able to achieve his aim of Ascent. But part of him also hoped that it wasn't a lie, and that even now Mallian and the Kin were starting to follow the winding trail he had led and retrieving those sad, dangerous relics.

If that were the case, their distraction might enable him to make it out of the Fold alive.

18

She runs, she races, and towards the place where she formed the portal between her world and the other, she even flies. Perhaps it's that brief moment of flight— her first for as long as she can recall—that does so much to drain her energy.

She lands within the portal, and as she takes a moment to gather herself, she assesses what she has done. The time delay between sensing the actions of the fairy girl and forging this new pathway between worlds is slight. The energy required is huge, and it all comes from within her. If she'd taken a few moments to consider her actions she might have prepared better, and might have constructed the portal in such a way that the power required was used and distributed more efficiently. As it was, her reaction was instinctive, and the doorway before which she stands quivers and shakes with seeping energies.

I'm wasting myself just by standing here, she thinks, and she walks through.

On the other side she is even weaker. This world has been bleeding her dry for as long as she can remember, and the terrible times at the mercy of that evil human woman are her own nightmares. She relives them again now as she re-enters that world—she can smell its rot and ruin, and taste sickness on the air like the breath of a dying animal. Coming back makes her realise why she has grown to hate this place.

Her legs quake and she staggers to one side. Falling to her knees, she is shocked by how colourless the real world is when set against her Fold. It is grey and bland, bereft of plants and grasses, the land seemingly seared clean by some cataclysm. She wonders whether a lot more time has passed over here than she anticipated. It could be that the humans have finally destroyed themselves and their world, and that the girl has become an old, old fairy, haunting the ghost of an uninhabited place.

If that is the case, she has come to rescue her.

She remains on her knees as the shakes and weakness begin to lessen. Her hand is splayed in the dry soil, and she squeezes her fingers and feels, rather than a dead nothingness, a rich and thriving fertility. That surprises her. She lifts the soil to her nose and breathes it in, and senses the true story of this place.

Peace and coexistence. Conflict and fear. Water and death.

She breathes in deeply a few times more, enjoying the feel of the afternoon sun on her skin, and tries her old wings again. They part from her body and slap at the air effectively enough, but she knows that to use them now would drain what little energy she has left.

She needs it for what is to come.

Standing slowly, she's aware of movement behind her. Something else is coming through the portal. She tenses, ready to dash across this grey land to catch any Kin that might be attempting an escape. She's disturbed by her lack of concentration, and the fact that she has not considered the full implications of her actions. Usually her plans are so considered that they have the clarity of recent memories, and they almost always play out the way she intended.

She saw and sensed signs of the girl and ran. She should have known that pushing a portal through from her Fold to the world might allow her Kin to escape. She should have taken measures.

But once I have her, it won't matter if I have the Kin or not.

She smiles. It's not an expression she uses lightly, or often. She has dreamed of sharing her time with another fairy for many centuries. They will nurture each other, make each other well. Given time, perhaps they will fly together. Her wings twitch at the thought.

She realises that it is only the human, skittering away from the portal like a startled deer. He sees her, pauses, then runs in the opposite direction.

She could chase him down and take out his throat in a heartbeat, but he no longer concerns her. She's glad that he's gone. He was a taint on her land, something she did not welcome, and now his blood will never again infect her soil.

As the human flees, the fairy stands and turns a slow circle. She sees the portal, like a hazy wound in the air. It is stable for now, but she will reassess its build and strength all the time. She sees a wide, shallow valley where a lake once stood, and senses the remains of a human settlement.

She feels madness on the air. It's a strange sensation because it is a Kin madness, and it makes her feel uncertain and sick. Three of them, she thinks, driven to distraction by a human-inspired insanity. If she gets a chance, she will put them out of their misery.

And then she finds the girl. Not far away, across the valley floor close to the remains of a ruined building.

She breathes in, tastes the breath of a fairy, and sighs deeply.

Feeling strong once again she begins to move.

"That's not her," Lilou said.

The Kin had started banging inside the cooler room again, louder and more violently than before. Angela guessed it was the appearance of the portal that had them agitated. It had her agitated, too. Her heart beat twice as fast as normal, sweat beaded across her nose and the back of her neck, and she had to fight the urge to run towards the shimmering place out across the valley floor. It looked like heat haze, a dust devil, a place where reality doubted itself. She had seen its like before, and last time it had slammed shut before Vince could escape.

The last time she'd seen him he had been facing up to Mallian.

"What the hell is that?" Bone asked.

Angela laughed. It had an edge of madness. *A gateway into another dimension created by a mad fairy*, she thought. She could not bring herself to say it, though she had the feeling Bone would believe her.

"That's not her, Sammi," Lilou said again. The nymph was standing atop the half-buried cooler room.

"What?" Angela asked.

"Take a look."

Angela scrambled up the fallen remains of the wall, hoping she would see him, hoping against all the hopelessness she had felt over the past two years. When Lilou reached out for her she took her hand and gripped, pulling herself up, and the two women—human and Kin—kept holding hands as they looked past the scattered ruins of Longford and towards the river.

And there he was, Vince, running awkwardly towards them, left arm held across his stomach, and glancing back every few steps. He was different—his hair was much longer and he wore a straggly beard—but she could never not know him.

She tried to speak but it came out as a deep, violent gasp. Lilou held her up.

"Something's chasing him," Lilou said. "We need to be ready."

"Ready with what?" she asked.

"Maybe ready with Sammi."

Angela looked down at the girl sitting in the mud, pale and wan and worn out.

"Sammi," she said.

"I heard."

More banging came from beneath them. Angela didn't like to think how little there was between her and the mad, infected Kin. They still knew so little about them, but the fact that they were dangerous was a certainty.

There's Vince, she thought, and it was a moment she had never truly believed would happen. She had seen him countless times over the past couple of years in daydreams—laughing at her, flicking food, scowling, the two of them drinking and walking by a river and making love—but however much she had hoped, the idea of ever seeing him again had been a remote, foolish dream. She might as well wish after someone who was dead.

Now here he was, and Angela lost herself. She jumped from the wall and landed on the bank of silt built up against the cooler room. Her feet sank in and she rolled, standing again, running, ignoring Lilou's shouts and Sammi's weaker cries, because this was Vince, the man she loved and the other half of her in this world, and she would not spend another second without him if she didn't have to. She had been incomplete for the past two years, her soul broken, and though Sammi had given her purpose she could never, ever fix her. Vince's loss had been so traumatic that sometimes it had given her physical pain, and she'd examined her body for signs. Some forms of grief were so deep and powerful that they could damage the flesh.

"Vince!" she called, but her voice was stolen by her panting, gasping breath. She ran harder and he saw her, and she saw him try to call her name as well. He was in pain, but she would wrap him in her arms and make him better. Whatever he had been through there in the Fold with Grace and Mallian, whatever he had done to survive, she would make him better.

As the distance between them grew less she began to fear it was all a hallucination. She was seeing things, her mind tweaked and stirred by this strange place and these weird events, she was imagining Vince coming towards her.

Would I really imagine the ways he's changed? The long straggly hair, bushy beard, drawn, thinner face? Could I really dream that desperate hope in his eyes?

Then they were close and she smelled him before they impacted with each other, barely slowing down as if trying to combine themselves and their cells, make two into one as they had been before all this chaos and craziness began. He smelled old and dirty, but beneath it all was the familiar Vince-scent she would know even in a gloomy, crowded room.

"Vince!" she breathed into his neck, and when she inhaled she caught a dozen untold stories on his smell. She only hoped he would have time to tell them.

He squeezed her as hard as she squeezed him. It hurt, and he groaned in pain as well, but she loved it, because it was the love of her life holding her so tight that she thought he might never let go.

"I can't believe it's you," he said. He moved back a little so he could look into her face. "You've changed so much!"

"*I've* changed so much?" she gasped. "Why did you think the beard was a good idea?"

"Camouflage. Against the dragons."

"There are dragons in there?" She looked past him towards the portal, and although he grinned and shook his head, the idea was not ridiculous. Nothing was anymore.

"We have to move," he said. He looked back, still holding onto her as if afraid she would vanish as soon as he looked away. "Grace. And Mallian."

"Oh shit, are they there?"

"More than ever before," Vince said. He grasped her hand and urged her to return the way she'd come.

"Your arm?"

"Mallian. What about Sammi?"

"Over there, with Lilou." She pointed.

"Who's the guy?"

"Bone."

"Nice name."

"Don't trust him."

"Even more comforting." Vince looked around as they ran. "Did I miss a war, or something?"

"It used to be a flooded valley. Long story."

"How long have I been gone?"

"Too long, Vince. You can't leave me again, ever. Ever!"

"I don't want to, ever. How long?"

"Two years," she said, and she feared she should have broken it more gently. Maybe over there it had only been two months.

"Feels about right," he said. "I must have missed some great TV."

There was so much more for both of them to ask, so many questions that might have no easy answers, but he pulled her fast, and she was surprised by how much fitter and leaner he was. It only inspired a dozen more questions.

He continued looking around as they ran, and as they closed on Sammi, Lilou and Bone, she felt Vince's hand close tighter around hers.

"There she is," he said, and for a moment Angela thought he meant Sammi. She was standing with Lilou's help, smiling at them both as they approached. But Vince was looking to their right, past the stumps of an old building protruding from the ground and towards the spiky remains of a clump of trees. She caught movement among their stripped grey trunks. She had seen that figure before.

"Grace," she said. "She's come for Sammi."

"Huh?"

"Sammi. She can do things, Vince. She's a fairy, or has fairy blood."

Confusion shifted to understanding on his face. And then fear.

They reached the ruin where the others waited only seconds before Grace.

Still weak and queasy from the strange magic she had used, Sammi tried to stagger away from Lilou as she saw Angela and Vince rushing towards her. She felt like the centre of the world and had no wish to be there. She had asked for none of this, and though the strange power she'd felt growing inside for some time excited her, right now it only made her tired and depressed. All she wanted was to be together with Angela, and now Vince.

Lilou did not let her go. Instead she grabbed and held her tight, and Sammi began to panic and struggle.

"I've got you," Lilou whispered in her ear, and Sammi realised that the nymph only ever meant her well. "I'll look after you."

Angela and Vince were almost with them. Vince looked different, like an older ghost of himself. Angela looked shocked and afraid. Further away, Grace was also running towards them. She moved so quickly that she left a haze of dust in the air behind her.

Everyone is coming for me, Sammi thought, and she struggled again, wanting only to turn around and run.

"It'll do no good," Lilou said.

"What can I do?" she asked. When Lilou didn't answer, she twisted a little so she could look into the nymph's face. There was no hope in her eyes.

Bone had moved closer to the cooler door, crouching down as if to hide from the people running at them. None of them knew his real story, and she doubted him. How could someone called Bone be trusted? Even Sammi could see that he'd been military, or still was. Noticing small tells was something her dad had taught her when they used to sit at sidewalk cafés in Cape Cod and people watch together. *Carrying a limp but trying to hide it. He walks really upright and stiff, proud. She still wears her hair short, and there's a regimental tattoo showing beneath her sleeve.* With Bone it was something more subtle and fundamental— the way he carried himself; the movement of his limbs; his voice and choice of vocabulary.

"What can I do?" she asked again. Angela and Vince reached them, breathing hard.

"Hey, Sammi," Vince said through a mask of pain. She could see that his left arm was broken and held awkwardly against his chest. "So you're a fairy now? I always thought you were more of an Orc."

And then Grace was there while she was still smiling. It made no difference that Angela and Vince had reached her first. Angela stood close and put an arm around her shoulder, hugging her in, and Vince hugged them both with his good arm. Vince and Lilou swapped a glance, a smile, enough for Sammi to think, *Secret histories between those two.* She wished she didn't think that. It would be easier if she couldn't see so much, but her senses were sharper than they had ever been. Her hands tingled, fingers throbbing. The scars on her arm simmered as if they were rivers of fire coursing through her veins.

"You can't have her," Angela said.

Grace came to a gentle halt ten metres from them, taking them all in at a glance. Sammi had been close to her before, when the fairy had come through from the Fold and dragged her across the threshold from this world and into another. Back then, though, Sammi hadn't known what she really was. She'd been a girl trapped in an adults' world, brave and resourceful, yet still experiencing a child's confusion and fear. Now she was older and wiser. Perhaps wiser than almost everyone here.

Almost, because Grace was a vision of age and wisdom, power and grace. She might have been a god. Shorter than them all though she was, slighter in stature, her diminutive build projected only strength. Her limbs were slender and supple, her body clothed in a finely woven one-piece dress. Her long silver hair was braided over one shoulder, and on her feet she wore seamless, laceless boots made of a material Sammi could not identify. If it was leather or hide, it was from a creature she did not know.

The fairy's face was delicate yet stern, her eyes a rich sparkling blue, deep with the weight of endless memories and ancient times. Sammi could look at Grace and fall in love, though she exuded nothing resembling Lilou's more basic animal allure.

"You can't have her," Angela said again.

"She's not yours to keep," Grace said. Her voice was surprisingly low, the words accented and awkward, as if she rarely spoke.

"I'm not yours to take," Sammi said. She felt some of the strange energy inside surging, and her left arm tingled as the lightning-strike patterns glowed.

Grace smiled. It did not reach her eyes. "Child," she said, "I take what I want."

Sammi felt the power roaring and raging, and yet surrounding it all, like endless space nursing a neutron star, was an infinity of hopelessness. She had never felt such a surge of despair. It brought tears to her eyes and a weakness to her muscles, and she knew without a shadow of doubt that she was utterly helpless in the face of this exotic, terrifying creature.

As Grace stepped forward her smile faded, her eyes dulled, and her mouth drooped open. She staggered two more steps and then stopped, as if she had forgotten how to walk. She became motionless.

"Oh, no," Vince said, voice quivering with fear. "Oh, no... he has her. Mallian has her."

Past Grace and across the valley floor, a tall, triumphant shape stepped out of the portal.

19

Lilou's stomach dropped and her heart hammered in her chest once, twice, three hard times, as if seeking to finish her there and then. So much was happening she could barely keep track of events. After two years spent wandering the woods, and wondering what vague destiny fate had in store for her now that Mallian was gone, the future was coming to her. It was happening now, and she felt the pressure of every small decision she was about to make.

Mallian was back. And though she had betrayed him and she feared him more than anything in the world—more than the fairy, more than death—she also loved him. Theirs had been an unconventional romance, a deep respect and love for each other that had rarely manifested as physical. Though brash and superior, she also knew that the Nephilim had needed her, and valued her company for the long, long years they had known each other. Her decision to go against him and his plans for Ascent must have hit him hard.

She doubted he had forgiven her.

To her left, Bone stood close to the partially buried

cooler room, hunkered down by the door as if to hide from everyone. Closer in front of her, Angela, Vince and Sammi hugged, and she had never seen a sight so right. The three of them were family. If the whole world and all its troubles were to envelop them now, they would still have each other, and their bond would keep them safe. She envied their closeness. However hard she had tried to help and protect them, she knew that she would always be an outsider.

Her own family was across the grey landscape and emerging from the portal that Grace had forced into the world. He seemed somehow diminished. Thinner than before, shoulders drooped, he was a withered husk of what he had once been, and Lilou wondered what the hell the fairy had been doing to him.

At least he's still alive, she thought. Vince also looked changed. The two of them would have stories to tell, but she didn't think they would ever tell them together.

Mallian had control of the fairy, which meant that his glamour had worked. From Vince's wide-eyed expression, she thought he might have been struggling against Mallian all this time.

The Nephilim strode out into the dusky sunlight and rolled his shoulders, clenching and unclenching his big hands as if reloading or rebooting himself. His gait was strange, uncertain. Perhaps he had not walked far for some time.

As he approached, Lilou caught a whiff of his body odour. Some of it was familiar, most not. There was dirt and filth and decay there, smothering his more familiar scents. She felt so sad for him.

Even though he smiled, she knew he had been through so much. Mallian was proud, and he would not take torture or mistreatment lightly.

Lilou walked past Angela, Vince and Sammi, skirted around Grace where she stood frozen to the spot, and stepped out to meet Mallian.

"Lilou," Vince said. "Don't mess with him."

She didn't reply. Vince was a friend, but she and Mallian had such deep history that the humans behind her seemed little more than smudges on time, fleeting patterns of thought and shape that would be gone with the next moon. She and Mallian were more permanent. They were part of the landscape, and this was a continuation of their long story.

"Mallian," she said as they drew close. "You've looked better."

"You never have," he said. "My sweet Lilou." She had never heard such affection in his voice.

"What did she do to you in there?"

"Nothing. Nothing at all."

Lilou frowned.

"She treated me as if I didn't exist," he continued. He looked past Lilou at the fairy, and grinned. "She knows different now. Watch this." He closed his eyes, frowning a little, and raised his chin.

Lilou sensed movement behind her. She glanced back and saw the fairy contorted, twisting in pain, her limbs drawn in and then hands slapping at the air around her head. Two shapes parted from her back with a delicate ripping sound, and Grace screamed.

"What are you doing?" Lilou asked. Mallian did not acknowledge the question. He remained in concentration, and he smiled as the fairy's tattered wings started flapping, creating first a swish-swish sound and then a light buzzing as her weight grew less and she lifted from her feet.

All the time, she was crying out.

"It's hurting her!" Lilou said.

Mallian's eyes snapped open and his smile turned into a grimace. "Good," he said, and the fairy rose higher, five metres off the ground and describing an uneven circle in the air above Angela and the others.

"I don't know what she did to you in there, but there's no need for this."

"There's every need," Mallian said. "And who are you to give me orders, Lilou?"

"I'm your friend."

"Friend." He blinked and the fairy fell to the ground. She landed softly, then staggered and fell onto her side. Then she was up again, as if hauled upright by invisible puppet strings. She swayed a little, wings tucking in against her back. She shivered, and the wings fluttered and shook as she pulled them close.

Lilou could not see her face.

"Yes," Lilou said. "I always have been, you know that. I've only wanted what's best for us, and for the

Kin. Ascent isn't for the best."

He chuckled. It was a deep throaty sound, like something was broken inside. Lilou realised that even though he looked thin and malnourished, even though he smelled of filth and decay, Mallian was as strong as he'd been the day he was trapped in the Fold. Perhaps stronger. His mind endured, and with it his aims and ambitions, enriched and refined by his time away.

Now he had the fairy in his thrall, and the possibilities were horrific.

"I'm not going to beg you," she said.

"Good."

"Mallian, I'm appealing to you with the memory of all the time we've spent together, and all the things we've seen and done. You hate humans, but you also know their power and might."

"Against her?" he said, nodding past her at Grace.

"A fairy who cries when she flies?"

"Pft!" He waved a hand at her. "Flying is just a trick. You know the things she can do, the powers she bears. They're mine now. The only limit is my imagination."

He's right, Lilou thought. She tried not to show it. *And he will never change his mind.*

She looked back at Vince and the others, hoping to steer Mallian's attention that way. As she did so she gripped the handle of the short knife in her belt.

"You betrayed me," he said. "Left me trapped in there with her. You know what she was doing to the other Kin she drew in, the sad mongrels like the girl there? She was eating them, one piece at a time. Chewing off chunks of Kin meat, letting them heal, then hunting and eating them again. Imagine being eaten alive for eternity? That was her aim all along."

"And you?" Lilou asked, trying to hide her shock.

"Maybe my old meat was too tough for her," he said. "But that's what the best of us, the most powerful, have come to. Eating each other. What do you think happens to the rest of the Kin if we do nothing to reassert our place in the world?"

"We fade away," Lilou said. "We've had our time. That doesn't mean you and I can't remain civilised and enjoy the time we have left."

"I was not born to fade away," Mallian said, and she saw the look she had been waiting for, the hooded eyes, the dreamy distance as he considered his long, turbulent past and the many wonderful, amazing, terrible things he had seen and done.

Lilou drew on every dreg of her power, lowering all the masks and shields she lived with day to day in the world of the humans, and projected herself as she really was and always had been many centuries before, when hiding was not so important.

From behind her she heard a collective gasp as the humans fell under her spell.

In front of her, Mallian's eyes went wide and his expression became open, almost childlike.

Lilou pulled the knife and stepped forward, sweeping the blade around towards Mallian's throat.

She would only have one strike, and it would have to be hard. The blade was keen. And although she hated the thought of it, and knew that his death would also be the end of her, it was the only thing left to do.

As the blade struck his throat it passed right through, and she stepped back from the imminent fountain of blood.

Mallian laughed.

In her hand, the blade had turned into a feather.

"Tickles," he said. His laugh ended as if sliced in two, and there was no second chance. "No more, Lilou. No more."

There was movement behind her, and in Mallian's eyes she saw a reflection of the end.

Vince felt Angela's hand close tighter around his own.

"No!" he shouted, tugging, struggling to get free so that he could run to Lilou's aid, even though there was no help he could give. White-hot pain scorched in from his broken arm and he welcomed it. It was nothing compared to losing Lilou.

"*No!*" he screamed again, his throat raw.

He loved Lilou as well as Angela, and the emotional pain he felt was proof of that.

The fairy drifted closer to Lilou, reached out a hand, and white fire spurted from her palm. It broke around the nymph, then curled in and struck again and again, a blazing snake-like heat with a mind of its own.

Lilou barely had time to struggle. Her arms waved and she took a couple of steps to one side, but by then her beautiful hair was singed to nothing and her smooth skin blistered off, flesh aflame. Her scream was terrible but brief. She fell onto her side, glowing with blue fire as the fats in her body ignited. The flames shimmied and spat.

Grace lowered her hand and became motionless once again, a puppet awaiting its master.

Vince twisted and pulled, but Angela's nails dug in, and her voice held him fast.

"Don't leave me again."

"She's gone, Vince," Sammi said through a blur of tears. He realised that she was holding onto him as well.

Lilou has gone.

Rage consumed him. Mallian looked down at the blazing, bubbling mess the nymph had become. His face was blank, and Vince so wished he could wipe that expression away.

"Bastard!" he shouted.

Mallian glanced up at him, then back down at Lilou's burning remains. Parts of her skeleton were exposed now that some of her flesh and insides had burned away beneath the intense, unnatural fire. One arm stuck up and her fingers were twisted in towards her palm. A leg shifted and kicked as tendons heated and snapped.

Vince could not believe such a beautiful, ancient mind could have been erased so quickly and so thoroughly. Where were her memories now? The things she had done, the few men and women she had loved and the many, many more who had loved her?

"We need to go," Angela said. "We need to get away from here now, while we still can."

"I can't," Vince said. "I can't leave her. Not like that."

"There's nothing left of her to leave," Angela said into his ear. "Please, Vince. We're together again, and it needs to be for however long we have left."

"Not long," he said. He saw Mallian for what he had become—a monster, a harbinger of hate. Lilou had known, and even through her love for the Nephilim she had tried to act against that. If only he could too. "We have to do something."

"What can we do?"

Vince had no answer.

"Okay," Angela said. She tucked his broken arm into his shirt, ignoring his groan, his cold sweat. "Okay, we *will* do something, but not here and now."

As Vince took the first few steps away from the awful scene, he heard something strange. It sounded like drums, but then he saw Bone struggling to open a metal door.

"What's he doing?" he asked.

"Oh, fuck," Angela said. "Does it never end?"

Father will help me, Bone thought. *Father will help all of us.*

He could barely compute what he was seeing. He'd

encountered Kin before, but fleetingly, never like this. The fairy thing, spewing fire from her hand. The tall beast that had emerged through the rip in the world.

And just what the fuck is that rip, doorway, thing? Where does it go? What more will come through?

As he watched, the steady *tap-tap-tap* from behind the door worked its way into his brain. Mohserran and the others had stopped banging and were now scratching, and it had the sound of something more deliberate. Maybe they were finding their minds again after waking, using their wiles, hollowing their way through to the outside.

Father can help us all against this.

Even as he worked at the metal chair leg securing the door shut he knew he was being foolish. They would still carry the Kovo, and perhaps they could spread it through bites, or saliva, or simply through exhaling the germ so that others could breathe it in.

He paused in his efforts, listened to the spitting of the burning body, then started again. He could smell cooking meat. It made his mouth water, and that made him retch, puke rising into his mouth. He turned and spat it out. It burned in his throat and around his tongue.

When he turned to the door something struck it hard from the other side. The metal chair leg, already twisted by him, bounced from the rusted hook and eye and clattered to the ground.

Bone stepped back and tripped over his own feet as the door burst open. He kicked back in the dust, heels digging in and throwing up dust as sunlight fell on one of the dark creatures inside. The werewolf Francine stood in the doorway, panting hard and squinting against the sun. Her pelt was burned on one side of her face.

She looked down at Bone.

"Francine," he whispered.

"Back!" he heard behind him. "What the fucking hell are you thinking?"

"They can help," he said. "Against that thing." He nodded at the tall shape still standing close to the burning corpse. He'd heard it called Mallian. It seemed transfixed by what had happened, staring down at the flames for so long that its eyes reflected the fire and burned themselves.

The woman, Angela, grasped his arm. "With us. Now! We're not waiting." She let go and he heard her and the girl and man start to run. He knew he should go with them.

Francine looked at him, then at the burning body. Mohserran appeared behind her, pushing forward out of the cooler, and behind him came the gargoyle. All three of them were shaking and sweating, their eyes yellow and alight, mouths slavering, and Bone knew that their madness was not something that would ever fade away.

Neither was their infection.

"What have I done?" he muttered.

His father, the creature Mohserran, fixed him with a stare.

"Oh, that's just wonderful," a deep voice said, and when Bone managed to rise and look behind him he saw Mallian standing close. He smelled of burning flesh. Beside him the fairy was swaying back and forth, her mouth slack.

"Grace," Mallian said. She tilted her head and the three infected Kin filed from the cooler and stood close together. Their eyes dulled a little, and their stance became less aggressive. More submissive.

"They're infected with—"

"They're a good start," Mallian said. "An army needs berserkers. They'll be a magnificent front line."

Bone started backing away. At any moment he expected the fairy to cast him down, burn him up, or slash him in half with a wave of her hand.

"Run," Mallian said. "Hide, human. Ascent is here. You'll know me soon. You'll all grow to know me."

Bone turned and ran, heading after the other three. He wished he was young again, and that his tree was still there, and he could find the hollow trunk and huddle away from the world forever. But he was no longer a child, and there were no hollow trees.

Everything here was exposed.

PART TWO
ASCENT

20

Lilou emerged from the woods one morning and surprised Angela while she was taking a bath. Sammi had woken early and disappeared on one of her regular long walks. It took a while to fill the bath, using buckets from the spring-fed well and heating saucepans on the wood burner, but Angela did it once each week. Cool showers were all right, but she'd always enjoyed a long soak. Back home in London, in the maisonette she shared with Vince, she'd bathed most evenings, sometimes with a coffee or a glass of wine, always with a good book. Jay had brought a selection of books to the cabin, but Angela had found she could only ever read when schooling Sammi. It was more to do with her own mindset than Jay's choice of books.

For most of the summer they had the bathtub beside the cabin, out on the rough timber deck partly sheltered by the overhang under which they stored firewood. Angela had developed strong shoulders and arms from chopping logs. Living a more basic life, she'd found her strength building month on month.

As the water cooled around her she heard the nymph's footsteps. She could instantly tell they weren't

Sammi's—the girl walked with a different pace, a heavier gait—and she crossed her arms over her chest and sat up.

"Oh. Sorry." Lilou didn't seem sorry at all. She smiled at Angela and sat on a pile of logs. "I brought breakfast." She held a rabbit in one hand, its neck broken. A drop of blood pattered onto her boots.

Angela grabbed her towel and stood from the bath, wrapping herself up.

"You could have warned us you were coming."

"You didn't hear me calling from the lane?"

"No. In a world of my own."

"It's hot," Lilou said. She eyed the bath, holding back from actually asking.

"You stink," Angela said. "What do you do when you're out there, roll around in deer shit?"

"It's good camouflage," Lilou said. "Actually fox shit is better, but then wolves want to roll in me."

Angela laughed. She couldn't help it. "Have a bath," she said, taking the rabbit. "I'll gut and skin this bastard, and cook it while you relax."

"What about Sammi?"

"That girl's got a good sense of smell."

Angela was right. By the time the rabbit was stripped, sliced and fried, Sammi had returned from her walk and Lilou had bathed and dressed again. They ate sitting on the porch deck, with insects buzzing around them and birds calling from the nearby trees. Angela realised that she had not felt so relaxed for some time. It was over a year since Vince had vanished into the Fold, and she and Sammi existed day by day. She was constantly on edge, waiting for a visit from the law or, even more worrying, a Kin. There was no saying that some of Mallian's followers hadn't remained in the area.

When Lilou was with them, she relaxed. Angela could never quite get past the tension between them, and the element of mistrust in her that was settled and solid. But the nymph had a way of making her feel that everything was going to be all right, even though she knew it never would be. Nothing was going to be all right ever again, but that day, when she brought a rabbit and stole her bath, Angela knew that, despite everything, she was a friend. Bringing peace and comfort was what friends did, with no thought of payback, no ulterior motives.

"She was my friend too," Angela said as they ran. "It was complicated, and sometimes I thought I hated her, but I didn't really."

"I know." Vince could hardly speak, broken arm held across his stomach. They held hands and he squeezed hers tight, but at that moment she could not tell what was going through his mind. Her own mind had never been put completely at rest about Lilou and Vince. The nymph had sworn that they had never slept together, but she had seen what Lilou was—had experienced some of that extreme allure herself—and she knew that in his own confused way, Vince saw her as more than a friend.

"I'm sorry," she said.

"He killed her. Right in front of us. Didn't care."

"She tried to kill him," Sammi said. She ran beside Vince. Angela was steering them, across the valley floor and up a very gentle incline towards the green landscape above. If they could reach the trees, perhaps they could get away.

There was something strange about fleeing. If Mallian wanted to catch and kill them he could do so himself, or send the raving infected Kin risen from their silty graves, or the powerful fairy now in his thrall. She could only deduce that he did not care about them, and did not consider them a threat.

Perhaps murdering Lilou had affected him more than it had appeared.

"We're going the wrong way," Sammi said.

"What do you mean?" Angela asked. "Any direction away from that mad fucking monster is—"

"She's right," Vince said, and he slowed them down. He was sweating and pale, and she couldn't imagine the agony he was going through. His left hand rested between the buttons of his shirt, and there was no saying how badly the arm was broken. At least she couldn't see bone protruding anywhere.

Angela glanced back and Mallian was out of sight, somewhere down in the remains of Longford and hidden from view by folds in the landscape. In some ways it was even worse not being able to see him.

They stopped and she could see the memory of Lilou's horrific death flickering behind Vince's eyes. It would play on a loop in his mind forever—and in hers.

They stood by the remains of an old wall on the beginnings of the valley slope, stones slumped down and mostly covered with dried silt. A few small plants had made a home in cracks in the silt, taking root in the short time since the reservoir had drained. Life found a way everywhere.

"I don't see what we can do," Angela said.

"Nothing here," Vince said. He looked at Sammi. "Right?"

"Nothing on this side," she said.

"You want to go back?" she asked, aghast.

"Not without you. Nowhere without you." He held her tight around the shoulders, half turned aside to protect his arm. It needed tending to, perhaps splinting, but there was no time. "But it's the last place he'll expect us to go, and we have to do something to try and stop him. This is what Mallian has wanted for years, the power to stand. This is Ascent, and he's not going to waste his time. He'll call his supporters to him, somehow, and with Grace on his side..." He shook his head. "Lilou knew. You must have talked about it with her."

"We didn't talk about much, really. Staying hidden. Catching rabbits to eat. You."

Vince blinked, and she saw a sadness that might never wane.

"He's cast a spell back in the Fold that gives him control over Grace, so if we've any hope of reversing it, it's back there." He looked at Sammi.

"We don't know what Sammi's capable of," Angela said. She feared for her niece, and their brief dash had revealed how weak she still was from the taste of magic she had already used.

"Neither do I," Sammi said. "Won't know without trying."

"What's in there?" Angela asked. She couldn't deny that part of her wanted to go into the Fold to see. She'd been in there before, briefly, but she'd been looking for Sammi, and in fleeing had no time to take in her surroundings. Grace might have made that place anything.

"It's a big valley. Green, lush, a river, some cliffs, meadows and forests. There are insects and birds and animals there, but mostly small ones. And there are Kin."

"Ones like me," Sammi said.

"Yeah, humans with Kin blood. Mallian calls them mongrels."

"Charming," Angela said.

"There's so much to tell you, show you," Vince said. "It might be the only place we stand a chance against him, and maybe some of the Kin will help us. None of them have any love for Grace, and if they know what she is now, who she's serving..." He shrugged, wincing at the pain it caused.

"What about that?" she asked, nodding at his arm.

"What about it?"

"Okay. So, what happens here?"

"Here? Now? I don't know. Nothing we can control. All we can do here is run, but in the Fold, maybe we can make a difference."

"For Lilou," Angela whispered, and as Vince's eyes grew moist, her own vision blurred.

"This way," Sammi said. "Across the valley side, then we'll approach the doorway thing from the other side, behind Mallian."

"What about Bone and those things he released?" Vince asked.

"I don't know how dangerous they are, but we can't do anything about them, either, not right now. As for Bone, he knew we were running," Angela said. "He's on his own."

Every step of the way she expected Mallian to appear from somewhere and stop them, stomp them into the mud, crush them to pieces. Maybe Sammi might be able to fight back for a short time, but she was only just sensing the strange powers she carried, accepting the blood in her veins and allowing it to feed her magic as it gave her life. Grace had been a fairy since the moment she was born. Any confrontation could only end one way, so they had to shift the balance.

Mallian did not stop them. Grace did not appear. As they headed back down into the valley, Angela was assaulted with doubts about what they were doing, and they all came from the fact that Lilou was dead. With the nymph alive she had felt insulation against the strange world of the Kin. Lilou had been a barrier between Angela's real world—the life she had left behind, with all its lost hopes and dreams—and the more fantastical place she now knew existed. Even when Lilou spent long periods absent, Angela knew she was out there, a friend with a foot in both worlds. Now she was gone, Angela felt naked and exposed.

The landscape of the reservoir bed was lacking in cover, and they had to search for wrinkles in the terrain to take them out onto the valley floor and towards the shimmering portal. *What if we go through and Grace shuts it forever?* she thought. It was not a consideration. They were in danger already, and putting themselves at more risk in order to combat Mallian was inevitable.

They might not have very long.

They might not have any time at all.

"There," Vince said, pointing ahead. His voice was flat. He held onto Angela's hand as they went, and Sammi led the way towards the place where two worlds touched.

I can't believe she's gone.

Saving Lilou from Mary Rock's thugs was how Vince had discovered the world of the living Kin. Before that they were merely relics to him, ancient remnants of obscure, ambiguous creatures that were worth a fortune on the collector's market. He'd become a relic hunter for the London gangster Fat Frederick Meloy, another man who had subsequently fallen under Lilou's spell, and who had sacrificed himself to save them all.

Now Lilou was dead, and Vince too felt exposed to the world of the Kin.

Angela was with him, gripping his hand. He had to hold onto that. Lilou would want them to be together, and she'd want them to continue the fight she had begun. The nymph's cause had been strong enough for her to go against the creature that had been her best friend for far longer than Vince had been alive. He would never betray that.

How could such a rare creature be snuffed out so easily? *She's still burning*, he thought. *Somewhere behind us, Lilou's corpse is still hot to the touch, because Mallian made Grace burn her to death.*

He would do everything he could to avenge her murder. It wasn't only about preventing Ascent and a conflict that might cost countless lives, both human and Kin. It was about taking revenge for the death of the *other* woman he loved.

There was no time to waste.

"Straight through," he said when they reached the portal, and he pulled Angela and then Sammi after him into the Fold.

A brief disorientation came and passed. He shook his head and looked around at the new landscape, and it was depressingly familiar. He supposed most people might consider it beautiful, its wildness something rarely seen back in the modern world. He saw it only as a prison, and this time Angela was incarcerated with him.

"She might have felt us come through," Sammi said, her gaze distant, not yet taking everything in.

"Maybe," Angela said, "but that doesn't mean she'd tell Mallian, or that he'd automatically know. Does it?"

Sammi shrugged.

"We need to find the relics," Vince said. "The ones Gregor collected, and a new one Mallian got in here."

"How did he get it?" Angela asked.

"He made a Kin bite its own tongue off for him."

"How the hell are we going to find them here?" Angela asked, and Vince realised that she was right. Even though he knew this landscape well, and had only escaped from here maybe an hour ago, something about it had changed.

Mallian and Grace aren't here anymore, he thought. *Maybe that's it*. But it was more than that, something deeper and more profound than an absence. The Fold had always been wild, and its air of wildness had always encouraged him to keep his head down and take care over every movement and encounter. Now, that wildness had come to the fore. Storm clouds played over the opposite hillsides, lightning arcing down. The river roared along the valley floor, apparently in flood and carrying clumps of dead trees and undergrowth with it. Rain was sheeting down at one end, its line visible as the clouds progressed across the whole terrain.

"It knows she's gone," he said. "The Fold's already starting to fall out of balance."

As if to illustrate his point a subtle vibration shook beneath their feet.

"Earthquake?" Sammi asked.

"There's a dwarf tunnelling in these hills. But that might have been anything. This is Grace's place, and it could be more an integral part of her than we can ever understand. Without her here, the edges might not hold."

"Maybe it'll fall apart if Mallian keeps control over her," Sammi said. "It takes fairy magic to make this place hold together. It takes effort. She's not directing her own efforts anymore."

"We might not have very long," Angela said. "Where the hell do we look, Vince?"

"Maybe where I saw him last." He pointed. "Down that way, I think. If not there, perhaps down by the river where Grace held him."

"You mean that river?" Angela nodded downhill, through the misting rain that was now falling around them. The river roared and surged, white water dancing in places, and it had already broken its banks in several areas. Where once it had provided the Fold with a gentle, timely flow, now it was a raging beast.

"One step at a time," Vince said. "Come on." He led them away from the portal and down the lush hillside, skirting a copse of trees and heading for the small clearing where Mallian had held him down, crushing him into the ground. His burning arm reminded him of how recently that had occurred.

So much had happened since then.

Rain fell harder, soaking his tattered clothing and causing a chill. He shivered, but the constant movement kept him warm. That, and fear. Fear of what would happen now that Mallian was free, had taken control of Grace, and would undoubtedly pursue his agenda of Ascent. Fear also of the Fold. He had survived this place for two years, but he realised now just how dangerous it was, perhaps more so because Grace was no longer here to maintain balance.

"It was here," he said when they reached the place. His voice was deadened by the rain, but Angela and Sammi were close enough to hear. He looked around, sweeping his foot back and forth through the long grass, and the hopelessness of what they were doing hit home. The relics were small, the largest barely the size of his fist, and even if they did find them, there was no telling whether simply disrupting their arrangement would do anything at all. He had no clue how the glamour worked. Maybe Sammi did, but probably not.

"Not quite here," Sammi said. "A bit further over there. Over by that pile of rocks. That's where he did it."

"How do you know?" Angela asked.

Sammi shrugged.

Vince hurried to the rocks to see if she was right.

As he and Angela paced back and forth, Sammi knelt and pulled aside an overhanging bush. Beneath it, hidden in the shadows, were the relics.

"Fourteen of them," she said. "Thirteen old and sad and filled with regrets. One fresh and still screaming in pain."

"You see what he's done?" Vince asked. He stood behind Sammi, looking over the kneeling girl's shoulder at the strange display. Mallian had placed them here to keep them out of sight, which hinted that there must be some danger in him leaving them alone. Would it be as easy as just kicking them asunder?

Angela stepped forward to do just that.

"No!" Sammi said. "It's dangerous. I don't understand how or why, and it'll take time, but I do know if we mess them up now, something dreadful will happen."

"How do you know?" Angela asked. "What will happen?"

"Something to Grace," Sammi said. "This pattern of relics has... it contains... some of her soul. She's been pulled in two by Mallian." Her voice was growing deeper and flatter, and Vince noticed she was sinking down onto her haunches, as if settling in for a long time.

"So what do we do?" Angela asked. Sammi didn't reply. She looked at Vince, raised an eyebrow, and he indicated that they should move back a couple of steps.

"I think Sammi's in charge here," he said. "Let's give her a moment, see what she has to say."

"We don't know how many moments we have left," she said, and perhaps some of the moisture on her face was tears.

"We never really do, do we?" Vince held her with his good arm and buried his face against her damp neck. He wished more than anything that the rest of the world would go away, and that they could stand like that forever.

21

Bone soon lost track of the other three as they ran. Instead he aimed up out of the valley, hitting the green line and continuing without pause. Being amongst colour again felt good. The greyness of the revealed valley had seeped into his soul, discolouring his vision of the future.

He knew that he had done wrong. Releasing Mohserran, the gargoyle and the werewolf Francine had been a stupid error, something a man with no sense would do, a man with no true path. After doing it, he could not recall his reasons. Was it really in the hope that they would attack Mallian and stop him doing whatever it was he had planned? Or was it simply because one of the infected was his father? His mind was fractured. Usually if he found Kin it was a simple matter of protecting their secret and letting them go again. Mohserran and the others were not a simple matter.

Fleeing through trees and grass, with bushes snatching at his clothing and startled birds taking flight around him, he might have been in another world. He still carried valley mud on his boots and lower trouser legs, and the dust of drying silt was thick at the back of his throat and in his eyes. He also bore the memory of the murder he had witnessed. He had seen violence before, and perpetrated it himself from time to time, but he'd never seen anything so brutal and inhuman.

Inhuman is what it's all about, he thought. He'd never thought of himself in such terms, because he had never allowed that strange, non-human part of him to come to the fore. He did not want that for himself.

He wasn't sure *what* he wanted, other than to know his father was at peace. Now, out of the valley, he realised that he should have listened to Angela and the dead nymph, understood what they were trying to do. In killing his father and those other tortured beasts, they were seeking the same as him.

Reaching a clearing and climbing a steep rocky slope, he stood and looked back down into the valley, and realised what he had to do.

He half expected the phone signal to be ineffective. The valley looked like another world, and what he'd seen today was not of the world he knew. But the buttons beeped with a familiar sound, and the ringing at the other end was answered within three tones.

"Jordan."

"It's me."

"I know who it is."

"I'm in Longford."

"And?"

"There's something here," he said. He couldn't keep the fear from his voice, and it translated through the phone line, because her prickliness dissipated instantly.

"What have you found?"

"It's more like what has found us," he said.

"There was something alive under the reservoir after all? One of *them*?"

Bone had spent his time working for Jordan doing his best to hide the Kin from her. This turnaround was not easy, and the enthusiasm and excitement in her voice somehow made it more difficult. He felt his betrayal of the Kin biting deep, but he didn't know what else to do. This was now far bigger than him.

"The gassing didn't kill everything. There are three creatures, not human, and as far as I can make out they're still infected. But they're not the only ones we have to worry about."

"There are more?"

"Yes."

"How many more? And where from?"

He frowned. He wasn't sure how to answer. The girl was Kin, that was evident, but what about the man and woman?

What about me?

"Uncertain. But one of them is... huge. Dangerous, powerful. And it came through some sort of opening, or portal."

He heard doubt in Jordan's silence.

"I'm telling you what I saw. Doesn't mean I believe it any more than you."

"So what do you suggest?" she asked.

"You have to send help before it escapes the valley," he said. "I'll do what I can to prevent that, but I'm not sure what I *can* do."

"What do you need?" The switch was amazing. He was now the man on the ground, and Jordan was efficient and professional enough to understand that. She was still his superior, but she had placed him in charge.

"The army."

"Be a bit more specific, Bone."

"The army. Send all of it."

He disconnected and stared down into the valley, at the distant remains of Longford. "And come quick," he muttered. "Though I'm not sure that will be enough."

22

He has always known it would come to this.

Mallian moves the burning corpse with his foot. Some of Lilou's white-hot fat sticks to his toes and scorches his skin, but he welcomes the pain because he deserves it. He has killed his closest friend. He did not wield the fire, but he breathed its creation and sent it on its way.

He touches his neck where Lilou's knife would have opened his skin, had the fairy not turned the keen metal blade into a feather. He feels his pumping blood, a rapid pulse because he is still fired up from his escape, his emergence back into the world, and the confrontation with Lilou.

"You should have listened to me, Lilou," he says. Her corpse spits in response. The remains of her right hand clasp at the soil, as if trying to hold onto the world for a little while longer.

Lilou is gone, her beautiful hair sizzled to nothing, her smooth skin blackened and split, her body twisted and melted into something horrible, and dead. There are Kin who might have been able to save some of her mind, absorb her memories and fears, her dreams and desires, but none of them are here. She died in this barren human place, knowing that her best friend did the killing.

He takes some comfort knowing that she experienced only a moment of pain before her brain was fried and everything she was turned to heat, gas and fire. He does not like to contemplate that moment.

Mallian does not have many friends left, and losing one like this is a harsh lesson on his journey to Ascent.

"You could have been here with me," he says. He looks at Grace, standing slumped and weak a few steps from him. She's also looking at him, but her eyes are vacant and hollow, staring into a place he hopes never to see. She appears weak, but he bears the weight of her great power inside, and understands that she is stronger than even he can ever understand. She is terrifying. He has already seen and used some of her strength, and in the days to come he will use so much more.

He has to take his time. Ascent is not about him, it is about the Kin, so he needs more of them here to shoulder the burden and share the glory. He cannot rush into a future he has craved for so long.

He blinks, and in that single moment he sends a message via the fairy and her vast, complicated mind. *Thorn, my old pixie friend, I'm back in the world and our time is at hand. I hope you've managed to fulfil your task. If you have, meet me here, and Ascent will rise from the dirt of a forgotten place.* He looks down at Lilou and touches her with his foot again. His toes sink in. He feels heat from fire, not from her living, striving flesh. That part of her is cold. *We will rise from the ashes.*

Grace twitches once and the message is sent. Mallian smiles. He has never experienced so much power.

He sends another thought, and Grace turns her gaze on the three Kin who emerged from the buried structure. He can feel their mindless rage, the frightening violence coiled in their shrivelled limbs and coursing through their old veins. Grace opens their minds to him, and he recoils as he reads the truth.

Humans did that to them.

They were poisoned and changed, turned from gentle creatures into the monsters that humans always see. Then they were gassed, buried and forgotten.

Humans will reap what they have sown.

Grace settles again, but he can feel and see her discomfort. Good. He possesses not an ounce of pity for her, even though she is the oldest Kin he knows. Grace was here at the beginning of everything, long before the Time when Kin walked fearlessly across the land, and she has seen and known so much in her long life. What is happening to her now is just another small part of her endless story.

He didn't even know whether the glamour would work. He is delighted. Gregor, that old human fool, did his job well.

"Shall we go to war?" he asks. Grace does not reply, and he senses that she does not understand. Whatever is left of the fairy is deep inside, and she was mad even before he took control of her mind. Perhaps she doesn't even hear. He thinks the same phrase, and she blinks several times, fluttering her eyelids as if to shoo away a fly.

"Shall we go to war?" he asks the three mad, infected Kin. One of them, the gargoyle, slavers and drools, its muscles knotted and primed ready to launch against any foe. Mallian understands that he would be as much foe as a human. These three are machines, corrupted and unclean. They are the Kin version of human missiles. He will set them on their course.

He looks around the strange valley. He's not sure what has happened here, but he can see that this used to be a human place, and now it has gone to mud, dust and ruin. He's excited, his old heart beating faster than usual. He feels a tingle of anticipation at what is to come. For two years he has waited, never knowing if or when the chance to escape would present itself. For many years before that he schemed and planned, again not knowing for sure whether his grand plans would come to pass. He looks down at Lilou's remains once more, and this time he does not feel sad. She is the first casualty in the battle for Ascent and will be remembered as such. A hero.

"Yes," he says, this time speaking to no one but himself. "Let's go to war."

23

Thorn hears the voice of his master, and knows that his whole life has come to this. For a while he is too giddy and excited to even think about what it must mean. He's been waiting for a long time, and even though his loyalty has never faltered, hope and expectation has. He has never been able to shake the conviction that Mallian was gone for good.

Now the Nephilim is back.

He jumps and dances and spins, filled with excitement that not only is Mallian alive, but he has advanced his cause to the point where he is calling for the Kin to join him and rise. Thorn hoped that he would see this day, but never assumed it would happen. Deep down, deeper than he would ever admit to, he has always believed the craving for Ascent to be folly.

Its reality will be something very different.

"What's up with you?" the man beside him asks. Thorn is in a small, scruffy bar in Boston, jigging at the counter and ignoring the many strange stares. He's used to people staring. He might be the smallest man any of them have ever seen. Usually he lets the stares slide from him, because he's Kin and he has to blend in to survive. Used to be that he was a kind Kin, too, but the years have bled that benevolence from him, and Mallian's outlook and cause drew him back from a precipice that might have swallowed him up in blackness and depression. Just occasionally he returns the stare loaded with the full weight of his years, and his experiences, and his deadly rage.

From time to time he lets that rage fly, but only if he knows he won't be caught.

Now his joy and rage combine. He dances some more, kicking over bar stools, knocking tables and spilling drinks. The man stands from his own stool and brushes both hands down his front, shaking them and splashing spilled beer to the ground.

"You freaky little fuck!" he says. He grabs up a bottle from the bar, smashes its neck, and comes for Thorn.

"Max, leave the little dude alone!" the barman says. He points at Thorn. "And you. Out."

Thorn barely hears. His old heart hammers, stuttering now and then with age and alcohol abuse and emotional misuse, but the blood pulsing through his veins feels young, and he is filled with more energy and joy than he can remember for many decades.

He takes the bottle from the man's hand and sticks it in his assailant's eye. The man screams and Thorn laughs, jumping to one side, snatching up a broken wine glass, shoving its snapped stem into the man's ear. The human's scream changes tone, catching in his throat as he drops to his knees. Thorn spins and slams the flat of his hand against the protruding glass base. It cracks against the man's ear.

Thorn laughs again. He smells the subtle oil of a firearm. He looks around and sees some men backing away from him, a couple coming closer. There are only a few women in this bar, most of them sitting in shadowy booths. One watches in terror, another with a strange smile. There are security cameras behind the bar covering most of the room, and Thorn leaps high and settles onto a joist, spinning around several times and maintaining his balance on one foot. He grins at the nearest camera.

See me! You can all see me now.

He's not sure this is what Mallian wants, but right now he doesn't care. The thought of what's to come, the anticipation of Ascent, has Thorn acting like the child he has not been for centuries.

A gun fires. He senses the bullet whip past him and bury itself in the ceiling. He hangs onto the joist and swings down, landing on a table without disturbing any of the glasses. A shadow turns and points something his way. The shadow stinks of body odour and fear, its breath fast and phlegmy, and Thorn kicks out and knocks the weapon from its hand. He snatches the spinning gun from the air and buries its barrel in the fat man's stomach. He pulls the trigger so quickly that three shots sound like one.

Panic begins to spread and Thorn soaks it up. He dances here, slashing a man's throat. He leaps there, shoving a broken pool cue into a woman's eye. People scream. They run and collide with each other, fighting to reach the door first, not understanding what's happening and struggling to flee the chaos.

Thorn *is* the chaos, and for a few seconds more he presents himself to the cameras, soaked in blood. He sticks up both middle fingers and grins.

"Hello, humans," he says. "Wait 'til you get a load of us."

A sandstorm rages in the playground of a school in Minneapolis. It's small and confined, manifesting as a twister two metres tall and hardly wider than two spread hands. It flits and zips back and forth across the yard, and at first the teachers on duty that afternoon smile and look at it as something of an oddity. The seventh-graders watching shout and laugh, rushing back and forth to pluck blades of grass or twigs from shrubberies around the yard to throw into the miniature whirlwind. It swallows them up, rips them to shreds, and spits them out into the air above. As it moves back and forth across the ground it leaves a trail of shredded plants behind.

The teachers' reaction turns from interest to fear when they see the face revealed in the twister's violent sands. It looks like an image drawn onto every page in a thousand-page book, then flickered into a moving visage. There are no real features. It's the white noise of faces, a convergence of every idea of what a face should be. Countless possibilities.

There is no sand here, one of the teachers says. The others have already thought that, but logic was displaced by fascination.

The face grins.

A child approaches to throw a handful of leaves into the tornado. The leaves are drawn from her hand, then her hand enters the swirling mass, her arm, and as she opens her mouth to scream she is swallowed away.

Every child watching screams for her.

When the red remains of the girl are spat skyward to patter down around the moving windstorm, the adults scream as well.

The children scatter in chaos, and as the teachers attempt to corral them and get them back into the building, the twister jigs back and forth, the demon within —its name is Ulb, and it ate thirteen knights and a prince during the Fourth Crusade—relishing this chance to take its fill without having to hide itself away.

Like a dog let loose in a butcher's shop, it only stops consuming when it is fit to burst.

The three women have been friends since they were girls. One is French, one Indian, the other from San Francisco, and over the past few years they have become internet sensations. Their greatest and most daring feat so far is base-jumping the CN Tower, for which they were all arrested and lumbered with hefty fines. They're careful to promote safety, and they always push the idea that they're vastly experienced at what they do. It's not just anyone who can parachute from a tall building, or kayak over waterfalls, or any number of a dozen other adventures they've undertaken together.

Today's might be the most widely followed yet. The three women have their trusted friends live-streaming the attempt to a select group, and several hundred people have gathered to watch. That no rumours have reached the ears of the authorities is something of a miracle, but also testament to how dedicated and passionate their fans are.

One day we'll end up in jail, they often say to each other. *One day we'll end up dead*. But their fires burn bright, and the same flames that brought them together also keep them safe.

Today, the flames come from a different place.

As they fly through the artificial canyons of New York, wing suits stretched to their limits, a shape appears and joins them in flight. At first they believe it's another wing suit, and the three women each experience a moment of annoyance that someone else is stealing their limelight.

On the ground, onlookers—fans and bystanders alike—are the first to realise that this is not merely another thrill seeker. The way the shape moves is different. Its ease in the air, its manoeuvrability, all indicate that this is not a man or a woman in a suit.

This is something else.

High above Times Square, heading north towards Central Park, a burst of bright yellow fire envelops the woman from San Francisco. She writhes, screams, and crashes into the side of a building, smashing glass and scattering blazing parts of herself into the streets below.

A high, ululating cry echoes through the streets of New York, a call that has not been heard by this many people in a thousand years. There's something joyous in the sound, and something terrifying. It's so non-human that it sends the crowds below scattering, even before the burning woman's remains strike concrete.

The Indian woman steers left to avoid the same fate, and flies straight into the boom of a crane protruding from the core of a building still under construction. Her head bounces across an intersection. Her body remains trapped aloft.

The third wing-suited shape heads for the ground as the French woman realises what has happened. Fate has caught up with her and the two women she thinks of as sisters.

She is the only one left.

Seconds later the winged creature—as big as her, but with membranous wings that stretch six metres to either side—emerges from behind a skyscraper and breathes fire into her face.

On the ground, the screams and panic are recorded by a thousand phones and sent onto the web.

In the sky, that delirious cry of joy echoes once more as the creature called Asher Vain glides out over the Hudson.

In Kansas City, a homeless man who has been begging outside a shopping mall for sixteen years pulls off his holed coat, shirt and trousers, then does the same with his long, knotted black hair and skin. His hairy chest makes a ripping sound as it parts from his body, and with several hard tugs he pulls the rest of the skin from his torso, arms and legs. He throws the wet coverings towards a cowering group of shoppers, who shout and flee in terror. Sweeping pale pink fluid from his glistening hide, he hops along the street on one large leg, shrieking at pedestrians, leaping into the road and causing multiple crashes, and finally disappearing into a side street from where witnesses later claim to hear insane, endless laughter.

In Idaho Falls, three children who people claimed to have seen living in the city's sewer system over the years come to the surface. They are filthy and blind, feeling their way along the ground until they reach a seating area outside a coffee shop. Here they ransack bins and steal bags and rucksacks, ripping them apart and chewing on leather and suede. As they chew, two police officers approach, hands held out and their voices calm and soft. The children fall to the ground and scream as wings extrude from their backs. They take flight, then circle around as one and attack one of the police officers. He suffers severe lacerations to his face and hands from their curled, filthy claws. His body-cam captures the entire event.

Several other strange incidents and sightings take place across the north-east United States, resulting in a dozen deaths and more disappearances. Social media catches fire with footage and eyewitness accounts. Theories range from terrorist incidents to meteor strikes, animal attacks to mass hallucinations.

As the Kin slowly begin to reveal themselves to a world much smaller than the one they hid away from so long ago, a shimmer of quiet panic is seeded amongst the human population.

Thorn washes himself in the restroom of a Greyhound station. His blood is still high, but he's already admonishing himself for his foolish display. He's not sure how many people he killed—three? four?—but he knows for sure he'll feature on the TV and internet news for his antics. And it's not as if he isn't easy to recognise.

Outside in the depot he practises the skills he's become used to for many years. He wisps through the waiting area like a ghost, moving from shadow to shadow, slipping a child's jacket from the back of a chair and pulling it on, picking up a baseball cap from atop a suitcase, and by the time he's sat on the floor with his back against the wall, close to a family but not so close that they'll question him, he is a child waiting for a bus. He is used to travelling, but usually does so only by night, and often trusting his own feet over human transport. Now, he is carried by an urgency that pulses at the back of his mind, sharpening his senses and preparing him for his journey. There isn't far to go. He's already looked up Longford on a map, and he reckons he can make it there within eight hours.

On the way he will contact and collect more Kin, and they will reach Mallian as a small army ready to fight. Others will prepare to rise and reveal themselves where they are, all in concert with Mallian and his plans. Some, he knows, have already jumped the gun and let their enthusiasm get the better of them. He cannot be angry with them, because he has made that same mistake. It has been so long coming that Ascent feels like a giant lake behind the flimsiest of dams. The leaks have already begun.

Thorn has made some calls, left messages on social media, and used more arcane methods of spreading his word. The seed of Ascent was planted many years ago, and over the past two years he has made it his duty to ensure it is nurtured and ready to bloom. He has been Mallian's silent general, a commander in the shadows travelling the country and ensuring that those already committed to the cause will be ready should the time come. He's also been recruiting, and Mallian will be surprised at how many more Kin he has found and talked around to their ideas. Thorn spent most of the past few centuries in Britain, and this larger, wider world came as something of a shock to him. The Kin here are different too, more independent and less reliant on support networks to survive.

But Thorn is nothing if not adaptable, and he has come to understand the American Kin. Their independence does not gloss over their past, nor their origins. If anything it makes them better placed to rise up and fight.

He has also met Kin who do not believe in Ascent, and he left them on their own. They will all have a second chance. When they witness the rise, some of them will change their minds. The others will find themselves more lonely and isolated than ever before.

What a glorious time.

Thorn looks forward to being reunited with his old friend.

24

Sammi had always wondered what it would be like to die. Now, she thought she was finding out.

When her mom died she had found it hard to quantify the loss and understand what had happened. Her dad had talked of her going to heaven, though he'd never really believed that and neither did Sammi. It was just a thing adults said to kids. It wasn't that strange explanation that had confused her, however, but the suddenness of absence. One day her mom was there, the next she was gone, she would never see, touch, or speak to her again. That had been a strange concept for her to grasp. Her mom had always been there for her, a presence in her life even when she was not in the immediate vicinity. She was a very personal gravity, a star around which Sammi orbited. Her death had taken that star away and negated the weight of her presence, sending Sammi into free-fall.

Her dad had saved her from falling too far, even though his own grief had been crippling. Now he was gone too. Sammi had been made to grow up quickly, and while her entire safety net had been ripped away, she'd then been opened to the world of the Kin.

The strange power she felt growing inside her was staggering, and yet she could not help feeling that it was gradually scorching away whatever it was that made her Sammi. Her life was bleeding away, sucked down by that power and let loose into the vast open space surrounding it. There was nothing she could do to hold it back. She could only make the most of things while she was still here.

I never wanted to be a fairy, she thought, and she chuckled, because what little girl could honestly say that?

"You okay?" Angela asked. Her aunt had stepped forward to help her when everything seemed lost, and in her eyes Sammi often saw a reflection of the woman her mom had been. Even though the sisters had not been close, and had spent long periods not communicating, the childhood they'd spent together meant that they'd had more in common than either of them would have admitted.

"I'm fine," Sammi said. They both knew that she was not.

"There's something coming," Angela said. "A Kin. Vince says he knows it, and he doesn't think it'll hurt us."

"I sensed it a while ago," Sammi said. "I don't know if it means harm. I don't know everything."

"I'm sorry," Angela said.

Sammi hadn't meant to sound harsh. The more she felt her senses expanding with the fairy magic settling around her, the more they would ask of her. She wasn't bitter about that, and she understood, but it hurt. It hurt all the time.

"You should go to meet it with Vince," Sammi said. "Maybe it'll help us. I think I'm going to need more time. Too much more time. I don't know if I can do this at all."

"I believe in you," Angela said.

"In fairies?"

"Yes. You know I do."

"You've been made to believe. Just like I have." Sammi heard what she was saying and sensed the hurt it caused in Angela, but she could not hold back. It was almost as if someone else was using her voice. They were her words, her thoughts, but something harsher spoke them. *The something I'm becoming.* She didn't look up at Angela, and when she moved away Sammi let out a sad, relieved sigh.

Sammi closed her eyes and took in a deep breath, catching hold of herself and maintaining her grip on the person she knew she was. Her mom and dad would want that, and she was desperate to hold on to reality.

For as long as I can.

She remembered shopping with her mom, her easy, kind laughter and willingness to talk to strangers. *Why wouldn't you want to talk to strangers?* she would say if anyone asked. *You never know what they're going to say, and mysteries are important.*

Sammi wished her mom could see the mystery she had become. She would likely never know why such a talent had not manifested in her mom, or even if she'd known what miraculous powers she carried in her blood, dormant and waiting. Perhaps Sammi's heritage had come to the fore because of the situation she found herself in. Exposure to the Kin might have awakened their trace within her, and Grace's lightning bolts had been well targeted. It was since the fairy's touch that Sammi had begun to really appreciate the differences she carried within her.

She remembered vacationing with her dad at the beach house. There had always been an empty space there with them, a hollowness where her mom should have been. Whether they were eating breakfast together, sunning on the dock or playing frisbee in the garden, that space had always been with them, making the house seem too large for just two people but too small to contain their grief. It had usually gone unspoken, but sometimes—in the evening when they sat on the patio and her dad had a glass of wine—they'd spoken about her mom, and sadness glittered in their eyes like reflected stars.

When she thought of the lightning strikes that had brought her into the world of the Kin, Sammi opened her eyes and focused on the relics laid out before her.

She felt, but did not understand, that they were held together by the arcane glamour Mallian had cast upon them. They were sad objects, each of them exuding the pain, fear and sorrow of the creatures they had been taken from. Gregor the Kin-killer had taken them, and in the end he had been betrayed by the one Kin he worshipped above all, Mallian the Nephilim. That was one death that Sammi did not mourn. The sum of Gregor's evil deeds were here, and she felt an overwhelming wave of sadness for those poor dead things.

The past was gone, and the future was uncertain. If she was to help she had to concentrate on that, forming her burgeoning skills and talents into a plan that might help them against Mallian. She had seen how powerful and strong he was even without Grace as his unwilling general. With the fairy on his side he might well be unbeatable.

Sammi understood that fighting Mallian was not the way to stop him, to begin with at least. Weakening him, taking away his advantage, was the first thing to do, and to achieve that she had to strip away his hold over the fairy.

Restrained within this rough circle of sad relics was a portion of Grace's soul. Mallian had stolen part of her and made it his own, and if Sammi could find a way of setting that fragment free—giving Grace's soul flight so that it could find its way back and recombine with her powerful, primeval self—she would break his hold over the fairy.

What Grace might do then, none of them knew.

Sammi glanced up after Angela and Vince. Angela remained close by, her back turned to Sammi but always aware of where she was. Vince had gone to meet the approaching Kin. They understood even less of what was happening to her than she did, but their presence was a comfort.

Seeking to embrace the frightening, growing power inside, rather than pull away from it, Sammi concentrated on the relics and let her energies flow.

Vince saw movement through the rain. It was darker than when they'd arrived—day and night had also been thrown into even more chaos by Grace's absence—and the rain caught errant light and cast flickering shapes across the landscape. The movement he saw was definite and determined, and as it came closer a form began to coalesce from the shadows.

"It's Dastion," Vince said.

Angela was behind him, still close to Sammi and the relics.

"Who?"

"He's a dwarf. I haven't seen him for a long while. A year, or more. Last time we spoke was the first time. He was drunk and depressed. Then he disappeared underground. He must have been digging ever since."

"How do you know?"

"Slag heaps all around the valley. Like giant mole hills. They're covered in plant growth pretty quickly, but they're easy to see if you know what to look for."

"All that time in the dark."

"Yeah."

Dastion was shorter than Vince remembered, but

also wider, stronger, like a boulder pulled out of the ground and now rolling across its surface. He heard the dwarf breathing as he paused ten steps away from them, a heavy sound like stones rolled in a bucket, but redolent of strength, not weakness. He wasn't breathless, but drew air in and out with hungry heaves. His hair and beard had grown wild, forming a complete halo around his dirt-smeared face. His eyes were narrow against the weak light, and Vince wondered what it must be like to exist underground for so long, the way lit only with occasional torches and fires. He wore heavy leather clothing, cracked and thick with dust, and on his hands were surprisingly light, tight gloves. They were made of a material Vince could not identify.

The dwarf nodded once, and Vince and Angela nodded back.

"Raining," Dastion said. He looked curiously at Angela, but asked no questions.

"It is," Vince replied.

Dastion looked up at the sky, eyes squinting tighter as his mouth opened to catch raindrops. He spat the water out and wiped his mouth.

"Euch. Plain. Water I drink is full of minerals. Takes days to filter down below, longer. One place I found, the water takes ten years to permeate down through the rocks. Thirteen strata, seven impermeable, it has to run down them, forms channels and dissolves salts and minerals. Best damn water you'll ever taste." His eyes opened wider, his stare much further away, and Vince thought he already wished he was back in his mines.

He must have surfaced for something.

"You know what's happened?" Vince asked.

"Why else do you think I came up? No other reason to come up here."

"Food?" Angela asked. "Company?"

Dastion snorted. "Enough food down there for a lifetime, if you know where to look. And my own company is best."

"Mallian controls her," Vince said.

"Oh," Dastion said. "Fuck."

"You didn't know?"

"I knew she was gone. There are cracks in the Fold, deep down in its foundations, and they've started growing wider. Tremors where there shouldn't be. I guessed it could only be that crazy fairy bitch has left us alone."

"She went of her own accord, but the Nephilim took control of her, back in the world."

"The world," Dastion said. "Haven't thought about that place in a while."

"So why come here, to us?" Vince asked.

"In the hope that we can go back," Dastion said. He nodded behind him, and through the rain Vince saw other shapes hiding in the trees. "We've all been a meal for the fairy at one time or another."

"Even you?"

"You thought me immune?" Dastion lifted his arm to display a pattern of deep, ragged indentations along his left underarm. "I believed I was safe down there, and it took her a long time to come after me. Maybe she'd grown tired of the hunt up here." He frowned, eyes distant and haunted. "Foolish of me to believe I might ever be safe from her. So we're here, all of us, in the hope that you can help us."

"Me?" Vince asked.

"Sure. We help each other, right? You've talked to most of us over the past couple of years, helped some after she took bites out of us."

"You know what Mallian plans?" Angela asked.

"I've heard whispers. We all have."

"So?" Angela asked. It was such a loaded word that Vince held his breath. If they sided with Mallian they'd instantly become enemies, and he didn't like the idea of going up against Dastion.

"So, none of us has any love for the fairy. She drew us here, gave us our freedom, and most of us have embraced that, despite everything we left behind. But then she started eating us. That's no saviour. We want freedom from the fairy, but freedom in the world too, not conflict and pain. We all left people behind." He frowned and looked past Vince, as if searching for a way back to whoever he'd left when Grace had marked him and struck him down with lightning. "It's strange, we've left them now, and moved on, and found the existence we were made for. But none of us wants harm to come to those we left behind. If Mallian has his way, they will come to harm."

"So we all want the same thing," Vince said.

"Peace for the ones we love," Angela said.

Dastion nodded. Behind him the mermaid Shashahanna emerged from a copse of trees, seeming to flow with the rain and make it her own. A fox followed, walking on two feet and flickering behind the downpour, features blurring uncertainly between human and animal. Fer, the shapeshifter, was also with them.

"Good," Vince said, although he wasn't sure just how good any of this might be. Could he trust them? Did they really all want the same thing? He didn't have the luxury of time in which to find out.

"So what's the plan?" Dastion asked.

"That's what we've got to come up with," Vince said. He glanced at Angela, and she gave him a nervous look.

"My niece is... she has certain fledgling powers, and she might be able to break Mallian's hold over the fairy," Angela said.

"What powers? Where is she?"

"Just back past those trees," Angela said. "She's one of you, struck by lightning, marked and brought here by Grace, but we rescued her before the Fold closed."

Dastion looked suspicious, then his expression softened. His more relaxed face crinkled, and streams of rainwater ran down into his massive beard. The water collected and dripped off like falling diamonds.

"Good for her," he said. "No one should go through what Grace has put us through. So, how did you and the girl get back in?"

"A portal cast by Grace," Vince said. "But we're blind until we go through, and I'm worried Mallian will see us. We'll walk straight into him, and Grace, and that'll be the end of it. When we do go back we need an element of surprise, and something to fight him with."

"Sammi needs time," Angela said. "Mallian used arcane magic, a glamour maybe only he knew. Sammi thinks she might be able to break it, but..."

"But she's young, and is still finding her Kin way," Shashahanna said. Her voice was low but loud.

"What is she?" Dastion asked.

"She's not sure," Angela said.

The three Kin fell silent, and Vince sensed their distrust. He almost told them. Honesty would be the best answer, surely? But if he told these tortured, angry Kin that Sammi was a fairy, they might trust her as little as they trusted Grace. And they might hate her as much.

"We *think* she's a nymph," Angela said. "We knew one, a friend of ours, and Mallian just murdered her."

"He did?"

"She was his oldest friend and she went against him."

Dastion looked past Vince and Angela towards the trees where they'd left Sammi poring over the relics.

"So she needs time," Dastion said. "How do we give her that?"

"Somehow we have to slow Mallian down," Vince said. "Do something that'll upset his plans, if only for a while. He'll have called other Kin to him—he has a cohort that has always believed in Ascent, and I'm sure they'd have been waiting for his return—and once they're there..."

"He'll go out into the world," Shashahanna said.

"Yeah, and with a fairy at the head of his army," Dastion said. He looked around him at the Fold slowly descending into chaos. "All I want to do is dig."

"And you will again," Vince said. "That's what we're fighting for. Your freedom to do what you want. And humanity's freedom to co-exist with the Kin, even if it doesn't know of your existence."

"Most of it doesn't know," Shashahanna said.

Vince smiled. "Some of us who do have given up our lives to fight for you." He looked at Angela and his smile fell when he saw the sadness in her eyes. *We've lost our old life forever*, he thought.

"We're still together," she whispered, and her tentative smile revived his.

"So we need to get back to the world and try to disrupt Mallian, stop him from leaving," Dastion said. "And the only way back is through a new portal, formed by the fairy that he now controls, and which will likely drop us all right into the hands of Mallian and his forces."

"That's about the size of it," Vince said. "I figure we run out fighting."

"And die." Dastion rubbed his beard. "Well, I'll throw this out there for starters—I've found something deep down I think might help us."

"Found what?" Angela asked.

Dastion smiled for the first time, and it lit up his face. His beard lifted and parted, his eyes squinted tight, and his ruddy cheeks peered through their hairy camouflage.

"Maybe another way."

25

Bone waited on the borders of green and grey for Mallian to rise, for death to come. He had always existed on the fringes, knowing he was different, sired by a creature few humans would understand or even believe in. From his traumatic childhood onwards he had never known how to handle that, so he had spent his life searching for similar creatures. As a child he had known three, so as he grew older he held onto the logic that where there were three there were thirty, and three hundred, and maybe many, many more.

When he found such creatures he never told the people he worked for of the encounter. A few times, knowing how dangerous the Kin were, he had killed them. Given freedom, they might eventually have been captured or revealed, and then the world of the Kin would have become a much more public affair. He didn't like what he had done, wasn't proud. He'd spent his life ensuring that they remained a secret, so that his own troubling, strange powers remained a secret also. It was ironic that to protect these creatures he'd had to kill a few of them, to keep humans safe from them, and to keep the world of the Kin a secret.

He hadn't told his handlers of those occasions, either.

He fed Jordan an occasional lead, sent her a relic here and there, collected eyewitness statements and accounts. He made sure that each year of his employ he gave them something, but never enough. Working for them gave him the freedom and funding to travel and search, but he always ensured that the truth eluded them. Once they knew for sure of the existence of living Kin, it would only be a matter of time before they came after him.

With Mallian, everything had changed. Bone had never seen anything like him. Even the most dangerous Kin he had ever come across were shadowy figures, perpetuating myth and legend and living beneath the radar of human perception, their murders spread out and irregular.

Mallian was something very different, and very dangerous.

That was why Bone had called Jordan, and why he waited now for the end to come.

Looking down into the stark grey valley, he tried to catch sight of any movement that might indicate what Mallian would do next. He felt an urgent, deep guilt at letting his father and the other two infected Kin loose from their containment. If the Kovo infection transferred to other Kin, Mallian's forces would be boosted even more. And with the fairy under his control, his capabilities were already difficult to gauge.

Seeing what she had done to Lilou made Bone sick with dread.

He glanced at his watch, looked at the sky. Dusk was falling, and in darkness the Kin became more confident. He knew that from experience. Mallian's confidence was already boosted, and there was no telling when he'd be ready to emerge from Longford valley to reveal himself to the world.

He'll have a plan, Bone thought. *He won't just march across the countryside. There are small communities nearby, but no city for twenty miles. He'll have an aim in mind.* And he was patient. If what Vince and Angela said was true, the Nephilim had been trapped in the Fold for two years or more, and he would not rush his plan for Ascent. He'd make sure it went just right.

Reinforcements. He'll make sure he has an army, not only for the power it'll afford him, but for the spectacle. He didn't know a lot about the Nephilim's intentions for Ascent, and Angela and Vince hadn't revealed much about it, but a revelation of the Kin would surely require an event that would shake the world. *The more reinforcement, the better.*

He paced along the defining line between green grass and trees and dried grey reservoir bed, knowing he should head back down to confront the danger, but terrified to do so.

His father had given him one of his last breaths to escape and survive. The last thing he'd have wanted was for Bone to return and die in that desolate place.

He'd wait and see what happened, and for the army to arrive. He'd wait for death to come to him.

When Bone saw movement, it wasn't from the direction he'd expected. He caught the glint of fading sunlight on glass from the corner of his eye, then spotted the vehicle moving slowly along a road higher up the valley side. It crested the top and started down, and Bone set out at a steady jog to meet it.

He edged uphill so that the colourless valley was out of sight to his left, but he could still smell the dust of that place, and still feel the weight of danger influencing his every move.

He aimed for the narrow lane heading down the hillside through the trees. Running, he experienced a sudden flashback that almost made him lose his footing—three trucks laden with army personnel heading down this same road many years and a lifetime ago, while the young Bone hid in amongst the trees, looking for a way out yet terrified at escaping. He'd left his mother and father behind, and no little boy really wants to run away from his parents, however certain he is that they are dead.

The memory brought him up short. This was the same road, though very different now, and the car heading his way was on its own. He started running again, and when he reached the road he crouched down beside a fallen tree, looking uphill at where the holed, weed-covered track disappeared behind a roll in the hillside. He could see the splash of headlamps dancing through the trees up there as the vehicle drew closer, and from where he was he could decide whether or not to reveal himself when it passed him by.

It was a police cruiser. Bone tensed, crouched down again, mind whirring. What the hell were the cops doing here now? As the cruiser drew close he stood and waited beside the road, hand held up in a friendly wave.

The car stopped, engine still running, and the passenger door opened. The man who uncurled from the car must have been six and a half feet tall and over two hundred pounds. He was anything from forty to sixty years old, and several scars across his cheek and nose showed that he had taken care of himself, probably several times. Bone didn't like to think what had happened to the people who'd put them there.

In the driver's seat was a female cop. The way she looked at him made Bone even more cautious of her than the huge man. He scanned the man's uniform for a badge, didn't see the one he sought, then saw something else. Body-cam. All cops wore them now, of course, recording footage on a rolling basis in case any incident needed reviewing. He looked at the driver again and caught sight of the sheriff's badge on her jacket, light from the dash reflecting off it.

"Help you, son?" the cop asked. It was strange being referred to as *son* by a man probably younger than him. Bone had been on the road for much of his life, and he'd had enough experience with strangers—and with the police—to know that this likely indicated a man who was not intending to be his friend. This was a business-like greeting, from someone who could snap Bone in half with one hand.

"Just wondering what the problem is, Officer."

The sheriff's face lit up inside the cruiser as she looked at a display screen. She glanced up at Bone, then back down at the screen.

"No problem. Just a routine drive-by." The man scratched his head and sighed, as if doing so was a great effort. "Our patch just grew a lot bigger when the dam went. The sheriff says we've gotta patrol the borders of the old valley, make sure no one's making off with any souvenirs."

Bone wondered what souvenirs he might be thinking of. Some mud, perhaps. An occasional dead tree. A rock.

"Me, I'd much rather stay away from the old place. Went under when I was a kid, but I heard stories about Longford made me want to stay away."

"What stories?" Bone asked, but the officer took no notice. He bent almost double to look in the cruiser window and exchange some words with the sheriff inside. When he stood again, he appeared more at ease.

"Guess you're Bone."

Bone blinked in surprise. Jordan wouldn't have called in the police, surely? Not after what he'd told her. But then it all came together and made sense, and he felt a sinking sensation in the pit of his stomach. She hadn't believed him.

Maybe he should have thrown her one or two living Kin over the years, after all.

"Been asked to check in on you," the sheriff said, leaning from the window. "Couple of my guys who were keeping watch over this place turned tail, said they saw and heard some weird stuff down on the valley floor. Booming noises, flashing lights... things that looked like people but acted like wild animals." She scrutinised him up and down. "That wouldn't have been you, would it?"

"What were you told?" Bone asked, and both cops hardened. They were used to doing the asking, not the answering.

"Thing is, I like being in charge," the sheriff continued. "Dane here, he likes me being in charge too. It's why I chose this district, 'cos it's small and the population's generally pretty decent. Had a bar fight last year, maybe the year before. Bunch of kids took to fucking in strangers' gardens for a thrill three years back. Let them, I say, but the law's the law, and no one wants to see teenagers bumping uglies when you're serving up dinner, right?"

Bone wasn't sure if she was asking for a response, so he said nothing.

"Dog," Dane said.

"Oh yeah," the sheriff said. "A dog was stolen a couple months ago. See, fuck all happens here, so I don't like it when there're strange sounds and things that upset my guys. And I don't like getting calls from people like your friend Jordan. It upsets my balance and gives me the shits."

"Sorry to hear that."

"So you just jump in the back with us, and we'll head down into the valley to see what's up."

"No," Bone said. "Bad idea."

"You wanna tell your boss that?"

"Yes," he said.

The sheriff and Dane glanced at each other then stared at him.

"Really, it's a bad idea," Bone said. "There are... dogs down there, wild dogs. With rabies."

"Dogs," Dane said.

"Not according to your boss," the sheriff said. "She reckoned there was a group of drug takers and thieves making the old Longford their home, and you'd got mixed up with them and needed our help. What are you, DEA?"

Bone shook his head.

Her eyes opened wider. "Fed?"

Bone sighed. He couldn't let these people go down there, not without a proper warning of what they were up against. And he didn't want to go there with them. He'd called Jordan to send the army, not two sarcastic cops who'd rather be eating each other back at their pissant little precinct.

"In the car," the sheriff said.

Bone tensed, ready to run. He saw Dane do the

same, the big man's eyes going wide in anticipation of the chase. His hand fell down to the taser on his belt.

"Car," Dane said.

Bone could run. He'd known these hillsides once, but he wasn't a young boy anymore, and there were no hollow trees for him to hide in now.

Besides, Jordan hadn't believed him. She'd sent these two to check his claims. If he went with them, maybe they'd have a chance of pulling back and getting the fuck out as soon as they saw what he had seen. They'd have Mallian on their body-cams, and he'd be able to show that footage to Jordan.

He nodded, walked to the police cruiser, and sat in the back. Dane slammed the door and got in, and the sheriff drove them on their way.

"You'll have to be careful," Bone said.

"Of the dogs or the junkies?" Dane asked, and he chuckled.

"What's your name?" Bone asked the driver.

"Sheriff," she said.

He sat back and closed his eyes. If Jordan was sending these cops to test the water, the army was not yet on its way.

He had to make sure it would be soon.

The sheriff parked the car at the edge of the old reservoir. The lane ended there, and though before it had wound down the hillside towards Longford, now it was part of the grey mass of drying reservoir bed and muddy pools. Further distant the river still meandered through the valley, and to their far right, shielded now by the falling dusk, the old dam cast a broken guard. Fading sunlight did little to give colour to the greyness. As shadows emerged and coalesced, it looked more like a moonscape than ever.

"Can't hear those dogs," Dane said, tilting his head through the open window. "Don't smell no dope."

The sheriff wasn't laughing. She was watching Bone in the rearview mirror, frowning. *Maybe she's starting to believe something's really wrong*, he thought.

"Take the shotgun," she said.

"Seriously?"

Still not taking her eyes off Bone, she nodded. Dane unlocked the shotgun secured between the front two seats. He held it awkwardly, as if he'd hardly used it before. He'd stopped making quips.

"Coming?" the sheriff asked.

"No," Bone said. He'd made a decision. To prove to Jordan that what he'd said about Mallian and the infected Kin was true, he had to prove it to these cops as well, and do so without getting them killed. Venturing down there would doom them all. "We can't go down into the valley."

"What have you really seen?" she asked. "It's not rabid dogs or drug users, is it?"

"Neither of those, no. We just need to get something on camera to show my superior and then—"

"Lily!" Dane said. "Something out there."

Bone's heartbeat immediately jumped. He stared through the security grille and out the front windscreen, past where the road ended and onto the flatter expanse of grey. Nothing moved.

"You better tell us what's out there quickly, Bonham, or we're straight back to the station and—"

"There!" Bone said. "Ahead and to the right." It wasn't Mallian, Bone knew that right away. Maybe it was what his father had become. The shape was small and fast, darting right to left down the hillside, little more than a shadow.

"Deer," Dane said.

"Deer don't move like that," the sheriff said. With one more glance at Bone, she opened her door and left the cruiser. When Dane did the same, Bone reached for the door handle and realised his error. He was locked inside. Of course he was.

"Don't go too far!" he called. "Just get something on camera and then—"

Dane slammed the door and walked into the cruiser's headlights. The sheriff was off to the left, aside from the lights and at the edge of the grey, shielding her eyes and looking down into the valley. Dane stood with the shotgun held in one hand by his leg, casual and confident.

Bone rattled the door handle.

Something flitted past the car. It scraped claws across metal as it went, causing a piercing shriek, and as Dane and the sheriff spun around it disappeared into the trees to the right.

Bone watched it go. It was Francine the werewolf. He wound his window down and beckoned Dane back to him.

"Quietly!" he said. "Quick and quiet, they're playing with you, you have to—"

"You damage my cruiser and I'll ram this inside you," Dane said, swinging the shotgun up and holding it across his chest.

The figure that rose behind him blocked the headlamps and cast a huge shadow, a towering, shimmering shape that danced across the valley as it stepped closer.

"Holy fucking—" the sheriff said, voice cut off as she was swatted to one side.

Mallian came himself, Bone thought. *Of course he did. He wants to be on camera as much as I want him to be seen.*

Mallian stood tall and proud as Dane turned around to see what stood behind him. The Nephilim glanced down at the sheriff as she struggled to rise, then took three quick steps and snatched Dane off his feet. Even such a big man looked toylike in the Nephilim's hands.

The shotgun fired into the night, then Mallian plucked it from the officer's hands and snapped it in half. Still holding Dane beneath the arms in his other hand, he held onto his legs around the thighs, raised him high above his head, and pulled. Muscles stood knotted in his arms, shoulders and chest, and Mallian roared with effort as he twisted and pulled the big cop in two.

If Dane made a sound, Bone didn't hear it.

Blood and fluids splashed down on Mallian's upturned face, and he opened his mouth to swallow them down.

The sheriff was on her feet fumbling for her sidearm, eyes wide and disbelieving.

Mallian stood bathed in light, a bloody, living sculpture holding two torn halves of the same man aloft. His head and upper body glimmered as he moved, and it shook everything he knew of the world, even though he had known of Kin since he was a little boy. It made everything darker.

He couldn't imagine what reaction the sheriff was fighting through.

She'd pulled her gun and was trying to aim, but her hands shook, her right leg quivering as she tried to keep her footing.

Mallian threw the upper portion of Dane's corpse at her. His head struck her right hip and she went down, and Bone thought, *Now he leaps on her and tears her to pieces.*

But the Nephilim was relishing this moment. He held the dead cop's lower torso and legs high and roared, remaining in the light. He knew what he was doing. This was Mallian's moment, a time he must have dreamt about for years, decades, centuries. This was the beginning of his personal revelation to humanity, and Bone knew that what the cops' body-cam and dash-cam images recorded would become the founding, early images of Ascent.

The sheriff had gone. Bone hadn't seen her run, and he felt a momentary fury at her cowardice. She'd left him here, alone, locked away and at the mercy of this beast. Seconds later, he realised he'd have done the same. She couldn't be thinking straight, and running blindly into the woods would be her first and only reaction.

Bone shrank down, peering between the front seats at Mallian as he turned a slow circle. The headlamps would prevent him seeing into the cruiser, and perhaps he'd simply leave now that his job was done. Slipping lower, holding his breath, he wasn't ready for the object that slammed against the driver's door.

Of course, the shape we saw just before, one of the infected Kin sent by Mallian to distract the cops, make his revelation even more mind-blowing, and now it'll rip the doors off and come inside and there's nothing I can do. All my fault. I let them out. I let my father out when I should have killed him.

The driver's door opened and the sheriff dropped into the seat, her breathing short and panicked, hands shaking as she reached for the keys. She didn't seem to remember Bone was in the back. He said nothing.

Starting the car drew Mallian's attention again, and he heaved the other half of the corpse at the vehicle. It slammed into the windscreen and slid down, leaving a slick trail on the glass.

The sheriff crunched her foot on the gas and reversed, twisting in her seat, catching Bone's eye then looking past him as she steered the car backwards away from the blood-soaked giant. Dane's body dropped from the bonnet and Mallian stepped on it as he came for them.

He didn't run. He took long, loping steps, grinning, and Bone couldn't help thinking he was performing for the dash-cam. *He won't stop us,* he thought. *I'm not going to die at his hands just yet.*

Maybe tomorrow.

The sheriff was a good driver. She slid the car into a spin, pushed it into drive and then powered away, keeping her eyes on the road and only on the road. Not on the beast that had stopped downhill, a few huge steps out of the grey and into the green.

Bone turned in his seat and watched Mallian recede behind them, his daunting shape revealed by the bloody dusk. He couldn't help feeling that the two of them locked eyes.

In the front, the sheriff began to groan with each breath.

"Can you send images from this thing?" Bone asked.

"Huh?"

"Can you send dash-cam images from the cruiser? To phone or email or something else?"

"Huh?"

"Pictures of Mallian."

"What's a Mallian?"

"That thing."

"It has a name?"

"Can you do it?"

She drove, weaving between trees and bouncing along abandoned tracks. The cruiser's suspension creaked and cracked, and Bone pressed one hand against the ceiling to prevent smacking his head.

"Sheriff! Lily!"

"Huh?"

He let her drive. She was still groaning, an exhalation with each breath that might have been disbelief, or fear, or grief, but was probably all three. A couple of minutes later they hit a smoother road and she turned left, towards the valley crest and the long road to the nearest town beyond. She was driving too fast. Blood smeared the windscreen, forced into cracks in the glass from the impact of half of Dane's corpse.

"Sheriff, I need to send those images to my superior," Bone said. "She'll send help."

"Help. Against that."

"Yes."

"What is it?"

"I don't know," Bone lied, because anything else would take too long to explain. After decades he still sometimes didn't understand himself.

"The images," he said.

"Yeah. I can send. But not here, and not yet. I'm getting the fuck out of this valley first."

Bone sighed and sat back into the cruiser's rear seat, every part of him in agreement.

"Holy fuck."

"I told you."

"What is it?" Jordan asked.

"I'm not sure." The same lie, for the same reason.

"I didn't believe you."

"I know. So, the army? You'll send them? It's not the only one, and some of the others... they're different. Worse."

"Worse than that?"

"Worse."

The phone line crackled, and Bone wasn't sure if some of it was Jordan holding her phone away from her head and taking deep breaths.

"Of course," she said. "They'll be there by dawn. I didn't believe you, but I couldn't take the risk. Longford already had a red mark against it, a watch notice, and the army mobilised when you first called."

"Thank fuck for that," Bone said.

"Will it do any good? Will they help?"

I don't know, he wanted to say. *I don't think so*, he thought. Instead he said nothing, and after a period of uncomfortable silence Jordan said, "Keep in touch," and ended the call.

The dead air sounded deep, dark, and filled with terrible futures.

26

Angela and Fer stayed behind with Sammi, and Vince accompanied Dastion across the hillside and down through one of the many hidden entrances to the mines he had been working on beneath the surface of the Folded Land. Shashahanna went with them, moving like mist, mysterious and silent.

Vince couldn't help feeling that they were working against time. The Fold was failing, its edges shredding, a tempestuous creation angry at its creator for leaving. Rain fell heavier as they entered the mines, wind blew harder. The ground itself shook with minor quakes. There was no telling how long it would hold together, nor what would happen once the edges began to give way.

Sammi was still struggling with the glamour cast over the relics, and her own burgeoning and confusing powers. Vince could see the pain she was suffering, and knew that Angela saw it too. It was awful to behold, but something they had to ignore, because they both knew that Sammi was doing her best. She was their only hope, and they had no choice but to let her do whatever was needed to break the spell.

Beyond the Fold, Mallian was marshalling his

forces. What would happen once Ascent began, no one could know. Vince imagined terrible things—cities laid waste, Kin fighting humans, modern warfare tangling with powerful fairy magic in the valleys and hills of eastern America and the wide skies above. Much of it was beyond imagining, but he knew that the death toll would be catastrophic.

No version of Mallian's Ascent would be peaceful.

The clock ticked, and with every step that Vince took, he felt an uncertain ending drawing closer.

Dastion had been busy beneath the ground. His mines were deep, the tunnels twisting left and right, up and down. Larger galleries had been carved from the rock of the land, with columns left standing to support the curved ceilings. Here and there he'd taken time to carve images into the stone walls, strange glyphs telling tales Vince had no time to understand. It must have been difficult for Dastion to adjust to his new life. As well as leaving his human existence behind, it appeared that a deep, complex race memory had been carried in his Kin bloodlines, and he was telling his own story through digging, tunnelling, mining and carving.

The dwarf moved with confidence, handing them torches stored at regular intervals. The brands blazed with a rich yellow light, pushing back the shadows, filling the space around them. Here and there side tunnels headed off into the depths, and Dastion glanced at some of them with a strange longing.

All he wants to do is dig, Vince thought.

Every now and then the tunnels shook. Dust fell around them, and grit; and occasionally larger stones and rocks broke away from walls and ceiling.

"Built to last," Dastion said, slapping a heavy timber bracing propped across the tunnel above Vince's head. He sounded confident, but looked less so. Or maybe it was the way torchlight reflected in his eyes.

Dastion led them deeper, down a series of spiralling staircases and across several narrow rock bridges that spanned cracks in the land. Vince was drawn by the dark spaces beneath these bridges, and he found himself pausing and looking down. On the third crossing he glanced up to see Dastion and Shashahanna watching him, his eyes full of understanding, hers unreadable. Vince looked back to the depths and dropped his burning torch.

It fell, turning slowly end over end and shedding sparks. Its light splashed across crevasse walls and fell with it, a ball of illumination that grew smaller as it went deeper. Vince expected the torch to strike bottom, break apart on a rocky floor or extinguish in an underground stream, but it simply kept falling until it was little more than a speck of light, a descending star that then became something he wasn't sure he could see at all.

"How far?" he asked.

"I don't know," Dastion said. "I've gone deeper than we are now, and that's where I found what I have to show you. But down there..." He shrugged. "I'm fascinated by it, but afraid as well."

"You don't seem like someone who'd be afraid," Shashahanna said, her deep voice echoing.

"You don't know me," Dastion said. "Neither of you do. Come on, we're almost there."

They left the crevasse behind and entered another series of tunnels. Skirting an underground pool, Shashahanna handed Vince her torch and slipped into the waters with hardly a ripple. He and Dastion edged around the pool, and as she emerged on the far side, water slipping from her body, her eyes were wide. She breathed in a chestful of air and exhaled slowly.

"So old," she said. "Older than anywhere I've swum before."

"How can this place be older than anywhere else?" Vince asked.

"I didn't dig all these tunnels, human," Dastion said. "I find the way, but sometimes the way is here before me."

"So old," Shashahanna whispered again, moving ahead of them away from the pool. She did not once look back.

During Vince's time here days and seasons had seemed to change at random. Down in the darkness it was even harder to follow the passage of time. He wondered how Dastion managed, but then realised he did not need to. For the dwarf, being down here was time on his own, and day or night, winter or summer, did not matter.

"We're close," Dastion said. "We'll wait here. Just for a while."

Vince couldn't tell if the dwarf was tired or scared, or maybe both.

"We don't have time to wait," he said.

"Just while I tell you what I found, because if I'm right, what's around the corner might be dangerous."

"So tell us," Shashahanna said.

"I found... a crack in the world."

Vince thought back to the crevasse, a few minutes or an hour earlier. He wondered if his torch was still falling.

"Not like that one back there," Dastion said. "This is something different. That crevasse is deeper than it ever should be. When I found it, I threw rocks in and never heard them hit bottom, but I've done nothing since. I'm worried I'll disturb whatever might be down there. But this place I've brought you to is more of an edge than a crack. An end."

"Of the world?" Vince asked.

"Of this world. You've tried walking out of the valley, I'm sure."

"Countless times," Vince said. "I get turned around without feeling it. A weird sensation. As if I've rebounded from a wall, but there's no wall there and no sense of changing direction."

"I've tried down here, too," Dastion said. "I've mined in a straight line for weeks on end, and eventually end up back in the cavern where I began. Here, I've found the edge of the Fold, and it's visible.

It's dark, like infinity. Like nothing."

"What good is that?" Shashahanna asked. "You've brought us all the way down here to see a wall?"

"I think the edge might be open," he said.

"What do you mean?" Vince asked.

"Grace has formed one opening out of the Fold."

"And you think it might be mirrored down here?"

"We've come down here on a supposition?" Shashahanna asked.

"I know the ground," Dastion said. "I know the rocks and the soils, the cracks between rocks, and the way it all holds together. There's a poetry to it, and a form. I haven't been living the life I was meant to for very long, but it's been a part of me forever. I think this is a place she forgot about, or maybe never knew about in the first place. And now that she's formed her portal up there, this down here might be another way out of the Fold."

"So let's go and see," Vince said. He nodded past Dastion and the dwarf turned and led the way.

The tunnel ahead of Dastion suddenly opened up wide, swallowing torchlight and giving nothing back. The blackness was deeper than any Vince had ever seen, a thick, physical presence rather than an absence, and he experienced a moment of dread that prickled sweat across his skin and shrivelled his balls. The tunnel was narrow, but this consuming darkness was suddenly wide, stretching across his whole field of vision.

"You didn't say how fucking scary it was," Vince said.

"Yeah."

Shashahanna crept forward and approached the endless darkness, reaching out her hand. "It's like the depths I've always sought," she said.

"I've tried touching it," Dastion said. "Took a while to pluck up the courage, but when I eventually did my hand just—"

Shashahanna reached forward and her hand pressed into the black wall. She exhaled softly, as if from pleasure, and pressed in deeper.

"There's no telling where it emerges, is there?" Vince asked. "There's no saying whether it mirrors the portal Grace made up above. We might walk through into Mallian's hands."

"One way to find out," Shashahanna said, and she took three quick steps forward and vanished.

Vince gasped. There one second, gone the next, without any shimmer in the black curtain, no sound, and no evidence that she had ever existed at all.

"I guess the mermaid's gone," Dastion said.

"We came down here for a reason," Vince said. He slipped his belt off. "How about you hang on to one end while I take a peek?"

"And I'll pull you back from the dark depths of infinity if it's too scary for you," Dastion said. He nodded. "Plan."

Vince let Dastion tie the belt through one of his belt loops and the dwarf held the buckle end in one of his big hands. He was strong, Vince had no doubt of that, but strength might count for nothing. The darkness was cool, sucking the heat from his body. It was silent. It gave the impression that it was indifferent to them, yet Vince thought he felt the regard of a great, unknowable consciousness.

He hated the idea that he was leaving Angela again, but events seemed to conspire to force them apart.

With a nod to Dastion he followed Shashahanna.

It was different from passing through Grace's portal. There was more pull and pressure here, his skin compressed from every angle, air forced from his lungs, muscles crushed into his bones as he walked, and his broken arm was shifted and tweaked so much that he opened his mouth to scream.

The darkness rushed in and put pressure on his insides, pushing out. He felt trapped, yet somehow he kept walking, two more steps, three, and then he fell to his knees on soft ground and he was out. The relief was immense. He drew in a startled breath, feeling lighter than he ever had before. He thought if he breathed too deeply he might drift up from the ground into the air, and maybe if that happened he'd never come back down.

"Quite a rush," Shashahanna said. She was standing beside him, and when he reached towards her took his hand and pulled him up.

Vince noticed that his belt hung limp from his jeans.

"The dwarf let you go?" she asked.

"Not sure he had a choice."

"It's okay." She went back through, leaving Vince alone.

He took in another deep breath and looked around.

They were still in the Longford valley. It was dark, the valley bathed in moon- and starlight, and the revealed reservoir bed was pale grey. This new portal— perhaps a crack in the Fold that Grace did not know about, a fault in her creation that had formed when her own new portal was initiated—opened onto the hillside, above where her doorway emerged down in the valley. The geographies were confusing, but then Vince didn't expect anything about it to make much sense.

A few trees stood around him, there was long grass underfoot, and heavy banks of shrubs hunkered like sleeping creatures in the moonlight. He felt very much alone, and he realised he was somewhere he had vowed never to be again—a universe away from Angela.

"Fucking hell," Dastion said behind him. He stumbled as he emerged from the deep shadow on the hillside, but Shashahanna held him upright.

"We're here," Vince said. "You were right!"

"For all the good it does us," Dastion said.

"It means we can see what's going on here while Sammi works on her powers, her spell, whatever, back in the Fold. No one knows we're here. And if needs must, we can do something to slow Mallian down."

"Something like what?" Shashahanna asked. "What can we do against the fairy?"

"I'm working on that," Vince said. "Come on, let's head downhill to see what's happening." He looked around for a while, locating this place as well as he could. The last thing he wanted was to lose his way back here. This portal was a deep dark shadow standing close to a wall of rock, and if the night grew much darker he wasn't sure he'd be able to find it again.

"I've got it," Shashahanna said.

"You're sure?"

She tilted her head to one side. "Trust me. I'm a mermaid."

He wasn't sure exactly what that meant, but he nodded and led the way down the slope towards the grey.

It took only ten minutes to reach the dividing line between greenery and greyness. They paused there, looking downhill to see if there was any obvious movement. Vince scanned the landscape until he saw what he thought was the remains of Longford, further along the valley to their right. That was where Grace had formed her portal when she'd sensed Sammi's use of her fledgling powers, and that was where Mallian would hopefully still be. Vince only hoped the Nephilim would not have already fled the valley to commence Ascent. For all his bluster and bravado, Vince had always known Mallian to have other Kin around him. Even trapped in the Fold he had welcomed Vince's occasional chats, and on occasions he'd seen him speaking with Kin. A powerful being, he was also one who enjoyed company, and Vince only hoped that was still the case.

The clock was ticking.

"Down," Shashahanna breathed, her voice like a rumble of distant thunder.

Vince and Dastion dropped, still and silent. Vince breathed through his mouth, listening for whatever had startled the mermaid. She touched his face, caught his attention, and pointed across the hillside.

Two figures moved from the shadow of the lush hillside onto the stark exposed reservoir bed. They paused at the divide, and Vince was sure he saw the glimmer of eyes staring his way.

He lowered his face so that the moon did not shine from his paleness.

When he looked up again the figures were walking down into the valley. They were all but silent, but they made no attempt to hide their progress. They were confident and calm. They were Kin.

As he exhaled something passed above them, a swooping shadow cast against the starlight with wide wings and a short, stumpy body. It glided above the hillside, following the line of the land down into the valley. Soon after it passed above the walking shapes it passed out of sight, lost to the darkness. Vince caught a dank and musty smell, an old smell like something unearthed after a long time buried. He rubbed his nose to try to rid himself of the scent.

He'd been expecting this, but not so soon. Kin were coming to join Mallian on foot and wing, ready for the uprising he and others had been planning for so long. Somehow he'd got word out. It was terrifying, but at least he was still readying himself for Ascent, not rushing right into it now that he had Grace under his control.

The ticking clock might have slowed a little.

Vince tapped his companions' arms and signalled that they should return the way they'd come. Shashahanna led the way, but moments after starting back into the trees, she froze.

Vince moved beside her to see what had brought her up short.

"Bone," Vince whispered.

"I lost you," Bone said. "You see them?" He nodded past Vince.

"Yeah. He's calling them to him."

"Who're your friends?"

"Shashahanna, Dastion. This is Bone. He's with us." *At least I think he's with us*, Vince thought. That he was a loose cannon was for sure—he'd let the infected Kin out, after all.

"He's already begun," Bone said.

"Meaning what?"

"He killed a cop. I saw it. Tore him to pieces in front of his sheriff, so she could catch it all on her body-cam. And the cruiser dash-cam. Horrible, just..."

"People saw it?" Vince asked.

"The army's on its way. I called them in. There's stuff about me you don't know, but the agency I work for can help. Maybe. And now Mallian's shown his first card and there'll be no going back. It's all going to hell."

"Maybe not," Vince said. "If we can break his control over the fairy, once the army gets here he'll recognise the overwhelming odds. He'll back down."

"You really think that?" Bone asked. "You didn't see what he did, how brutal he was." He sounded shocked, haunted.

"I've seen him do worse," Vince said.

"So you believe a thing like that will put its arms up and surrender?"

"Maybe, if he sees he has no other choice."

"You have a plan?" Bone asked. "Because time's ticking."

"I can hear it," Vince said. "Yeah, we've got something of a plan, and maybe you can help. When will the army arrive?"

"Six, seven hours."

"We can't let him leave," Vince said. Beside him, Dastion nodded.

"He won't wait for very long," Bone said. "His blood's up."

"We'll make sure he stays."

"How?"

Vince shrugged. "That part I'm still working on." He looked at Dastion and Shashahanna in the darkness, vague shadows, exotic and amazing creatures who he could smell, feel, touch. Sometimes he forgot how incredible these beings were. He hated that events took away their wonder. He wished he could simply be with them and enjoy their company, rather than pitching one Kin against another, or watching while the maddest of them declared war.

"Will we find help?" he asked, and they both knew what he was asking.

"I'm sure," Dastion said.

"I'll try to talk them into it," Shashahanna said.

"Help from where?" Bone asked.

"Somewhere else," Vince said, because there wasn't time to explain. He didn't really know *how* to explain. "A place we have to get back to. You wait for the army to arrive and guide them in. Though by then, I reckon they'll know where to come."

"Just follow the fight, right?" Bone asked.

"I think so," Vince said. "It makes my skin crawl, but I think that's the only way this can end."

27

Angela hated being alone with Fer and Sammi. Sammi was distracted, kneeling close to the relics and silent, concentrating on whatever was happening inside her young head. Angela wanted to hold her, drag her away from all this and find some way of giving the girl normality once again, but she knew that was a foolish hope. Normality had left them years ago, and it could never return. The irony was, Sammi seemed much more adaptable than Angela, and more ready to make the most of the way things were.

That would be the fairy blood in her veins.

Angela was cold, wet, and she couldn't remember the last time she'd eaten. Food seemed so unimportant compared to what was happening, but her stomach ached with hunger. Fer, the shapeshifter, didn't appear hungry or cold. It seemed to pulse with countless forms, its visage never quite the same each time Angela looked at it. She couldn't tell its sex, and didn't ask. They hadn't swapped a word since Vince left with the dwarf and the mermaid, but Fer had stayed close, circling the clearing where Sammi pored over the relics. It returned from time to time, looked at Sammi, looked at Angela, and then left again. She liked to think it was keeping watch for any dangers approaching, but it could just as easily have been keeping watch on them.

She hated Vince being away from her again, exploring somewhere deep beneath the Fold with a mining dwarf and an enigmatic mermaid, neither of whom she knew enough about to trust.

She hated every single thing about this situation, and over the course of the last half hour she had thought of ways to take action. Sitting, standing, waiting was not in her blood. She'd been doing that for too long since Vince had disappeared into the Fold, a stagnant existence with Sammi at the cabin in the woods, broken only by occasional visits from Lilou.

Poor, dead Lilou. Now she was gone, Angela realised how much she had grown to like the nymph, despite the doubts and suspicions she still had deep down about her relationship with Vince. She had been one of the most relatable Kin Angela had met, and the one with the most refreshing, open outlook, passionate about her causes and reasoning. That passion had resulted in her death.

Angela could no longer stand around and let events pass her by. Every heartbeat dragged them towards further tragedy, and there was no telling who might be the next one to die.

"Sammi," Angela said, "we need to act, and now."

Fer drifted in from the left, passing through the misty rain and catching starlight from unknown constellations.

"I need more time," Sammi said. "It's confusing."

"How much more time?" Angela asked, and she sounded angry. She hadn't meant that, but the pressure bit at her, the sense of uselessness just standing here in the rain.

"Angela," Sammi said, turning around. "I don't know. I feel lost. It's all coming so quickly, all the knowledge, all this magic, and I'm getting smothered, and I don't know..."

"I'm sorry, Sammi," Angela said, kneeling beside her niece and holding her tight. "I'm sorry. We're asking so much of you." Sammi laid her head on Angela's shoulder, but there was a tension there, and a distance that Angela had not felt for a long time. She thought they had grown close, and been pulled closer by the pain of their loss. Sammi's new life, dawning on her only now in ways both painful and troubling, was pushing her away once more.

Angela hugged her tighter, hoping to hold onto some of the past.

"I'm working it out," Sammi said. "But it needs to work first time. Otherwise if I do something, cast a spell, whatever it is, and Grace isn't freed right away, I'm afraid Mallian will kill me."

"He'll have to get through me first," Angela said. So full of bravado, it also sounded foolish.

"He will," Sammi said. "You know that. You won't even break his step."

Sammi pulled away and looked into her aunt's face.

"I know," Angela said. "Do your best, Sammi. I don't think we have very long. But I have to do something, find out just how long we have. I'm going through to see what's happening."

"We can't use Grace's portal! Vince said we might walk right into Mallian's hands."

"None of us knows. And I'll be careful. Hopefully Vince will be back soon. But I can't just stand here watching you trying to do whatever you're doing." She nodded down at the scattered relics, mere shadows in the darkness, but probably so solid and bright in Sammi's vision. They all came from something alive, and their presence made Angela feel sick. The Kin were incredible, but like humans they had their dark sides.

"Good. I'll work better alone," Sammi said, and Angela couldn't help feeling it was a snub.

"I don't like to leave you on your own. But from what I've seen..."

"I can look after myself?" Sammi raised an eyebrow.

"I won't be long." Angela smiled at the hint of humour, the shred of Sammi. "I love you," she said. She wasn't sure she'd ever said it to the girl before.

Sammi's face went grim. "I know," she said in a deep voice, and they both chuckled.

Angela stood, Sammi turned back to the relics laid out before her, and Fer was by her side, naked and in human form.

"What's happening?" it asked.

"You and I are going to see the lie of the land."

"We're going through?" Fer asked.

"Only for a peek." Angela frowned, looked Fer up and down, and then smiled. "You're very beautiful."

"Thank you," Fer said, smiling.

"So what else can you be? I have an idea."

Angela and Fer stood close to the portal. It was a strange, shimmering space, like a blur on her vision. The darkness and shifting curtains of rain made it ambiguous, a reflection of Fer and its own ambiguity. She hoped Fer would go through. It had not shown fear, but its movements were less certain.

"You think you can do it?" Angela asked.

"It doesn't hurt?"

"No. It doesn't hurt."

"Last time I was brought through, I was someone else."

"You're stronger now than you were then. You're what you're supposed to be."

"But *she's* through there," Fer said.

"You don't have to fear the fairy anymore," Angela said. "There's worse, now. What Mallian plans will destroy the Kin, just when you've found your way to become one. Don't you want a future? Time to grow into yourself?"

Fer looked at her, and Angela could not read its expression. Even in human form there was something alien about its face, animalistic, and it might have been smiling or grimacing.

Fer lowered its head and crouched down. Its shoulders hunched, limbs snapped straight and bent again, and it let out a low growl as its back arched. The sounds were sharp and damp, painful and ecstatic, and in moments Fer was a wolf, head lowered as it stared at the portal.

"Can you... understand me now?" Angela asked. She didn't know how this worked. Was the Kin still a shapeshifter, or was it now a wolf with all of a wolf's senses, abilities and understanding?

The creature didn't even look at her. It stalked towards the portal and entered, disappearing from shadows into darkness.

Angela waited ten seconds and then moved forward herself. She was tensed and alert, ready to act as soon as she pushed through—hide, fight, or run. She tried to keep her eyes open but she could not. She was afraid of what she would see passing from the Fold into the world.

She emerged into cool, dry darkness. There was no rain, but a chill breeze made her shiver, drifting across the dusty reservoir bed and picking up silt to blow at her face. She crouched down and looked around, alert for movement. If she'd been seen, she would have only seconds to push back into the Fold and run.

A growl came from her left, and the wolf trotted into view. It inclined its head and set off, and Angela ran after it. Soon they were moving quickly up the gently sloping reservoir bed, the wolf's nose to the ground.

After only a couple of minutes the creature stopped, head down low, belly brushing the ground. Angela fell onto her front beside it. She was panting hard, yet she could hardly hear the shapeshifter's breathing.

They were close to the first ruins of Longford, and just ahead she could see the low slumped shape of an old building. Beyond, further up the slope, a shape wandered back and forth.

We've come too close! she thought, and she wondered again whether Fer had actually chosen sides. Then she saw that the shape was further away than she'd thought, and larger. Mallian.

Around him other figures stood or sat, shadowy outlines catching moonlight on their skins, pelts or scales. She counted five but there might have been twice that number.

Fear bit in, cold and sharp. She touched Fer's hairy back and nodded behind her the way they'd come, but Fer growled softly and pulled away.

"You'll be found!" Angela said, as quietly as she could.

Fer leaned in close, pressed its face against hers, then jumped up and was gone. Angela did not even hear it go. She was left alone in the darkness, and with only one course of action—to return back through the portal and into the Fold.

Mallian was gathering Kin to him already, preparing for Ascent.

They didn't have long.

* * *

Left alone in the darkness and the rain, feeling no eyes upon her and allowed to concentrate fully on her new self, Sammi realised two things.

First, the old Sammi was already gone. The memories and emotions were still there, along with the regrets and the deep, dark sense that she could never be the same again, but she was not that girl anymore. Her memory of Sammi was of an innocent life, one marred by tragedy yet still retaining hope for the future. This new existence forced upon her— perhaps dragged up out of her, where the truth had been in hiding for so long—told a different story.

There was no hope, only a promise of conflict and pain. And with power came a great, heavy dread.

The second thing she realised was that it would take her lifetimes to fully master this power, not simply minutes or hours. She had come to understand that a shard of Grace's soul resided within the spell cast by Mallian over these objects, and to set it free would be to release the fairy. But that didn't mean she knew how to do so. She could sit and stare at the relics for as long as she wanted, but the knowledge of how to combat Mallian's spell would not come to her unless she took aggressive action. Kneeling here and waiting for the answer to arrive would do her no good, and in the end they would all run out of time.

She had to take the fight to him.

Gathering up the relics into a small pile, she felt how sad and cold they were, and how lonely and forgotten their previous owners. Scattered around the Earth, murdered and left in shallow graves, these Kin were long since vanished into the past.

Sammi would ensure that Mallian, the cause of their murder at the hands of the Kin-killer Gregor, would remember all their names one last time.

"Come back," she whispered, and she sent the words towards their targets as hard as she could. "You have to come back. I need you."

She sat in the darkness, face turned up to the sky instead of down at the ground, and let the cool rain wash over her skin.

Angela heard the call and ran. It left a stain in her mind, like old pencil marks on her brain that would take a while to rub away. It was not a nice feeling, but it was Sammi, so she heeded the words.

A Sammi she no longer knew.

"We have to run," Vince said. He leaned against the wall of the tunnel, swaying as the wooziness left him. Sammi's urgent words echoed in his mind. She was calling him back, and he had to know why. "The fastest way up and out, Dastion. Now!"

Dastion nodded and led the way.

* * *

"I have to go back to the world and do it there," Sammi said. "If I even can. I'll have one shot, and it'll be a weak attempt, but if I can take him by surprise it might work."

"Mallian's already murdered," Vince said. "A cop. He let the other one go, and the whole thing's recorded on their body-cams. Ascent's begun, whether we like it or not."

"But he's still waiting," Angela said. "Gathering his forces."

Sammi looked around at the small group and wondered what they could do. She realised that their willingness to try against much greater odds was their finest weapon, but she was also terrified that it could only end in death and defeat.

"I wish I thought I could do it now," she said. "I'm useless. Useless!"

"No!" Angela said. "This is all of us, not just you. We work together and it'll happen. Vince?"

"Yeah," Vince said. He was covered in dirt and dust and Sammi couldn't read his expression, but the doubt was evident in his voice. "The army is on its way."

"And that's when it'll get out of control," Angela said. "Mallian will set Grace against the army, and the whole world will see what she, and he, can do. We have to stop them before that happens. Before this all goes too far."

"So let's come up with a plan," Vince said. He moved closer to Angela and Sammi saw them holding hands, and in that small expression of love she found hope.

28

Angela insisted that this time, she and Vince remain together. He didn't disagree. They both realised how unlikely it was that their plan would work. They were probably going to die, and after everything they had been through, they didn't want to die alone.

They split into two groups. Vince, Angela, Sammi and Dastion went down into the mines, descending towards the crack in the world that emerged up on the hillside above the remains of Longford. Sammi carried the relics with her, wrapped securely in her jacket. She moved silently through the darkness, unfazed and unamazed. Her focus was internal, she let them guide her but took little part in the journey herself.

Vince walked at the rear of their group, carrying a torch and turning around every minute or two. He was jumpy and nervous, certain they were being followed, but he embraced those nerves, that level of alertness, and readied himself for the confrontation to come.

They had all armed themselves. Dastion carried a heavy metal pike that he used for mining, something that Vince was not sure he would have the strength to even pick up, let alone wield in anger. The dwarf carried it as though it was a wooden stick. Angela had fashioned spears for herself and Vince out of lengths of wood. Sammi carried the relics and had refused a weapon of any kind. If this all worked out, she would be their weapon.

What Angela had said up on the surface had been a lie. This really was all about Sammi.

Shashahanna had recruited another Kin from the Fold, a cat woman called Fellian. They would slink through the main portal and perform their own distraction. Fellian said there were more Kin from the Fold who might join them, but Vince couldn't be certain whether any of the others would help. Perhaps some of them had already tried escaping through the portal, either joining Mallian or, if they refused, being put down. There was no time to wait because the clock kept ticking. Vince hoped they could do what Shashahanna claimed. This whole day was built on hope.

As they passed by the deep, dark crevasse down in the mines, Sammi stopped and stared downwards.

"What is it?" Angela asked.

"I don't know," she said. "Something not of our world, and not of the Fold. I think Grace would know."

"I don't want to know," Vince said. "Let's move on. We're almost there."

They reached the deep place, and Angela paused and stared at the expanse of nothingness ahead of them. Sammi seemed unperturbed.

"I've been through," Vince said to Angela, pulling her

close so that their heads touched. "It's fine. It's safe."

"I'm worried about what happens on the other side," she said. "We could just stay here, build a cabin, live naked in the woods."

"Just the two of us," he said, nodding. "I'll grow my beard even longer and be Grizzly Adams."

"I always liked you with a bit of stubble."

"That dude had a hedgerow, not stubble."

"You talking about me?" Dastion said. He glanced over his shoulder smiling.

"You, it suits," Angela said.

The four of them stood in silence for a moment, gathering themselves for what was to come. Angela reached for Sammi's hand and took it, but Vince saw that Sammi did not seem to notice. Her hand lay limp in Angela's, like a landed fish. She stared into the darkness ahead as if she could see beyond, and her eyes were wide, tears streaking her face. If she *could* see, what she witnessed was only bad.

Vince kept hold of Angela's other hand and led them through.

In the darkness, it was easy to imagine that nothing was wrong. The bushes and trees around them were still, and other than the rustling of small night creatures, the valley slope was silent. Any curious sightseers would have gone home, away from the rain and the darkness.

Downhill, the expanse of grey silt caught the starlight like a scar on the world.

"Maybe you should stay here, hidden away," Angela said to Sammi.

"I need to come. The closer I am, the more chance this will work. I think I'm almost ready now. I think I can do it, but we need to get close."

"We stick together," Vince said. "Angela, we don't want to leave her under a bush. There are things out here that have come to join Mallian, and one of them might find her."

"Strength in numbers," Dastion said, wielding his heavy pike and slamming it into the ground. It entered with a heavy thud. Sparks flew. The dwarf's strength was humbling, and Vince felt a moment of hope.

"Okay," Angela said. "Let's move down the hillside and wait."

They edged through the trees, with Sammi taking the lead. She said she could feel ahead of and around them, probe outward for other Kin.

Vince wished he had a way of staying in touch with Bone. The older man might have been mad, but he also now seemed to have the same end in mind as Vince and the others. His connection with the Kin was strange and Vince had yet to fully understand it. He hoped that he would soon.

They reached the line between lush ground and the exposed reservoir bed. Down the hillside and beyond the remains of Longford was the river, and it was this that they had come to watch.

"Shashahanna should have reached it by now," Angela whispered.

"If she hasn't been caught," Dastion said.

"And if Fellian is what she claims," Vince said. "She might come through and then side with Mallian. Dastion?"

"You're asking me?" the dwarf asked. Even in a whisper his voice was like a rumble through the ground. "I know her as well as you. As well as any of them who were in the Fold. I spent most of my time underground, you know that."

Vince nodded. "You okay, Sammi?"

"I'm good." She hardly sounded like Sammi anymore. Her voice was older, heavy with trouble and devoid of a teenager's lightness.

"There!" Angela said. "That's it, isn't it?"

Vince held up his hand, and a moment later they heard a percussive, deep hiss. Down at the river a silvery spray of water still hung in the air, spreading and falling softly just as another column rose up further along the course. It pounded into the night air, illuminated by moonlight and expanding as the second boom sounded across the valley. Another column rose, then another, sounding like mines exploding in a regulated pattern along the river.

"Nice, Shashahanna!" Vince said.

"They'll be going for her now," Angela said.

"Some of them. Others will be more on guard. We do our bit now, and Mallian will put his plans on hold until he finds out what's happening." *And then he'll stomp us into the ground*, Vince thought. The pain from his broken arm was a reminder of what was to come. Next time, Mallian would crush his head, or his chest, or small bits of him one after another.

"Tell us as soon as you're ready, Sammi," he said.

"I will."

"I mean it."

"I'll tell you, Vince!" For the first time in a while she sounded like the old Sammi. Vince wasn't sure if he was pleased or not. The old Sammi deserved to live past all this, but it was the new Sammi who might save them all.

"Let's go," he said. Wielding his sharpened spear in one hand, he led the way from the soft grass onto the damp, dusty silt. It was like stepping from one world into another.

The impacts from the river continued as they advanced towards Longford. Vince thought he could hear shouts from that direction, but none of them paused to listen. As they reached the first hump of a ruined building, Dastion dashed ahead and swung his pike from across his shoulder.

Before Vince knew what was happening Dastion was leaping back from a hissing, spitting thing, pike held across his chest. It advanced quickly, feet silent against the soil, a sleek humanoid shape, its snake's head filled with countless sharp teeth that gleamed pale in the moonlight.

Dastion danced left and jabbed with the pike, but the Kin was faster. It jigged to the right, dashed past Dastion, and came for Vince.

"Down!" he heard, and he fell to his knees with his spear held out before him, ready to impale the charging beast. He heard a swish above his head, and Angela's spear slashed across the creature's chest.

It cried out, a surprisingly human sound, and fell back with a scaly hand pressed to its wound.

Vince felt sorry for it, and he was about to engage it with a plea to surrender when Dastion's pike slammed through its neck from behind. The dwarf heaved and twisted, and the figure's head snapped to one side. It was dead before he shook it loose from his weapon.

No one spoke. They'd known what was coming, but the sudden killing still struck them all hard. Vince glanced at Dastion, and the dwarf averted his eyes. Vince was glad he saw no glory there, no gloating. Killing should never feel good.

They went on, Dastion first, Vince and Angela behind with Sammi between them. She walked quickly with the relics bundled up against her chest, and Vince wondered what she was thinking. She'd said nothing about the slaughtered Kin. He hoped she would be ready soon. If not, this would all be for nothing.

Another shape darted towards them from the shadows and Dastion lashed out. He missed and went spinning, and the shape faded and then reformed closer to them, a shimmer in the darkness, a shadow in shadows.

Angela cried out, jerked to the side, and slapped at her head. Vince went towards her and felt something stinging against his own scalp, like a raking of invisible claws.

Sammi whispered words he could not hear and the assault ended as suddenly as it had begun. He and Angela went close and checked each other, hands bloodied from their wounds. Her head was cut beneath her hairline, his left ear was scraped and tattered.

Dastion came at them with his pike raised, but Sammi held out her hand.

"It's sleeping," she said. "Not for long, but I found its dreams and called it down."

"What is it?" Angela asked.

"Wisp," Sammi said, and Vince immediately thought of Ahara. None of them had seen the wisp since the Fold had formed and closed two years before, and they were still unsure whether it had been for or against Mallian even then. Now, perhaps this was Ahara showing its true allegiance.

"It welcomes the dreams," Sammi said. "It's confused."

"It's not the only one," Vince said. "You can do this to any of them?"

"The ones whose dreams I see, I think so," Sammi said, frowning. "But don't rely on me, Vince. Not yet. I've got more important things to work on, and I'm almost there."

From lower in the valley, down by the river, they heard a long, high howl of pain. It sent a cool shiver down Vince's spine.

"We're close," Angela whispered. They were nearing the last place they'd seen Mallian, where the three infected Kin had been released from the old cooler room. Vince gripped his wooden spear and realised how ineffective it would be. Blood trickled down his face, and his broken arm pulsed with pain.

"Look over—" Dastion said, and a shape burst from cover and came at them. Growling. Snorting. It was Francine the werewolf, gassed and buried underwater for forty years, poisoned by humans, a perfect manifestation of unbridled rage.

Dastion dropped and rolled, his pike swinging up and around, but Francine avoided it and fell on him, straddling his wide chest and raising her front paws ready to tear him into shreds. The moon reflected in her mad, blazing yellow eyes. Foam speckled her jaws.

Just as she was about to drop down and claw Dastion's face from his skull, Fer bounded from cover and leapt at her. The shapeshifter was still in the guise of a wolf, and perhaps seeing something that might have been her kind gave Francine a moment's pause.

Fer powered into Francine closing its jaws around her throat, clasping and biting hard as they both fell away from the dwarf.

Vince grabbed Dastion's hand and helped him up, then stalked after the fighting Kin. Fer rolled and writhed, never loosening its grip on Francine's throat even as the werewolf raked its sides with her claws. Dark bloody lines opened in its hide. Fer only bit harder.

Francine slowed, limbs still lashing out, but heavier now, less strength behind the impacts. A dark flower of blood bloomed around the shapes, splashing the air, staining the ground. The moment Fer eased back to gain a better grip, the werewolf shoved with her shrivelled legs and caught Fer in the chest. The shapeshifter fell back and struck the ground hard.

Vince darted in with his spear, jabbing it towards the werewolf. Its point pierced the creature's left shoulder and she turned on him, bloody mouth yawning wide, eyes wild and flaming.

A hand closed around his arm and pulled him back, just as Francine leapt at him. He stumbled away and fell, dragged along the ground, kicking with his heels to gain purchase, and Fer fell on the werewolf's back and pushed her into the soil.

The beasts rolled and tangled, hissing and gnashing and growling, and then Fer was on top and pressing down with its mouth around Francine's throat once again. The shapeshifter shook its head, and this time when the werewolf's movements began to slow, Vince thought it was for real. Fer growled and pushed down, twisting its head left and right, and the werewolf shivered one last time.

Fer pulled back and away, panting hard. Its eyes were wide. Blood coated its mouth, face and neck. It stretched, crackling and snapping, twisting as it transformed into a humanoid form once again.

"Are you—" Angela asked, stepping forward, but Sammi grabbed her arm and held her back.

"It's not right," she said. "Fer's infected now, too. If we wait too long—"

Fer went from seeming to be in pain to grinning, and then growling as it crouched down onto all fours, hairs sprouting from its smooth skin, face deforming from human to bear-like. Its mouth foamed, and in its eyes Vince saw the same madness he'd witnessed in the infected Kin. They went from dark to a soft burning yellow as the fires of infection were stoked deep within. It shivered and shook, muscles squirming beneath its skin as they shifted from form to form. More hairs sprouted through its skin, and then dropped out. A thick scale-like growth smoothed across its neck and fell away again. Its limbs lengthened and grew thick, then shortened again, strong and sleek.

As Fer lowered its head and took a couple of shambling steps forward, Vince knew what it was asking of him.

He pressed the point of his spear to the back of the Kin's neck, ready to jam it through into its spine. His heart hammered in his ears, matching the creature's heartbeat. He tensed. Blinked. He wasn't sure he could—

The spear jarred down, piercing the shapeshifter's hide and protruding from its throat. It gurgled and twisted, started thrashing, and then blood gushed from the wound where the makeshift weapon had struck an artery.

Shocked, hands still gripping the wood, Vince looked around.

Angela stood behind him with both hands folded and pressed flat against the spear's upper end. She was close enough for him to smell her breath, warm and fast. The smell, the feel, gave him a sudden and jarring flashback to lying in bed one Sunday morning in their maisonette in London, both just woken from their own dreams and looking forward to the day before them, not talking and not needing to.

"We can't hesitate," she said, and he blinked to bring himself back to the terrible present.

"I know."

"Not with them. Not with the Kovo. It stays in the valley and we put it down. If we don't, Mallian and his cronies will mean nothing. If this infection gets out..."

"What about us?" he asked. Fer was dead now, still impaled on the end of his spear. Its blood had splashed his hand. He wiped it on his jeans, knowing how ineffectual the gesture was.

"Fer had that poor thing's blood in its mouth." She nodded at the dead werewolf, a shrivelled and skeletal thing. "Her saliva was in its wounds. And... I think that's something we worry about if and when the time comes. Don't you?"

Vince nodded, but the truth was already out there.

Last time the powers that be needed to cover up the infection they had released, they gassed the whole valley and then flooded it to keep it hidden away. What they would do this time was anyone's guess.

And the army was on its way.

"Mallian," Sammi said. "He's close, and coming closer."

"How near are you?" Vince asked, nodding at the bundle in her arms.

"I could try," she said, but her doubt was obvious.

"Not yet," Angela said. "We have to be sure, Sammi."

"Maybe we should hide, then?" Vince said.

"Fuck hiding," Dastion said. "I think we're long past that."

Vince tugged the spear from the dead shapeshifter, stuck it into the ground a couple of times to try and clean some of the blood from the wood, and looked around at the people he loved and the dwarf he'd grown to like. He didn't want anything bad to happen to any of them.

From the direction of the river another dull explosion rang out, and a geyser rose and spread in the moonlight. Three more followed, and they were like strange trees blooming in this alien, desolate landscape.

"Looks like Shashahanna wasn't the one doing the screaming," Angela said.

From closer, footsteps approached. Vince expected Mallian to emerge from the darkness, and he crouched down with spear at the ready. Had they made a foolish mistake coming here too soon? Preventing Mallian from leaving the valley had seemed a priority, but breaking his hold over Grace was much more important. If they lost Sammi now—if Mallian came through them and took her—then *everything* was lost.

The footsteps halted. Nothing appeared.

"Where?" Angela whispered.

"Can't see," Vince said.

"Quiet," Sammi said. "Low... quiet... still. I'll make us sleek and unseen. Like your friend Bone."

Bone? Vince thought. His confusion could wait. Sammi was doing something, dipping into her fledgling powers once more, and as he, Dastion and Angela crouched down together, with the bodies of Fer and the infected werewolf close by, he felt the world moving away from them. It was a strange sensation. He was still fully connected to his surroundings—he could feel the ground beneath his feet and knees and the cool kiss of the night air, and he could smell the death and blood, and the bodily aromas from Dastion and his own unwashed, rain-soaked clothes—but he knew from outside he was barely part of the world anymore. Dastion was kneeling ten feet from him but he was less than a shadow, like a memory of once being there. Even Angela, so close that he could touch her, was a ghost.

The darkness came to life and Mallian appeared. In the night he seemed taller and more solid than before, stronger, as if he had never spent two years trapped against the rocky ground to wither and waste away. He was the size of a mountain, and Vince remembered the agony of the Nephilim stepping down to crush his arm. His broken bone and bruised flesh roared in sympathy.

Mallian had others with him. One small shape was familiar, and Vince felt a renewed anger at Thorn, the pixie who he had seen cause so much pain.

They paused close to where Vince and the others crouched, hidden by Sammi's growing fairy powers.

If Grace is with them she'll know, he thought. Sammi was taking a dangerous risk.

They were all taking risks.

29

If she's with him I'm going to try, Sammi thought. *I think I'm ready. I can't tell them yet, because I'm not sure I can take the weight of their expectation. Everything I've learned is too precarious. It's like a bridge made of glass, or cotton, or dreams, so weak and thin that it'll break under one false step.*

She didn't like keeping secrets from the people who loved her and were risking their lives to protect her, but she also recognised the reality of this fresh, strange existence. She was building delicate and precious pathways between the new parts of her and the old, and she had to ensure they remained as strong and stable as possible.

I'm sure I'm ready... but she needs to be with him. To break the bridge between the Nephilim and the fairy, I have to be able to see it and touch it.

Mallian was less than twenty metres from them, standing tall and proud and letting the moonlight reveal him like a living statue. He was shameless in his nudity. She would not see him hunched down low again. He was free and ready to ascend, rise to the might he thought he deserved in the eyes of the world, both human and Kin. She couldn't help but admire that.

She could also hate him for it. That was easier. He had killed her friend Lilou. And even though it was the fairy who had killed her father and ripped her life apart, it was Mallian who sought to keep it torn.

If he had his way, he would take her under his control as well. He would make her his soldier, stand her alongside Grace and force her to slaughter, destroy, paint the grey land red. Sammi would never accept that. She'd die before it happened.

She had no intention of dying

Grace was not with Mallian. But as he stood there close to them—sniffing the air, suspecting some subterfuge, but not seeing through her small fairy spell—she took in the measure of him. Being so close helped her prepare herself even more for what was to come. The relics wrapped in her jacket grew warm at his nearness, and she fed on that warmth and let it propagate the spell she needed to cast.

I'm ready now, she thought. *Definitely now.*

Mallian stared down at the two dead Kin and his anger was rich and bloody in the colourless shades of night. He kicked at the ground, as if suspicious of her spell and searching for them. Sammi held her breath. But the kicking was simply an expression of his rage, and he, Thorn, and two other Kin who had come with them turned and stalked back into the shadowy remains of Longford.

Sammi felt her glass bridges strengthening, her power

settling, and the void around the small core of what she had once been grew denser and more complicated than ever before.

I'll take everything from you, Mallian, she thought, but at the same time she knew that in doing so, she would be taking every good thing from herself.

Bone had imagined them coming to the valley with a great show of force. Chinooks *whacka-whacka*ing across the countryside towards Longford, searchlights splashing the ground ahead of them, bellies full of troops and armour. Smaller helicopter gunships escorting them, low and quiet and ready to unleash hell. Ground troops in transporters, deployed at speed and with complete efficiency. Tanks, troop carriers, trucks, field artillery set up at a distance and zeroed in using laser spotters, jets flashing high overhead with heavy ordnance ready to drop at a moment's notice. He'd never seen anything like that, but he expected it. If he were Jordan, that's what he would have sent.

Instead, a single car approached him along the road that followed the ridge line to the west of Longford valley. It was a Toyota, big but not ostentatious, and if he'd not received a call from Colonel Miles telling him where to meet and when, he might have hidden away and let the car drive by.

It slowed to a halt, and Bone only revealed himself when the colonel stepped from the back seat. He was an average-sized man, grey hair, and though he wore a uniform, he didn't seem like a military man on duty. He gave the impression that he'd just woken up, one that was reinforced by a yawn. Bone went to shake his hand but the man did not offer his to be shaken.

"I thought the army was coming?" Bone asked.

The man appraised him with narrowed eyes. It might have been thirty seconds until he spoke.

"Colonel Miles, 3rd Group out of Fort Bragg. You Bone?"

"Yes." He had the pressing desire to salute. "Yes, sir." The colonel's eyes bore into him, sharp points of light in the darkness, as if they gathered starlight and fired it back.

"You've seen these creatures?"

"I have. They're... very powerful."

"So am I," Miles said. "Your superior put a lot of faith in you, Bone. I've seen the footage, and quite frankly it's hard to believe, but believing's not my job. Containing the threat is, and retrieving as many of the items as possible."

"Retrieving?" Bone asked. He was confused. Which items was the colonel talking about?

"You know the lie of the land, so I'm told, so I'll want you to brief my logistics team."

"Sorry, which items?"

"The threats," the colonel said. "I'm instructed to use lethal force only if absolutely necessary."

"You're here to *capture* them?"

The colonel frowned, his first sign of not being in control.

"You can't capture these things!" Bone said. "You said you've seen the footage. Don't you understand how dangerous they are?"

"How many are there?"

"The one you saw is Mallian. Tore a man in half with his bare hands."

"Let him try doing that to a Humvee."

"There are others worse than him. Three of them, they're infected with some sort of virus or nerve agent, something that—"

"I know about the infected," Miles said. "They should be dead. If they *are* still on their feet they'll be weak and ineffective."

Bone shook his head, snorting laughter. "You don't understand. None of you understand."

"I understand that I'm here with orders, and you're here because you know what these things are."

"Yes, and I know what they aren't. They aren't just target practice for you. They aren't creatures that will come quietly, or sit by while you coax them into cages. They aren't anything you've ever seen or imagined before. They have a fairy that—"

"A fairy?" Miles said, and his bright eyes sparkled with laughter. Bone also heard someone in the Toyota chuckling.

"Oh, God," Bone said quietly.

"Look, your superior said you were here to assess and

keep tabs on what was happening, and I'm sure you've done that to your full ability. Now the army's here."

"Where?" Bone asked. "I see you and a car!"

Miles smiled, a lifeless expression that didn't touch his eyes. Bone realised they were actually the same height, even though he'd first assumed the colonel to be a few inches taller than him.

"They're coming," he said. He looked past Bone, and for a second Bone thought the Kin had made themselves known, following him up out of the valley, stalking him, and now they would pounce and make a show of slaughtering this blinkered military man just as they'd killed the poor cop who'd come on ahead. But the colonel smiled again and slapped Bone's shoulder a couple of times. "In fact, they're here."

Bone felt it first—a low, gentle vibration in the ground, transmitted up through his feet into his legs. Then he heard it, a rumble in the distance, almost too low to perceive. Way behind the colonel and across the windswept hilltop, the sky lit up. Moments later the first set of lights appeared over the ridge and dipped down as they followed the narrow road into the valley. Behind them, higher up, clouds began to glow as the aerial contingents of Colonel Miles's force made themselves known.

Bone should have been pleased. Here was power and might, the finest of America's military come to face up to the strangest, most obscure threat they had ever known. He should have felt some form of comfort.

All he experienced was dread.

"I need you to talk to my people," Miles said.

Bone nodded and forced a smile, but already he was planning his escape back down into the valley. The time for talk was long gone, and nothing would persuade the colonel from his mission.

Bone had to find his father and end his unnatural existence himself.

"Up there," Angela said. "What's that?"

"That's war," Vince replied.

"The military. Bone really did get them to come."

"You doubted him?"

"I wasn't sure what to make of him," Angela said. "He's strange."

"He's Kin, like me," Sammi said. "Half human, half Kin, still finding his way."

Angela was hardly surprised.

"So what happens now?" Dastion asked.

Angela and the others looked uphill towards the ridge where lights played through the darkness, cutting swaths across the hillside and down into the valley. She counted a dozen vehicles, maybe more, and there were at least six separate helicopters buzzing above them, describing wide circles over the valley, probably scanning the terrain with radar, or heat-sensitive equipment, or whatever the hell else those things carried.

"Now Mallian gets what he wants," Angela said. "War between Kin and humanity." She turned to Sammi, and the change in the girl shocked her. Just ten minutes ago they'd been huddled down together while Mallian stalked nearby. She had kept them silent and hidden from his view, but still seemed nervous and afraid. Now, Sammi was something else. There was a confidence in her eyes, a power, that had never been there before. There was also a weight of sadness, as if they had already lost.

"Sammi?"

"I'm ready to try," she said. "I have to be close."

"We just *were* close," Vince said

"Close to Grace," Sammi said, and Angela realised where the sadness came from. To free Grace from Mallian's control was to put herself at risk. Grace had sought out Sammi to drag her into the Fold, to be with her forever, and now Sammi would be presenting herself at the fairy's feet.

Angela also recognised that there was no choice, and seeing that realisation in Sammi's eyes made her so, so proud.

"Then let's move," Angela said. "All of us, together. If we reach them before the army does, maybe we can end this before it's really begun."

Vince nodded, and Dastion wielded his pike.

Angela was the first of them to rise and follow the route Mallian and the other Kin had so recently taken. The valley came alive to the sound of motors and helicopters. Lights flashed through darkness.

From somewhere ahead of them she heard a deep, ground-shaking roar of triumph.

Mallian's throat hurts but he continues to shout.

"Go!" he commands. "Kill them! Let them see you. No hiding, no scampering in the dark. Be yourselves, and then *kill them all*!"

From around him come growls, howls and shouts as Kin launch themselves through the darkness and towards the lights closing in on them. Thorn the pixie dashes away into the shadows, ready to commit his own acts of violent mischief. The harpy that brought several Kin here, making fast, silent trips through the night carrying them in her clawed feet, launches herself up towards the stars. A gremlin runs, a smoke-ghost flows, a leprechaun scampers and a chupacabra sprints, and all of them have their blood up. All of them share his blood and his desire to live in the open once again, triumphant and in control.

This is everything he has ever wanted.

Grace is beside him, small and shivering. Power radiates from her like a constrained sun, and he concentrates, dips in, touches that power and uses it to exert his control over the two infected Kin. The third has gone and not come back, its body lying not too far away, and he suspects the humans and the fairy girl are also back in the valley, come to cause him trouble. He is not concerned. He will finish what he began with Vince and crush him into the ground. He will pull Angela in two in front of her niece. And the girl Sammi will fall under his command. First, Grace will be controlling her and then, when this first battle is over, he will cast a similar glamour to make her his own.

He is prepared to launch the fairy at the forces coming for them, but he's going to hold her back for a while. First, he wants his Kin comrades to blood themselves, redden their hands, sink their teeth into flesh to ignite their taste for humanity.

Then, when he's prepared himself mentally and is ready for the concentration and effort required, he will unleash Grace.

There is not a future he can see where he is not triumphant.

Mallian shouts again, and he hears his voice go up against the echoes of engines and man-made things, and win.

30

As Bone returned to the valley, he heard the first explosive gunshots from behind and above him. They were too heavy for small-arms fire, and glancing back he saw a bright tracer arcing across the valley from one of the helicopters. He wondered what it was shooting at. Its flight path was erratic, engine sounding strained. Moments later there was a snapping, whistling sound, and the dark shape shuddered and dived into a violent spin. The shooting ended, but the sound of the struggling rotors reverberated across the slopes.

Bone knew he should be running, but he could only stand and watch as the aircraft's deadly plummet ended in a shattering crash and explosion. It shook the ground, sending a fiery mushroom boiling into the night sky and illuminating the hillside for hundreds of metres in every direction. The sudden action and almost immediate explosion had ripped the night apart and changed the valley to a place of noisy chaos.

Bone gasped in shock and ducked down low, then when the initial fireball faded he continued his flight downhill.

Now Colonel Miles and the others knew what they

were up against. And once that fairy entered the fight...

More shooting erupted behind him, starting in several scattered locations and escalating until it seemed the whole hillside was on fire. Small arms joined in with the heavier, deeper sound of aircraft machine guns, and moments later he heard the screams and shouts of men, women, and maybe Kin dying.

The army had never confronted an enemy like this. By the time the arrogant colonel realised that traditional combat rules must change, this first contact would be over.

Bone reached the grey and edged left to avoid Longford and the area where Mallian and the fairy might still be. He realised that his father was possibly already employed in the fight, controlled and sent by Mallian. He hated the idea. His father had not exactly been a creature of peace, but he had been fair, a creature concerned with the wellbeing of others and the differences between right and wrong. Now he was being used to fight innocent humans.

He felt like he was floundering, rushing around blind with no real plan. He'd come here looking for signs of his father, and had found a deadly infection that might spread if it escaped the valley, and a conflict the likes of which he had never imagined. In many ways, Mallian and his Ascent mirrored Mohserran and the contagion he carried. Both offered a terrible threat to humanity. Neither could be allowed to escape—or be captured and taken—beyond Longford and its dead valley.

Events were now much larger than him. His had become a private affair in an increasingly public incident, and he had to return to the only people he thought might help. With all that was happening, he could no longer find and confront Mohserran himself.

"He's moving forward for the fight," Sammi said. "He must be, because I sense Grace going forward too. It has to be now. We have to go to them now!"

"You're ready?" Vince asked.

"We'll soon know," Sammi said. "Come on!"

There was no doubt which direction they had to take. The initial scatter of gunfire had increased, and the rattle of small arms echoed around the valley. Two more choppers were twisting and diving, venting long bursts of gunfire at enemies unseen. Sammi thought she caught a faint glimpse of a winged thing, but it might have been a shade in her eye, a shadow crossing the stars.

Dastion took the lead, his heavy pike held across his chest. Sammi felt bad for him, because Grace had taken him to the Fold for one thing only. Now he was still helping them save a Kin who had taken bites out of him. She didn't understand how such madness could have overtaken a creature with so much power.

I only have a little of it, she thought. *There's no saying how much more there is, but maybe I'll learn, and maybe I'll have no choice. Maybe it'll drive me mad too.*

The sound of the battle changed. An engine

coughed, roared louder and spluttered, and a second helicopter spun down in a crazy spiral, spitting flames from its engine and lashing at the air with its traumatised rotors.

"Everyone down!" Vince shouted, and Sammi realised the plunging shape was far closer than she'd thought. They hit the ground just where silt gave way to grass, and seconds later the stricken aircraft made impact in the woods above them. Trees snapped and shattered with a deafening crunch, then the helicopter exploded, the detonation thumping up through the ground and winding her. A chunk of debris—perhaps a spinning rotor—smashed through the trees above and around them, showering them with fragments of split wood and bark. A wave of heat washed over Sammi and she squeezed her eyes closed, curling into a ball and thinking, *I just heard people die.*

Every second that passed, every moment between now and her freeing the fairy, might doom more people and Kin to a fiery death.

Screams came from ahead. A shape emerged from the shadows, running at them, and Dastion raised his pike.

Vince caught the dwarf's arm at the last moment, and Bone skidded to a halt before them.

"We have to get close to Mallian and Grace," Vince said. "She can help." He pointed to Sammi, but Bone barely glanced her way.

"They've come to capture them," he said. "The

three infected Kin. The army's no idea how dangerous they are, and they've come here to catch them, take them away."

"Only two now," Dastion said. "Fer killed one of them."

Bone's eyes went wide.

"The werewolf, not Mohserran," Vince said. "He's still out there somewhere."

"He'll be fighting," Bone said. "Will you help me?"

"We have to help each other," Angela said. "Grace first, and then stopping Mallian. Everything else is secondary."

"Even if the infected Kin escape the valley?" Bone asked.

"While there's still a fight here, they won't," Sammi said, but none of them could know that for sure. Even after all this time, none of them really knew anything.

"So we're going back towards that?" Bone asked, pointing behind him. The fighting was taking place uphill from them in the woods, past the blazing scattered remains of the crashed 'copter in the dark and shadowy places that Kin called home.

"We are," Sammi said. She nursed the relics wrapped in the coat in her arms, felt their warmth, and when she blinked she imagined what it would be like to try and cast the spell.

It was going to hurt.

In the end, Mallian found them.

Vince saw the shadow just as it burst from a copse

of trees. Time slowed down. Panic bit in, and fear, but also a sense of relief that the confrontation had been brought to them here, and now, and that their future would be decided soon. He turned and raised his spear one-handed, looking up at the looming shape.

Mallian waved one arm and swept him aside. Winded, Vince hit the ground and rolled, crying out when his wounded arm folded beneath him. He lurched over onto his back and Mallian was above him, blotting out the moon and ready to stomp on him one last time.

Dastion swung his pike and slammed it into Mallian's leg. The Nephilim grunted and overbalanced, going down on one knee not two metres from Vince's head.

Vince grabbed up his spear and rolled again, prepared for the white-hot agony consuming his arm. He cried out but kept rolling, because now Mallian meant to kill him, and against the Nephilim there would be no second chance.

As he struck a tree and pulled himself upright, he saw Grace in the darkness beneath the trees behind Mallian. She was touched by starlight, slack-jawed and staring, her eyes out of focus, body and limbs slumped as if there was a single invisible thread holding her upright.

This might be their only chance.

"Sammi!" he shouted.

Sammi had already sensed their arrival. She knelt and placed the wrapped bundle on the ground before her, pulling the jacket open and exposing the relics to the night.

Mallian's attention went from Vince to Sammi, and then to the relics displayed before her. His eyes went wide. Grace had seen too, and now her vacant stare was not quite so vacant, her stance no longer that of a puppet. She took a small step in Sammi's direction, then froze, her face a rictus of pain. Mallian's hold over her was total.

The Nephilim rose and turned towards Sammi.

Vince, hauling himself upright in turn, saw a flicker of movement to his right. Angela dashed beneath tree cover, and at first he thought she was going for Mallian. He wanted to scream at her to wait, hold back, because the Nephilim would kill any of them who went close enough, and he could not bear to see Angela killed.

Anyone but Angela.

As he opened his mouth to shout, she ran into the fairy and sent her sprawling in the long grass.

No, Vince thought, but then he realised what Angela had done, and why. Mallian froze and frowned, and as he turned back towards the fallen fairy, Sammi set to work kneeling amongst the relics.

"Hey!" Vince called, standing and waving his spear at Mallian. "Hey, you big ugly fuck!"

Mallian did not take the bait. He didn't even glance back at Vince. Instead, all of his attention was on the fairy, and the woman wrapping her arms around her to hold her tight.

"No!" Vince shouted, and he ran. It felt like he was moving in slow motion, but his brain shifted at the speed of light. Bone crouched to his right, motionless and powerless. Dastion was beside Sammi with his pike raised, ready to protect her. Other shadows moved beneath the trees and above them, Kin that were friend or foe. Further away were shouts and shooting, explosions and roars, screams.

None of that mattered now.

"Let go!" Vince shouted, and he and Angela locked eyes. "Let her go," he said again, quieter, and he raised his spear.

He was ten metres from Mallian, and ten seconds too late.

The fairy seemed to pulse. It was a heavy, single throb, smacking through the ground and air with the power and impact of a giant heartbeat. Angela was thrown across the clearing, too fast for the movement to be followed.

Vince heard rather than saw her crash against a tree.

He shouted in rage and grief, a wordless scream, and closed on Mallian with his spear raised. The Nephilim must have been momentarily distracted by what he had done and the effort it had taken to control Grace. Vince plunged the spear into Mallian's left side, shoving as hard as he could, feeling it grind against bone and then snap as Mallian roared and turned. He slammed one arm into Vince and sent him spinning, breathless, bouncing across the ground towards where Bone crouched in the shadows.

Pain sang in from all directions—his broken arm flopped against his stomach and side, he heard a crunch from his ribs, bruises and cuts rose and bled. His head felt like a solid metal chunk that had been pounded and bent out of shape. Bone grabbed him and helped him sit up.

"Angela," Vince whispered.

"Sammi," Bone said. "Look."

Sammi was on her knees and bent almost double over the relics. She was shivering, and Vince was sure there was a gentle glow emanating from her head and hair. Either that or his vision was damaged, his eyes shaken by the violence inflicted upon him.

He looked for Angela and saw her twisted and motionless at the base of the tree. *Oh God*, he thought. If she was dead then so was he.

Sammi shoved and felt the glass bridges beginning to break. It hurt her to push, but she could also now sense the agonies being endured by Grace, and they were far, far worse.

As links began to fracture, she saw the great shadow of Mallian towering above her. Coming for her, not Grace. Knowing that *she* was the danger.

She took in a deep breath and pushed one last time.

* * *

Angela, barely conscious, saw her niece become the centre of things, and felt the power thrumming out from her. They all did. Even Mallian, standing over her with hands raised and Vince's broken spear still sticking from his side.

She blinked, and an eternity seemed to pass before she opened her eyes again. Her senses were distant and vague. Pain bit in from everywhere, so intense that it became one raging fire.

Her pain did not matter. The moment when everything changed was all that mattered. She saw that moment, when Grace came back to herself. The fairy stood taller, shook like a dog shedding itself of water droplets, then glared at her surroundings as if seeing them for the first time.

Her gaze fell on Mallian. Her expression changed from one of confusion, to utter, outright fury.

"Be with me," Mallian said to the fairy. The first time it sounded like an order, but when he spoke the words a second time they were a plea, and they might have come from the mouth of a child. "Be with me."

Sammi slumped over the relics, and Vince grabbed her by one arm and dragged her away. He groaned with each step. Angela could hear him above the gunfire and shouting coming from further away, and in his voice she heard her own pain also. *We're losing each other here and now*, she thought, and though she tried with all her strength to hang on, darkness came and took her away.

The last thing she heard was the fairy, speaking furious words she did not know in a voice she hoped she would never hear again.

"We'll rise ascendant," Mallian says. "We'll be special again! I was going to release you, soon, when you realised that standing against the humans alongside me is the way. The *only* way."

Grace glares at him, and speaks those words again. He does not understand them—she's speaking in the old fairy tongue, and he hasn't heard it for aeons—but he does recognise the look in her eyes. He's felt such rage in his own expression many times before.

"Please," he says, and he's aware that he is begging. All around him are the sounds and sights of his plan only just beginning—gunfire and fighting, and human cries of pain as they die beneath the hands, claws and teeth of things they do not yet understand; the triumphant roars and songs of brave Kin finding their footing in the world once again; humans scattered at his feet, broken and afraid. It is all he's ever wanted. It's all within his grasp.

"*Please,*" he says, taking two strides towards the fairy.

She raises her hand, whispers more words in her old tongue, and Mallian freezes to the spot. Every muscle vibrates, knotting into cramps that bring a muted roar of pain from his constricted throat. He shivers as he tries to tear loose of her hold, and knowing what her power over him entails—he had two years held pressed to the damp ground to consider it—he directs every ounce of his strength into ripping free.

He is a butterfly pinned to a board.

He feels the eyes of the humans upon him, and some Kin as well, traitors to their kind.

"I... never... lose," Mallian says, and then the world around him blurs, blackness falls, and when he next opens his eyes it is raining, and the Fold has him once again in its grasp.

The fairy is there as well. She lets him fall free and slump to the ground, his muscles settling and strength returning. When he looks up again she is gone, and there's only him.

She didn't bind me to the ground, he thinks, but there is no comfort in that realisation. He looks around the Fold and sees only what he has seen before—the same views, the same skies, the same alien stars.

She left him free because there is nowhere for him to go.

31

Sammi was weak but conscious, and everything about her had changed. Vince didn't want to touch her anymore. Once he'd dragged her back from Mallian he let her go, and they watched together and yet apart as Grace and Mallian slipped out of sight back through a portal the fairy created for less than the blink of an eye.

There, and then gone.

"So is that it?" Bone asked.

"They could have gone anywhere," Dastion said.

"No," Vince said. "We know where they've gone." Battered and bleeding, hurting in a dozen different places, he staggered across the clearing to where Angela still lay slumped against the base of a tree. She was in a shape she should not make, arms and legs all wrong, head tilted to one side and resting on her shoulder. Blood leaked from her ear, nose and mouth. Moonlight painted it black, but the sun smeared the eastern horizon now, bringing some hint of dawn colour to the grey, dead valley. Mostly red.

He knelt beside Angela and reached for her, afraid to actually touch in case he found her too still, too cold. He couldn't take that. Not now. It didn't matter if they'd won or lost, didn't matter that Mallian had gone and his Ascent forces were now fighting a battle with no leader. All that mattered was Angela.

Her eyelids fluttered. Vince's heart did the same.

"Angela? Baby?"

Her left eye opened and swirled in its socket, until it focused on him. The panic left it, though not the pain. She lifted her left hand and reached for him, and he held her hand. Even his good arm hurt.

"She'll live," Sammi said. She was standing behind him, a presence he did not recognise.

"Who's that?" Angela asked, and she frowned and closed her eyes. It broke Vince's heart. She'd spent two years with Sammi, the only family she had left. Now she did not recognise her own niece.

"It's me," Sammi said, but even the girl's own voice did not sound convinced at who she was. Vince saw her confused, troubled tears, and that also broke his heart. Was it possible that drawing together had driven them all so far apart?

He realised that the shooting and shouting from deeper in the woods had grown less intense, and instead there were cries of confusion. Helicopters circled above, sweeping the hillside and valley back and forth with powerful probing searchlights. Bursts of gunfire still chattered here and there. Shadows skittered through the trees nearby, and then fell still and silent.

A series of lights flickered on down on the valley floor, and the sound of engines broke through from a different direction. Shooting rattled through the dawn. Lights flashed left and right. Shadows darted, shapes stalked.

"What's happening?" Bone asked. He held Dastion up, the dwarf favouring one leg and bleeding from a gash on his cheek.

"They're leaving," Sammi said. "They're running. Now that their leader has gone they're adrift."

"They know he's gone?" Vince asked.

"They must." Sammi looked around, then focused on Vince and Angela again. "We should go. I don't know what's going to happen here, but none of it will be good."

"We can't let them capture the Kin," Bone said. "Vince. You know what'll happen."

"Ascent, just in a different way," Vince said.

"How's that?" Dastion asked.

"Whatever happens now, this fight will go public," Vince said. "Too much footage to keep secret. There'll be leaks, and if they capture the Kin like Bone said they were aiming at... experimentation. Vivisection. Humans will know about the Kin, and we all know no good can come of that. We're just not built that way." He looked at Angela as he said this and her good eye was open. She shed a tear, because she knew he was right. However much he and Angela had tried to protect the Kin and keep their existence hidden—Bone too, if anything he said was to be believed—wider human nature would not be so benevolent.

"We can't take on an army," Vince said, but he'd already seen Bone glancing at Sammi several times. *We can't ask that of her*, he thought, and he was about to say it when everything about Sammi changed.

She grew stiff and still, like a statue. Even her breathing stopped. Her glittering eyes were pale and static.

"What is it?" Vince asked. He began to panic, fearing that Mallian—or perhaps even Grace—had somehow taken control of her, and her next action might be something terrible.

Then she seemed to slump. She drew in a deep, gasping breath, then looked around them, wide-eyed and terrified.

"Sammi?"

"We have to run," Sammi said.

"We can't run. Angela's badly hurt, Dastion can barely walk, and I'm not sure—"

"Vince!" She came forward and grabbed his shirt, ignoring his broken arm and his groan of pain. He recognised the staggering strength in the young girl, and the undeniable alienness. She was more fairy than human now. She was terrifying. "We *have* to run."

"Why?"

"Because she's coming back."

She realises that she cannot have the girl. She's become too strong too quickly, and she understands that the

Fold is not a place for a young fairy. She could try to take her by force, but there would be no love in that, and no future. And eventually the girl would become stronger than her.

If she is destined to spend eternity on her own in the Fold, she will need food.

And she will need to leave her mark so that no one tries to follow.

32

Dastion carried Angela, hobbling on his bad leg, grim faced but determined. His beard was heavy with blood. Bone went ahead with Dastion's heavy pike held across his chest. Vince kept close to Dastion, and Sammi was sometimes behind him, sometimes lost in the trees, a shadow avoiding the rising sun. Dawn coloured the horizon and it was beautiful, and the colour of spilled blood.

They passed a crash site where a helicopter had come down. It had blasted a hole in the forest, splintering trees and gouging a furrow in the soil. Shards and burning fragments were scattered around. Half of one rotor had slammed into a tree and hung metres above the ground like a giant axe. The whole area smelled of fuel and cooked flesh.

When they heard a group of soldiers approaching, Sammi came close and told them to huddle around. Vince saw the pain and tiredness in her eyes, and the frustration as she tried to cast the same sleek spell she'd used to hide them from Mallian down in the valley. She snorted in frustration. She was glancing at Bone and, as her shoulders slumped in defeat, she outright stared at him.

"Try," she said.

"What?"

"We don't have long. They're coming through the trees, up from the valley, driving Kin before them. They're scared and they'll shoot us on sight. Try!"

"I don't know..." he said, but when he looked at Vince, Vince saw that he did know very well. Bone knew what he was. He probably always had.

Sammi reached out and held his hand, a surprisingly gentle gesture from the girl who had become so distant. "I'll help if I can," she said.

Vince felt the distance growing around him, a vagueness, and even though they were huddled so close they could all touch, the others became ambiguous shapes in the dawning day. Soon after, a dozen soldiers hurried past. He could not make them out properly, but they were running instead of walking, and their manner seemed more panicked than organised. He wasn't even sure they were all carrying weapons.

After they had passed, he heard a long, slow sigh from Bone, and the world closed in around them again. Bone smiled, looking into the middle distance. Sammi squeezed his hand once and then let go. No one said anything as they continued across the hillside, aiming upwards but avoiding the route the soldiers had taken.

In a couple of places they saw soldiers through the trees and in clearings, huddled around bodies on the ground. None seemed eager to approach the Kin they had killed or wounded. Perhaps each of them was reliving childhood dreams and nightmares, and forming new ones to haunt their adult imaginations.

When they were close enough to see, Vince made out something common in all of their expressions— fear. He thought that was a good thing. If they were afraid, perhaps they would not feel so inclined to go after the Kin.

But he knew that was a vain hope. After what had happened here, the Kin were now out in the open. Mallian might have failed, but in a way his dream of Ascent had been seeded and bloomed here. A slower Ascent than he'd wanted, but an exposure nonetheless. Footage of the fight would be analysed, kept secret, inevitably leaked onto the net, and the whole world would see a mothman taking down an Apache attack helicopter, a pixie caving in the skull of a soldier, and other strange creatures killing and running and rejoicing in a newfound freedom.

Just a few minutes after they started uphill away from the greyness of Longford behind and below them, a massive detonation reverberated around the valley. Breathing hard, Vince and the others came to a halt on a rocky outcropping and looked back down into the valley.

Where the old town of Longford lay, a fire bloomed. It was a strange fire, gushing horizontally from a fault in the air, not vertically as if from an explosion. Vince knew that this was not something the military had done, but the act of the fairy.

Grace was furious, and she was illustrating that fury in flames.

"Run," he said. The conflagration spread quickly, powering across the landscape as if forced from a giant blowtorch. Wind roared before it, stirring up dust into swirling tornadoes, dark twisters that caught dawn's early light and then burst aflame as dust turned to fire.

"Up the hill," Bone said. "Up!"

"No more running," Sammi said. "It's too late. She's here, it's happening, and we can't outrun whatever she intends to do now. All I can do is protect us if I can."

Vince did not doubt her ability to protect them all.

The conflagration spread, becoming more furious as it expanded, scorching the air and setting alight everything it touched. Even the silt seemed to erupt into flames, and soon the entire valley floor was a blazing scar upon the land. The fire struck the river and the water exploded into a great, steaming geyser blasting water, rock and soil skyward. Vince hoped Shashahanna had escaped the flames. She'd probably disappeared into the shadows along with some of the other surviving Kin.

Waves of superheated air started to reach them, taking their breath away. Sammi cooled them. Smoke caught in their lungs, and Sammi gave them fresh air. It all seemed effortless, and Vince realised her inability to hide them earlier had been feigned, so that Bone could find his true self. Yet with each act he saw something sad in her eyes, as if she knew that every magical step she took carried her further and further away from who she had once been.

They saw a Humvee downhill to their right, crashing a path up between the trees with several soldiers hanging onto its exterior. The fire swept past it and consumed it with a dull, inaudible explosion.

Many smaller shapes ran, scampered, and fell before the rising flames and were swallowed up. Vince could no longer tell the difference between Kin and human.

"When will it stop?" he asked.

"Maybe she's burning the whole world," Angela said. Still nursed in Dastion's strong arms, she rested her head against his chest and watched.

"Not quite," Sammi said. "Even she doesn't have that much power."

"Look," Bone said, pointing downhill. "Look!"

"Oh, no," Vince said, because the shape rushing at them between the trees was unmistakable. Its limbs were thin, its movements jerky but strong, and even with the light and fire filling the valley he could see the glimmering yellow spark of its eyes.

"That's my father," Bone said, and he did not hesitate. Without pause, and without once looking back, he left Sammi's protection and dashed downhill, dodging between trees and heading directly for the Kovo-infected Mohserran.

Vince tensed to go after him, unsure whether he was going to hold him back or help him grapple with the selkie and bring it down. But Angela somehow reached out and grasped his arm, despite her injuries, and her eyes bore into his. *Don't leave me ever again,* they said.

He watched Bone sprinting downhill. Now fully exposed to the waves of heat rolling up the hillside, his clothes began to singe and smoke, and he waved his hands at his head as if his hair was already aflame.

"He'll expect us to go with him," Vince said, feeling a terrible shame at leaving the man to tackle the infected Kin on his own.

"No, he won't," Sammi said. "He didn't look back even once. This is what he came here for."

Bone shimmered in his vision, and for a moment Vince thought it was heat haze. Then he realised that he had truly found himself. As Mohserran saw him and ran at him, Bone became sleek, slipping between trees as he darted past the Kin and sprinted downhill.

For a second Mohserran stood rooted to the spot, glancing left and right as if trying to catch something from the corner of its eye. Then Bone appeared again down the slope and closer to the flames.

That was the last Vince saw of them. Bone the son, running towards flesh-searing fire. Mohserran the father, changed and made monstrous, chasing him as the conflagration grew in strength and violence.

Flames boiled and rolled, rising up the hillside like glaring water refilling the emptied reservoir. Sammi kept them sheltered from the effects, but around them leaves shrivelled on branches, bark was singed, and grass withered and died. Even beyond the scope of the flames, the effects of Grace's furious return to the world were being felt.

The advancing fire eventually slowed and stopped, and as the sun broke the horizon and cast its rays across a whole new world, the lake of fire began to settle. Its level became constant, a little higher than the reservoir had been before and scorching its shores, burning trees and undergrowth, sending plumes of smoke spiralling skyward in chaotic thermals. A column of smoke hung above the valley, spreading into a huge mushroom cloud that caught the most beautiful sunrise Vince had ever seen.

"It's staying like that?" Vince asked.

"Who knows," Sammi said. She smiled. "She's certainly made her mark."

Vince held Angela's hand and she squeezed back.

"I feel like shit," she said.

"You look it."

"Nice," Dastion said.

"We still don't know what's happened to them all," Vince said. "They could still be a danger."

"I don't think so," Sammi said. "They're in chaos."

"How can you know?" Angela asked.

"Because I can tell you who escaped and who didn't," Sammi said. "If I closed my eyes and really concentrated, I think I could see where they all are now, hiding or running."

"Or caught by the military?" Vince asked.

"Oh, very few of the humans survived the fire," Sammi said. Vince was shocked by her dismissive use of the word "human". She'd used it without even realising what she'd said.

"So which ones?" Vince asked. He was thinking of Mallian, even though he'd witnessed the Nephilim and the fairy flicker out of existence. There one moment, gone the next, slipping through the briefest of portals created by the blink of a fairy's eye.

"Thorn the pixie is still running," Sammi said. She was silent and contemplative for a while, and Vince thought perhaps she was remembering the cruel deeds she had seen the pixie perform. "Shashahanna crawled over the ruined dam and swam down the river beyond. She's gone too far for me to see. Fellian died at the river. Two of Mallian's Kin held her down and drowned her. She and her partner adopted three children and lived in Ottawa. They only have one mother now, but Fellian always remembered them, even though she found her real life in the Fold."

"Having a new life doesn't mean you shed your old one," Dastion said.

"A harpy is still circling the valley, high up, bloodied but delighted. Its name is Foxon, and it once ate a princess in front of her family, and killed torturers in an ancient war. Others died in the flames. I sense them, but I can't fix their names or their histories. They're just shades now. Ghosts. Like most Kin who have ever lived."

"Bone and his father?" Vince asked.

"Their story is finished," she said, and as she looked out across the valley her eyes were filled with fire.

* * *

Bone's skin was stretched and scorched and felt like it would split and burst aflame. His clothing smoked, and he could smell the tart tang of burning hair. He ran past smouldering trees, and piles of fallen leaves and sticks that had ignited, heading downhill towards the lake of fire where once had been his home. He sleeked past Mohserran and kept running, because he knew there was only one way he could lure his father to his end. This was his chance, now. This was the final chapter of his story. He had returned to Longford to find whatever might remain of his father, and though Mohserran ran after him—screeching, growling, promising pain at the end of his ragged claws or infection-laden teeth—Bone knew that in truth nothing remained.

Tears blurred his vision but the heat quickly cleared them away.

He heard rapid footsteps behind him and sleeked again, changing direction and then revealing himself once more, hearing Mohserran skidding after him. And for a while, unexpected and delightful, Bone was a child again, running across the hillsides while Mohserran chased him with a friendly growl and a scary roar. The trees were full and lush, the valley wide and bathed in beautiful sunshine, and somewhere uphill stood a hollow oak that had not yet become shelter for a small, terrified child. Everything was as it should be, and Bone called out a cry of unbridled delight.

That is how every day should be, he thought, and he turned his face up to the sky as the flames came closer.

He was finding it hard to breathe, and he could hear Mohserran closing on him, clawed feet pounding at the ground, disease-laden breath panting in and out, in and out. He could not risk a glance behind because he knew where he was going, and to not reach his destination was unthinkable.

He didn't want to die beneath his father's teeth.

He sleeked one last time and leapt down into a narrow ravine, switching left and heading for where the crack in the ground ended. Where once this place would have offered a wide view of the valley, there was now only fire. The air surged and simmered with heat haze, and every breath Bone took scorched his lungs. His vision blurred. His father was close.

At the last moment he skidded to a stop, turned around, and opened his arms wide.

Maybe he'll know me now, Bone thought, but as Mohserran barrelled into him there was no recognition in that mad, wretched creature's eyes. Only hunger.

Bone stepped quickly backwards and closed his arms around his father. Teeth snapped close to his face. Claws raked his back. Yellow fire burned in Mohserran's eyes, reflecting the whole world.

When Bone felt only air beneath his feet, he pulled his father closer and tighter as they fell into the fire.

33

Angela opened her eyes and Vince was there with her, sitting beside the bed, eyes closed and snoring softly. She looked around in a panic. Her breath came faster, and she peered at the closed door, expecting to see the hulking shape of a policeman standing guard.

"Hey, hey," Vince said. Her troubled fidgeting had stirred him. "Take it easy."

"Where are we?"

"Hospital."

"But—"

"You needed attention," he said. "We both did." He tipped a bottle of water against her lips and she took a few grateful sips.

"They'll arrest me. Put me in jail."

Vince smiled. "If they did, you could blame it on the Angel of Death."

"Huh?"

"That's what they're calling Mallian. Some of the press is, anyway, and the name's stuck."

"Angel of Death. He'd like that." She tried to calm herself, but the fear was still there that after all this, her fate lay in a prison cell for the London murders that Mallian had committed.

"How bad am I?" she asked.

Vince's eyes flickered to the side, then back to her. "I thought I'd lost you. You stopped breathing three times. They brought you back, but I'm not sure... I think Sammi had something to do with it, too."

"My... legs?"

"Battered, broken. It's your spine that's the problem." He paused, frowning. "They don't know if you'll walk again."

Angela closed her eyes and took in a deep breath.

"But Sammi!" Vince said. "She thinks she'll be able to help, but just not yet. Not until she's really found herself."

"Heal me?" She opened her eyes again, sad to see tears in Vince's.

"I hope so. That's what she thinks."

"Where is she?"

"She's outside somewhere. She comes in sometimes, looks at you, then leaves again." He looked uncomfortable.

"What?" Angela asked.

"She's not really Sammi anymore."

Angela felt a profound sadness, but also a strange sense of release. She'd taken Sammi's wellbeing onto her own shoulders after rescuing her from the Folded Land, but now it seemed that relationship had switched.

"She's making sure they look after us without telling the authorities," Angela said.

"Yeah. She calls it 'subtle suggestion', but she says

it can't last long. We'll have to leave soon. They've patched you up, pumped you full of drugs, sewn up your wounds, and we both have these." He lifted his arm to show his cast, and she felt the same around her left arm, and saw the cast on her left leg. She couldn't feel it.

"I should have died," she said.

"But you didn't." Vince leaned over to hug her tight. She felt the drip of his tears, and the room blurred as she cried her own.

"How long have we been here?"

"Two days," Vince said. "You've also fractured some ribs, bruised your kidneys, and you've got cuts and scrapes and a minor concussion."

"Did I break any nails?"

Vince snorted laughter. It was good to hear, and good to inspire.

"What about the others?"

He pulled back from her and wiped his eyes. The old Vince—the Vince of London, before she knew he was working for Fat Frederick Meloy and mixing with creatures she could never have imagined—would have been embarrassed at those tears. This new Vince was unashamed.

"Dastion went deeper into the hills, looking for somewhere to start a new mine, I guess. He'll mix in well enough until he finds the right place. He still remembers what it was like to be human."

"Mallian? The other Kin?"

"She took Mallian through with her," Vince said. He shivered. "I hate the son of a bitch, but the thought of what'll be happening to him—"

"Deserved," Angela said. "Every bite, earned."

"The military have got a couple of dead ones," Vince continued. "Plenty of images have leaked online and the news is all over it. I can pretty much guarantee it's on a channel somewhere..." He picked up a TV remote from beside her bed and pointed it at the screen up in a corner of her room.

It opened on a rolling news report about the Longford lake of fire. It was an incredible sight, and though the military was attempting to secure the area, the boundary between the blazing lake and the surrounding hillsides ran for more than twenty miles. Various experts spouted opinions about what was happening, but the news anchor kept referring back to the several clips of film they had managed to procure of soldiers fighting strange, unknown creatures, some of them very humanoid in nature. One of them was impossibly tall and monstrous. It was daytime TV and the warnings came thick and fast, but within minutes of turning on the TV they were presented with a clip of Mallian ripping the cop in half.

"Do they really need to show that?" Angela asked.

"Of course not, but they'll keep showing it again and again." Vince surfed the channels. "Hang on, let me find the Pentagon guy. They're showing this clip on a loop, too." He settled on a channel with an amused-looking presenter and a grey-haired man on the screen in the corner. The spokesman from the Pentagon chuckled at the stories put to him and said they were dealing with a mass delusion brought on by electrical discharges following a seismic event.

The interviewer responded by playing footage of a chopper brought down by a winged humanoid creature, and asked if camera technology was also susceptible to mass delusion.

And so it went on, and on, and would go on for a long, long time. Footage of Mallian killing the cop and other stuff from the attack and the fight on the hillside. Choppers going down, soldiers being killed and killing. The dead things that no one could explain.

"And there's the lake of fire," Angela said when the footage ended and returned to what looked like rolling coverage. "Grace's constant reminder of the power of the Kin, and why we should leave them alone."

"It's a good warning," Vince said.

"Yeah, but humans are inquisitive. We've always been tempted to play with fire."

They watched for a couple more minutes, then Angela reached out—groaning when pain bit in all across her torso—and fumbled for the remote. She turned the TV off. She'd seen it all first-hand, and hearing so-called experts arguing and offering theories, and military spokesmen calling it fake news, did nothing to detract from the ordeal she and the ones she loved had been through.

Were still going through.

"Sammi," she said. "She'll be staying with us?"

Vince looked aside, then back at Angela. "I think she'll be gone soon. I don't think she *can* stay with us, do you?"

Angela didn't reply. She wasn't sure. She didn't know if she even wanted the girl, the young fairy, to be part of their lives. Not after what she'd seen her do, and not after what they'd all seen Grace become.

"I'll get some food and coffee," Vince said. Angela grasped his good hand before he could stand.

"No!" she said.

"Hey, I'm only going to the restaurant. I'm here to look after you—forever."

"Stay with me just for now," Angela said. "And promise to never leave me ever again, and I won't leave you. Ever again."

Vince sat down and held her hand. He smiled and said, "Deal."

Later, when Angela was asleep, Vince slipped outside to see Sammi. The girl was curled up on a chair in the waiting room, eyes closed but not asleep.

"I'll be leaving later," she said as Vince sat beside her. "I'll be back to help her, but I have to help myself first."

"She'll want to see you before you go."

Sammi opened her eyes. Their shade had changed, and their shape, as if to take in the view of a wider world.

"I'll go in now," she said. "You need to make that call."

"Sure. And, Sammi?"

She looked at him.

"Take care of yourself."

"You know I will."

"No, I mean... I know you're going out there to take care of others. Kin like you, and maybe Kin who don't even know who or what they are yet. But you have to take care of yourself, too."

Sammi's eyes softened as she understood what he meant. She smiled, and for a while she looked the old Sammi again. "I'll be fine. I might even look in on you from time to time."

Vince nodded, stood, and went outside to make his call. He wasn't at all sure he'd want her to do that.

After speaking to Jay and ensuring he and Angela could return to the cabin in the woods, he went back inside. When he realised Sammi was not in the waiting room he expected to see her sitting beside Angela's bed, both of them saying their goodbyes.

But Angela was asleep again, and there was no sign of Sammi.

As if she'd never been.

In her Fold, closed off from the world forevermore, she takes stock. She brought the Nephilim through with her and for now she lets him run wild. He's no threat to her anymore. He's raging and raving, but she stays away from him, lets him work that rage from his system. Over the days and weeks to come he'll calm a little, and then he'll start considering his position. He'll drink from the river. He'll eat. He'll start to fatten up.

She also brought a handful of other Kin through with her, before she blasted fire back through the portal and then closed it forever. None of them are the ones she brought here originally—they are all dead, or gone back into the world—and that frustrates her. But on the other hand, these new Kin are mostly pure, and she senses that one or two of them are very, very old. Perhaps she will approach some of them and converse. She might even pass time with them.

When her hunger returns, they will provide much better game.

One of the Kin troubled her the moment it came through, and she knows it is from the drowned village. The gargoyle is wild and animalistic, not like Kin at all, and she also senses a dangerous human taint on and in it. An infection, still simmering even after it has spent a long, long time beneath standing waters.

It's unnatural. It's undesirable, and possibly even dangerous, if not to her then to the other new inhabitants of the Fold.

It is this gargoyle that she deals with first. She will never again open a portal back into the world, and she is already forcing herself to forget how to do so. There is one place in the Fold, however, where she believes it will be safe.

She herds it before her, using subtle glamours to steer the way. It scampers and runs across grasslands and up the valley side, leaping from rock to rock, running before her even though in its mind it is actually on the hunt. She edges it towards the caves where Dastion the dwarf once made his home.

The infected Kin darts into the cave mouth and she holds back. It takes some concentration, but after a few heartbeats the ground around the caves begins to shake, crack and tumble.

She senses it going far deeper, fleeing the rockfalls that seal off the tunnels behind them. The ground ruptures, and half the hillside falls into the network of tunnels and halls that Dastion spent his time hollowing out beneath the Fold.

She searches, sending her senses out wide. She's content that there is no way for the gargoyle to return to the surface. It will remain down there, that Kin with human stains, for as long as she remains up here, and as long as the Fold persists. Perhaps over time it will stop wandering those deep tunnels and sit down to die, or maybe it will persist, becoming motionless but still extant, still infected with the dangerous contamination that even she wants no part of.

Whatever happens, it will be safe.

There's no way out.

* * *

He sees her coming again and there's nothing he can do. Sometimes she lets him run, and he does so, because over the time he's been trapped in the Fold—months, maybe years—Mallian has never shaken the belief that one day he will better her. So he runs, and she hunts him, and after hours or days of cat and mouse, she always catches him.

One day, though...

Although this time, as she casts her glamour and freezes him against an old tree, the first doubts begin to sprout.

He struggles but cannot move. He can't even squirm. His heart beats, but at her behest. His blood flows, but only because she wants to taste it.

The fairy peruses his body, looking for a part that is not too knotted with the scars of healing bites. There aren't many. She finally settles on his left thigh, crouching down beside him and exposing her small, sharp teeth.

She looks up and locks eyes with him before she clamps her teeth onto his flesh. That's what he hates the most. She waits until he's looking so that he can see her pleasure in every bite.

ACKNOWLEDGEMENTS

I couldn't have written the Relics trilogy without the help and support of Team Titan, and special thanks go out to DEO Steve Saffel and Editor-at-Large Cath Trechman.

ABOUT THE AUTHOR

TIM LEBBON is a *New York Times*-bestselling writer from South Wales. He's had over forty novels published to date, as well as hundreds of novellas and short stories. His latest novel is *Blood of the Four* (with Christopher Golden), and other recent releases include *Relics*, *The Family Man*, *The Silence*, and *The Rage War* trilogy.

He has won four British Fantasy Awards, a Bram Stoker Award, and a Scribe Award, and has been a finalist for World Fantasy, International Horror Guild, and Shirley Jackson awards.

A movie of his novel *The Silence*, starring Stanley Tucci and Kiernan Shipka, was released on Netflix in early 2019, and the movie of his story *Pay the Ghost*, starring Nicolas Cage, was released in 2015. Several other projects are in development for television and the big screen.

Find out more about Tim at his website
www.timlebbon.net

and follow him on Twitter
@timlebbon